HORSEMAN
AWAITS

J. J. ALLEN

outskirts
press

Outskirts Press, Inc.
http://www.outskirtspress.com

Paperback ISBN: 978-1-4787-9380-9

Outskirts Press and the "OP" logo are trademarks belonging to Outskirts Press, Inc.

PRINTED IN THE UNITED STATES OF AMERICA

CHAPTER ONE
SOMEWHERE IN PAKISTAN

AUGUST, 2009

The drone pilot swore he felt the desert heat seeping through his monitor. The ground, the village buildings, the vehicles—every-thing--seemed to be oozing heat in the white afternoon sun. A lonely dust devil wandered outside of town. The airman had seen dirt swirl like that when the devastating drought hit his Texas Hill Country home. All grass dried and the dirt became dry, silty, powdery, like talc on a baby's bottom. The water tanks got lower and lower and hotter and hotter, and the fish floated to the top and the vultures feasted; then the stock tanks turned to mud and eventually simply baked clay. Suddenly thirsty, he reached for a water bottle, and in doing so saw a colonel – a full colonel – standing beside his captain. "Hot damn!" he thought, "High priority." He fixed his gaze on the target building, eager to demonstrate that he was ready for combat.

He flew the Predator drone over the building again. He'd flown around the village twice now – the target building was easy to find, sitting on the edge of town. He had seen no activity. Who'd want to be outside in that heat? He had seen a couple of men under a canopy on the roof of the house across the street. He thought it unusual to see people on the roof of a building that time of day, even under a canopy, but those people had lived their entire lives in that heat, so what did he know?

Two men walked out of the target building and got into a faded green Toyota light pickup covered in dust. The driver appeared young and energetic; the passenger looked older, with a slight stoop. He was carrying two bags, perhaps a briefcase and a bag of clothes.

The Colonel, tall, erect and forceful, spoke, "Be alert, Airman, this may be our target."

"Yes, Sir," he replied firmly, concentrating on his controls, keeping the visual sharp and the drone at an appropriate distance.

The pickup began moving out of town into the desert.

The Colonel listened intently into his earpiece. "We have confirmation," he said. The airman thought the Colonel sounded uncharacteristically excited. "Our target is in the pickup. When it gets out of town, destroy it."

"Yes, Sir" replied the airman. He brought the targeting mechanism of the Predator to bear. As the pickup neared the top of the hill, he calmly fired. The pickup was obliterated in a flashing explosion. "No one could survive that," the airman thought to himself, pleased with his success.

"Good work, Airman," the Colonel said, then left the room.

"Thank you, sir," murmured the airman as the door closed.

Under the canopy the bearded man spoke a word of thanks to the martyrs already in Paradise, then turned to his companion, an older man with a slight stoop, a renowned nuclear scientist, and said, "Congratulations, Dr. Husain. You are now officially dead."

CHAPTER TWO

HOUSTON

A SUNDAY IN SEPTEMBER, 2016, 5:02 A.M.

Two minutes after the scheduled call failed to come, Mohammed Aziz, the Saudi Consul in Houston, began to get anxious. He glanced at his Rolex, holding the silent phone in his hand. He realized many things could cause a delay, but because he was so close to achieving his dream of destruction, anxiety rose in his chest. He forced himself to submit to the will of God, even if it meant failure in his planned attack on America. His anxiety subsided with prayer, and after waiting for a few more minutes, he called his driver to bring the limousine. The truck should be on its way now, he thought. He wanted to be close to the bomb, to become a martyr. He delighted in the thought that when it was learned that he, a Saudi Prince, had died in the explosion, the American news media would treat the attack as terrorists indiscriminately killing even a Saudi Prince. They would never know it was his plan, that he would be the one who would take the Great Satan to its knees. Then it would be up to other believers to finish the job. God would know it was his plan, that was what mattered. The Prince blessed all who had helped him, his trusted drivers and his fellow believers. Nothing would have been possible without Dr. Husain. Blessings on him. Only a few people in the entire planet had that man's knowledge of nuclear weaponry, but he needed motivation. Blessings upon Husain's family killed by the Crusaders, those whose deaths had driven Husain to join their holy war.

Abdul Faisal had also been invaluable. How he had been able to smuggle that bomb into the country the Consul did not know, but he was grateful for the ability. It had been Abdul's idea for the well-logging truck, too, the type of truck that oil companies drive to wells to determine what rocks they've drilled through. A sight common in Houston, it would raise no suspicions and most importantly mask the radioactive material, Abdul had said. Brilliant, thought the Consul. His consulate drivers, Mohammed al-Omari and Mohammed al-Ghamdi, would drive the truck to the top of the bridge over the Ship Channel near the oil refineries. Dr. Husain would be in a second truck with whatever he needed. In a few hours, or a day at most, there would be an immense conflagration. It would bring the destruction of half of America's refineries, plus the destruction of downtown Houston, what Texas claimed as "the oil capital of the world." The Prince inwardly laughed at that absurdity. All the oil ever found by the Americans was dwarfed by what lay beneath the sands of Arabia. In the blast, Houston's famous Texas Medical Center would not be destroyed, according to Husain, but would be overwhelmed by casualties in the hundreds of thousands.

The Consul ordered his driver to take him to the warehouse district, to determine why Al-Omari was late checking in. He should be behind the wheel with the assembled bomb by now, according to the plan. The silence of the phone caused his anxiety to rise again, and again the Consul forced it down. Such anxiety was not proper for a Muslim who submitted to God's will, he thought. Best to go and determine the reason for the delay.

His emotions volleyed between anxiety and excitement. He could force down the anxiety by submitting to God, but no need to hold down the excitement any longer. He'd been working on this dream for seven years, trying to fit together all the pieces, large and small. Everything had to fit. Everything had to work. Everything had to be kept a secret. Only those whose contribution was absolutely necessary had been told what they were trying to accomplish. Every detail had to be worked out in advance, as much as possible so that there would be no snags. Still, he knew no matter how careful a plan, the end remained in the hands of God. That was a lesson one learned over and over in the harsh environment of the Arab world. Basic life was difficult. You planned and worked for something expecting success, "God willing." But so much failed, and you would shrug it off. "Never mind. We'll try again tomorrow, God willing." Aziz reckoned that was why Islam took such a strong hold on the Arab world — because living in such a climate as theirs was so difficult, and it was easier to accept when you realized it was God's will for you to suffer, so, submit to the will of God and be at peace, "Islam". But you never stopped trying to make life better. And striking this great blow against the Crusaders would make life much better for Muslims throughout the entire world, especially those in the Middle East. Without America, Arabs could band together and finally drive the Zionists from the Holy Land. Arabs could finally live their lives without American interference.

What a blow the atomic bomb would be! Most Americans did not realize that oil was their country's lifeblood. Virtually all transportation ran on gasoline or diesel. Certainly, all transport of food and goods did. Americans should understand that, he thought, but if so, how could they have left their refineries so vulnerable? Fuel for vehicles was just part of their demand, though. Americans wanted synthetic shoes and clothes, special plastics for cell phones and computers, the list was endless. Equipment of all kinds was made out of plastic. All plastic came from oil.

The first psychological blow would be the destruction of America's 4th largest city. The economic blow would be the severe shortage of gasoline and plastics. Americans would be fighting each other with their precious guns to get gasoline, and there simply would not be enough to buy. He wished in a way that he would be able to see the fruits of his plan, but he would rather have martyrdom. The lack of fuel would mean a lack of food in cities, and people would starve and riot and fight. Chaos would rule. The Prince was overjoyed at the thought.

The limousine left River Oaks, the wealthiest neighborhood in Houston, and sped down curvy Allen Parkway following alongside the course of Buffalo Bayou toward downtown, then through downtown to the warehouse district. Even on a pre-dawn Sunday morning, the lights of downtown were bright and contrasted strongly with the dimness of the warehouse district. There, no buildings were lit, and only the occasional feeble street light provided illumination. As they pulled onto Leeland Street in the warehouse district, the driver turned off the lights and they slowly drove several blocks in the darkness. There was no traffic but he wanted to draw no attention. The area seemed empty except for an occasional overflowing dumpster, or a person sleeping in a doorway or under a tree. Nothing was stirring. The limousine stopped at their warehouse. No lights were showing inside. The driver got out, began to remove his driving gloves, thought better of it and put them back on. Even at five in the morning, the heat and humidity of Houston struck him when he got out of the air-conditioned limousine. He began to perspire immediately. He grabbed a flashlight from inside the car door and walked warily to a side door of the warehouse. He was struck by the strong aroma of bread baking and coffee brewing in factories several blocks away. The warehouse was dark, but condensation on the windows meant the air conditioning was working inside.

The door was locked, and no one responded to his knocking, so he used the end of the flashlight to break the window. Glass clattered on the floor and the driver cautiously listened. All remained still and quiet. He reached through the window, unlocked the door and stepped inside. The place seemed empty except for some cranes that loomed over the space, a couple of engine hoists, and two bodies on the floor. He walked over and lit the faces with his flashlight, avoiding a touch lest the bodies were booby-trapped. Returning to the limousine, he reported to the Prince. "Al-Omari and al-Ghamdi are dead. The place is empty."

"What?" Aziz gasped, not believing, not comprehending. Dead? His drivers both dead? They should have been helping Husain construct the bomb! His gut churned with dread, his mouth filling with the bitterness of betrayal. He sprang out of the car, wanting to go see, wanting to leave, so aghast that he was virtually paralyzed. Dead! What happened? Where's the bomb? He was confused and had no idea what to do. The limousine driver, recognizing the difficulty his boss was suffering, reminded the Consul to breathe deeply, and to pray. The Consul slowly calmed, and his mind began working again. The sky would soon be getting light and the sun would rise. "Let's leave," he commanded.

"What about the bodies?"

"We can't do anything. Let's go."

The Consul boiled with consternation for the apparent failure of his plan, but he had not become a success by wasting time on what might have been. He needed to concentrate on the situation now. Right now. Slowly he began to fear that someone had betrayed him. The only reason to kill those two men, it seemed, was to steal the bomb, his atomic bomb.

Aziz told the driver to head home. Where is the bomb now? Who could have taken it? Perhaps Abdul? He'd been in on the plan almost from the beginning and had heartily endorsed the idea. He'd strongly agreed with the Consul's concepts of using the bomb on Houston and the refineries. Abdul had argued such in the committee meetings. Had that been false? Aziz didn't think so. Abdul was his nephew – the only one of his nephews who had meaningful accomplishments. He had seen Abdul's talents early, had encouraged him, had favored him over all the other nephews, even more than his own sons. Certainly not Abdul.

Husain? Aziz quickly focused on Husain the foreigner as most likely the traitor, even though the man's motivation was the slaughter by the Americans of his entire family. Still, who knows what goes on in the mind of an egghead? The physicist thought about things differently. He thought about other things than most people — always talking about science, physics, and things like that. He seemed to be the weakest link. Besides, he was Pakistani, the one most likely to change his mind. Finally, he was the person most critical to Aziz's plan, and would be critical to the thieves, whoever they were.

Still in the car, Consul dialed Abdul. A recording began, so Aziz dialed again, in order that Abdul could see he had called twice and might then call him back. Then, Aziz had an inspiration. He excitedly told the driver to head to the Beltway 8 Bridge, a major artery of eight lanes looming 175' over the Houston Ship Channel, near the center of all the refineries. His mind was racing. Perhaps Abdul or Husain had to kill the drivers for some reason and still were in the process of setting up the explosion. He had to be there.

Unimpeded by traffic, the limousine raced down I-45, the glow of the refinery lights growing brighter. After they swung onto Highway 225, the lights along the Ship Channel dominated his vision. 'Refinery Row' along the Ship Channel was a miles-long giant chandelier whose light consumed the night, turning night into perpetual day. Each refinery was comprised of towers and boilers and separators and tanks. Each piece of equipment was lit with several bright lights from the ground to the top, until there was no room for darkness. Mohammed was delighted in the idea, his idea, that soon the entire industrial complex would vanish in an instant. It took 20 minutes to get to the Beltway 8 bridge, and by then the sun was lightening the horizon. "What a beautiful morning to die," he thought.

With no sign of the bomb truck on that bridge, Aziz told the driver to go to the Loop 610 bridge. Maybe plans had changed, or something more terrible had happened in the warehouse. But they found no sign of anyone at that bridge, either. Deflated, his anxiety rose. Then Aziz remembered that Abdul was going to fly his private plane to Denver. Abdul had said, several times, that he would be a facilitator but not a martyr. So be it. He'd done a great job getting the bomb here. Now what? Did he have the bomb with him? If he did, why?

CHAPTER THREE

HOUSTON

7:25 A.M. THAT SAME SUNDAY

Riley Callahan felt the cool air on his naked body as bedsheets were pulled off.

"C'mon, Riley! You promised you'd go to eight o'clock Mass with me."

Callahan put his feet on the floor, stretched his aching back over his legs, and looked sidelong at the woman in the bathroom applying her makeup. He realized this was the woman he'd likely spend the rest of his life with, and he liked that idea. She was good for him in many ways. She was lively, and strong, and pretty and sexy, although somewhat shorter than he expected his life-companion to be. He felt lucky. Dark brown eyes, dark brown hair cut short, framing her round face and fitting her determined business-like demeanor. Special Agent Camille Richard of the FBI. He loved her; determination seemed to define her. Even her hair cut denoted that she would not be distracted from her goals.

He stretched his long lanky body and stumbled clumsily out of bed. "I'm coming, I'm coming," he said entering the bathroom. He wondered how he could have ended up with such a religious woman. He, Riley Callahan, 100% Irish Catholic, Catholic high school, Catholic college (as much as any were these days), who'd spent his whole life trying to rid himself of the foolish religious ways of his teachers and parents and grandparents (whose parents were from the Auld country), and now he was in love with a full-blooded Cajun as religious as anyone he'd ever known. Even his Great-Aunt Virginia, the Sisters of the Incarnate Word nun, seemed no more devoted to

God than Camille. "God, if there is one, has a mean sense of humor," he thought. He knew that having a family with Camille would bring it all back – the Catholic schools, and mass every Sunday and church rituals and an endless array of fundraisers. He moaned at the thought, but that was irrelevant to how he loved her. She was worth it, he thought; he hoped. He was pleased with his life, with being with her, with being an agent for the Department of Homeland Security.

Riley felt lucky: who could have failed to fall in love with Camille? She was engaging, energetic, a great cook, loved to hunt and fish. A much better shot than he, as proven many times shooting skeet and ducks. Firing a shotgun was as easy and natural to her as making a roux. Riley had never touched a firearm until he joined the Army, while Camille's father had been taking her hunting in the marshes of South Louisiana since she was maybe ten. Riley was completely baffled, though, by Camille's occasional flash of anger or temper. She was warm and loved to cuddle, he knew that, but sometimes she could be angry and laugh in the same sentence. He did not understand and definitely did not like that side of her, but it certainly kept life interesting.

Camille loved this man. His face was long—he said he was the only one in his Irish family without the familiar potato face. Dark brown hair and dark brown eyes were different from what she'd expected from an Irishman. He was strong and purposeful at work but playful and energetic at home. She couldn't believe her good fortune to find him, and the fact that he loved her in return. Life was good with Riley, and she was ready for him to ask for her to marry, expected the question any day. Everything seemed wonderful about life. She loved her work with the FBI, Criminal Investigation Division, even though right now Bureau morale was low after FBI Director Cormier's press conference about Secretary of State Hilliard a few months ago. He'd laid out the facts of how she'd broken the law but had said he did not see enough to prosecute. FBI agents knew it was not the Director's decision to make about whether to prosecute; that decision belonged to the Department of Justice and the Attorney General. It seemed like a political move, and it stank, in her opinion. She believed the FBI should be above politics. However, despite the low morale now, she loved being in the FBI and being useful in a job that demanded her concentration and talents.

Camille loved being back in Houston, too. It wasn't Lafayette, but close enough that she didn't have to continually correct people's pronunciation of her name. In Washington, she'd always have say "it's French, Ree-shar; not English, Richard", and doing that over and over irritated her. In Houston, in East Texas, people knew French names. The dining in Houston was fabulous, too, as Louisiana cuisine had migrated to the oil capital. They could eat anything from Brennan's to Cajun Po-Boys, plus food from around the world, thanks to the presence of the port and the oil industry. People from all over the world lived here, and that made life more interesting, more delicious. Indeed, anywhere Americans had drilled a well provided Houston with a new culture to add to the mix: Venezuela, Brazil, Australia, Norway, the Middle East, and so on. Because of the port, every country with a shipping business had sent people to Houston: Greeks, Dutch, Portuguese, South Africans, Taiwanese and more. More recently medical and business people from India and from China were being added along with the million or so immigrants from Mexico and Central America. All that made Houston the most diverse city in the country, despite New York City's boast. Camille felt comfortable in Houston. When people learned she liked to hunt and fish, they didn't raise eyebrows and sniff as if she were an odious creature. Houstonians generally were friendly—much friendlier than Washingtonians. In the Tax Day Flood and the Memorial Day Flood a few months before, Houstonians of all colors and ethnicities had worked together as neighbors. She knew lots of people in the oil business, mostly friends of her geologist father or acquaintances from

Lafayette. Life was easy, and she felt Riley was about to take them to a place where she knew she'd - they'd - be happy: a family.

While Riley drove through the trees of Memorial Park on the way to St. Theresa Church, Camille watched the tennis players and joggers, all trying to get their exercise done while the temperature was only in the 80's, before the day got really hot. The church was cool and welcoming, and Riley enjoyed hearing Father Phil's lovely British accent, despite his own ambivalence toward religion. Camille relished the fact that, around Houston, Mass was conducted in sixteen different languages. The one she'd most enjoyed was in French, a congregation of mostly West Africans. The music had been rollicking and uplifting, and she was eager to take Riley there some Sunday.

After communion, as they were returning to their pew, Riley's phone buzzed. "Don't answer it," Camille said. "Pretend we didn't hear it." Riley knew she didn't really mean it. She had as strong a sense of duty as he and would walk out of church to answer her phone if a call came from her office. He grabbed his phone out of his pocket and headed to the back of the church while Camille slid through the pew to get her purse, then joined him. She noticed that the head of the Houston office of the FBI, Robert Perez, had texted her to go to a warehouse on Leeland Street near downtown.

Riley listened to the voice on the phone and grimaced. "Looks like we're both on duty. Sounds like foreign nationals have been murdered." Camille realized it probably was more than merely foreign nationals. Both FBI and Homeland Security wouldn't be called for common drug dealers from Mexico or Colombia. She wondered what would draw them both. Since there might be little chance to eat once they got to the crime site, Riley headed down Washington Avenue to El Rey Taqueria. Camille wished Velvet Taco was open at that hour— what a delightful mixture of Mexican, Indian, and Cajun cuisine. It was emblematic of Houston, taking the best from everywhere and mixing it together. *E Pluribus Unum.* Riley smiled at Camille, then turned his attention to the drive-thru lane. When he lowered the window, warm humid air rushed in. He leaned his head out the window and began to order, "One black coffee, one coffee with cream," when he felt a sharp poke in his rib. He looked back at Camille.

Her face showed a big smile that crackled her eyes. "Didya have fun this weekend? Didya?" He slapped at her poking hand and turned back toward the speaker.

"One Cuban..." She poked again.

"Well, Didya?"

He squirmed and tried to order. "One egg and chorizo taco..."

She poked again, enjoying his discomfort. "Well, didya?"

Riley turned to her, and grabbed her leg halfway up her thigh, squeezing hard. Camille squealed and yelled with laughter. "Okay, okay," she said, pushing his hand away, and let him finish the order.

Camille settled back into her seat and wondered to herself, "Irish, when are you going to ask me?" She knew he loved being with her. "Is something wrong?" she thought. "Should I ask him?"

Sitting in the drive-thru line, Riley calculated that they had spent thirty consecutive hours in bed, arising only for bathroom breaks and refrigerator raids. And that was after four hours of zydeco dancing at the Fais-Do-Do Friday night. He remembered the old saying that if you put a bean in a jar for each time you had sex in your first year of marriage, and then began taking them out each time you had sex after the first year, that you'd never empty the jar. He couldn't believe that was true, but if it counted, they were sure putting a lot of beans in the jar already.

On Shepherd Drive, he crossed over Buffalo Bayou to Allen Parkway so he could enjoy the benefit of the Camaro along the winding road. Driving along Buffalo Bayou was an easy trip on Sunday morning, with the sun peeking around the downtown skyscrapers. Trees and grasses along the bayou were lush, reveling in the warm and fecund climate. The curves along the bayou and the dips of the underpasses made Allen Parkway the most fun stretch of road to drive in Houston. Riley loved the feel of a well-engineered automobile as it confidently slipped though the dips and accelerated out of the curves. Camille smiled to see her man revert to boyhood for a minute. He hit downtown, maneuvered through the streets using the timed lights, and headed toward the warehouse district southeast of downtown. As they passed Toyota Center, they noticed a stage being erected. The Rockets' first preseason game was scheduled to be today at noon, and there'd be a party beforehand to excite the fans. Riley felt sorry for any performers in the heat and sun.

The warehouse district was busy with police vehicles, so Riley parked in front of a Chinese restaurant supply store, a relic from the time before Chinatown moved from that area to the west side of Houston. The building looked strangely familiar to Camille; then she realized she had been here when she was maybe 15, when her mother drove the two of them from Lafayette to this store to buy a duck press for her kitchen. They had laughed and joked and her mother had shocked Camille, telling her startling things about life and men now that she had "become a woman." That trip was one her favorite memories of her mother, naturally coming from the time before Camille began challenging authority at every turn.

When they exited the Camaro, the humidity and warmth of the morning hit them. Riley could feel sweat already begin under his arms just by walking toward the cordoned area. The heavy air seemed to dare him to breath; he was simply not acclimated to this climate yet, after three years here. How long would it take? Camille, who'd grown up in south Louisiana, was comforted by the way the humid air cuddled her like a warm blanket.

The emptiness of the building struck Camille when they entered. A cavernous space, like an empty airplane hangar, nothing in it but a couple of cranes and hoists, the police milling around and two bodies lying in blood. The place looked impeccably clean, except for what appeared to be paint streaks and a crack in the cement floor. Camille approached a short grey-haired black man with stubbled chin in street clothes who seemed to be in charge and whom she took for a police detective, introduced herself with credentials and waited for Riley to do the same. The detective looked at her as if he were trying to remember something. Camille blushed, realizing her screwup last winter had made her infamous in HPD. He shook their hands and stated his name, "Detective Tom Dickerson, HPD." The two men looked at Camille, silently acknowledging that, as an FBI special agent, she automatically outranked them. She felt ill at ease, wearing a floral church dress rather than the normal FBI uniform.

"What do you know, Detective?" asked Camille, but her mind immediately leapt back to the first time she'd been in this situation, and she'd not handled it well. She remembered what Perez's advice after that incident, "Ask everyone's opinion, but follow your gut."

Dickerson responded, "The night security guard was making his rounds after sunrise, noticed a broken window and entered to find the bodies, then called HPD."

"So why call DHS?" asked Riley.

"They look like foreign nationals to me. How about you?" He pointed at the two bodies. They were short, of thin build, with thin sharp noses, and skin the color of sand. They wore ratty working clothes with blue paint stains the color of the streaks on the floor.

"I see what you mean," Riley said.

Camille interrupted. "Do we know who owns this place and who was leasing it?"

Dickerson waved over a man with a slight hunchback, who limped over. Camille's immediate reaction was that this security job might have been the only work he could find, but scolded herself for the put-down. Dickerson introduced the man, "This is Ron George, the security guard for several buildings here. He says the CIA leased this space."

"Not likely," blurted Camille. "Only the GSA rents buildings for the government."

George said, "I have the leasing document. It's back in my office in the next block."

"Please get it," said Camille. George limped out of the building, then she continued, "What do you think, Agent Callahan?"

Riley flinched but understood the need for formality. "You're the chief investigative agent. What do you think?"

She swept her hand around the room. "Looks like they were painting something blue, from the spill on the floor." The shade of dark bright blue painted splattered on the floor looked familiar, but she couldn't recall why. "Looks like our victims walked in wet paint, from the streaks of blue on their sneakers."

The Detective nodded. "Yes, the security guy says he doesn't remember the blue stain when the place was leased."

"What do we know about the victims?"

"Nothing concrete yet. But to me they look like Middle Easterners. Maybe just druggies. I imagine the fingers were cut off so we'd have no fingerprints."

"So, why'd you call us?"

"I have our interpreter coming – he might be able to figure out where they're from. He's from Iraq. He helped the American forces over there, at some cost to his family. He's in Houston now, has become a citizen, and is eager to help us however he can. Since he speaks seven languages, he's quite helpful to the police department." He turned to Camille. "But I have to warn you: his name, Farman, means 'danger,' and no one ever had a more fitting name."

"What do you mean?" asked Riley.

"You'll see. Let me put it this way; he's a kept man. He's very good looking. He's so good looking some big-time female lawyer keeps him in Dildo Towers and provides him money and takes him all over the country."

"Dildo Towers? You mean Dunlavy Tower downtown?"

"Yeah. The place where all the bigwigs keep their mistresses. He lives there. He's like a mistress, only for a big-shot woman. Can you imagine all those gorgeous young women living there with time on their hands, and he lives there, too? Naturally, a lot of partying going on. He's found his Paradise on earth already." Dickerson winked and laughed when he said it.

Just then the door opened and an immensely attractive muscular young man strode in, strutting like a rooster. His face had strong features, with dancing dark eyes. Most striking, though, was his hair. Long black curls glistened across his head, falling in ringlets down to his neck. Camille admitted to herself that this was perhaps the most handsome man she had ever seen. "A Greek statue come to life," she thought to herself. Riley thought the same with a trace of regret. The Greek statue walked directly to a pair of female officers who giggled and smiled and laughed nervously.

Dickerson yelled at the man, "Farman! Over here! And take off that ridiculous hairpiece."

"Sorry, sir, but it works." said the cocky man as he walked toward them. He slid off the hairpiece to reveal short-cropped black hair. "What do you need?"

Dickerson said, "This is Farman Yousif, consultant to HPD. Farman, this is DHS Agent Callahan and FBI Agent Richard." Yousif's dramatic eyes lingered on Camille. She flushed with embarrassment, felt foolish. She stopped herself from saying something regrettable. "You must get a lot of women throwing themselves at you," she thought to herself.

"Take a look at these two bodies," ordered Dickerson. "No ID, but I suspect they're Middle Easterners. What do you think?"

Yousif spent several minutes looking closely at the two bodies until he was pushed away by the coroner. Again, Dickerson inquired, "What do you think, Farman?"

"Not certain, sir, but I'd guess most probably Saudis — at least from the Peninsula. Maybe Yemeni."

"Why do you say that?"

"General body type, facial features. Just a gut feeling from my time in Arabia."

"Thanks, Farman. Hang around for a while."

Camille looked at Riley. "What next?" She realized he might take that more than one way, but she meant with the mystery at their feet.

Dickerson answered his cell, then looked at the two federal agents. "Patrol talked to a homeless guy in the next block who said he saw a big blue truck driving down the street early this morning."

"Truck?" asked Riley. "What kind of truck?"

"He said, like an oil field truck."

"Big Blue!" Camille exclaimed, surprising herself when the recognition struck. "Big Blue — that's oil field trash for Schlumberger. That's why the shade was familiar."

"Hold on there, Agent Richard," Riley puzzled. "Explain yourself."

"I thought the blue looked familiar — that's because it is Schlumberger blue. All their trucks are painted that shade of blue. Even their workers on the rig wear blue coveralls. That's why they are called Big Blue. I've seen them my whole life when I'd go to the drilling rigs with my daddy."

"Ok, I get it," said Dickerson, "I'm thinking we have some smugglers, drugs or whatever, and two dead, probably foreign nationals whom we can't identify. I'm guessing a drug deal gone bad, but Saudis have never been involved in smuggling drugs in my experience. If these two are Saudis, then I reckon they were smuggling something other than drugs. Our guys are sweeping for fingerprints but the way they took care of these two, I doubt we'll find anything."

"Okay, Detective. We're both in a difficult place," said Camille. Riley flashed his eyes at Camille, struck by her saying "both" instead of "we're all", but she continued. "You work on your murders, and we'll try to work on the smuggling."

"Fair enough," replied the Detective. "Stay in touch, will you?" He asked, but doubted he'd be kept in the loop, no matter what the federal agent said now.

"I'll try," said Camille, "But you know how that goes." Riley flinched again about not being included. Camille was acting as if she were his superior. Technically she was, but why act this way? Would she treat all non-FBI agents the same? He bristled.

"Unfortunately, yes," said Dickerson. He hesitated, then said, "Where's the security guy? He left but hasn't returned. This way!"

The three of them scrambled toward the open door and ran down the street a block, and burst into the security office. George was sitting in a swivel chair, looking at a screen, when Dickerson yelled, "What are you doing? Where's that document you were supposed to bring us?"

The man jerked his head around, mouth agape at the angry officers. "Ah, ah, ah," he seemed dazed. Finally, he blurted, "Sorry, sorry. I'm trying to help. I pulled up the cameras. Look at this." Dickerson, Callahan and Richard realized the man was sincere. He'd gotten the idea of loading security footage and forgotten to bring the leasing document to them.

Sure enough, on the camera was a big Schlumberger well-logging truck going down the street with lights off. "Can't see any license number," the man said.

"Anything else?"

"Yes, I've been fast forwarding from midnight. There are several people walking into the building and a big SUV, maybe a Suburban, that was here and left before the truck."

"How many people?"

"Can't tell you yet – going too fast, but I can slow down now. I've only looked at last night so far. I do remember a flatbed truck was there a day or two ago."

Riley spoke first. "Ok, Detective, this is your show now. Do you want to take the tapes downtown or bring a man out here?"

Dickerson sighed and shifted his feet. "God, we're so short of manpower since Ferguson and Baltimore. I'd have to go to the chief to get priority. It's Sunday – he's probably golfing with some big cheese. Do you have the manpower to work on this today?"

Riley turned and addressed Camille. "Does the FBI?"

Camille regretted having to say, "I'm afraid I don't have jurisdiction yet to claim manpower. Perhaps the DHS could provide some." She meant some jurisdiction but Riley took her to mean manpower.

"I think I can grab a guy to get down here," he said, and looked inquiringly at George. "but I need you to stay here and help my guy."

George assented.

The three headed back to the warehouse, and each pulled a cellphone. While Riley phoned the Houston headquarters of the DHS for a person to help George, Camille began to call Robert Perez, head of the Houston FBI office, but hesitated, then phoned her father in Lafayette.

"Daddy"

"Bonjour, Cherie"

"Bonjour, Papa, I have a question for you."

"Yes, Cherie, what?"

"Why would someone use a Schlumberger truck to smuggle something?"

"Hmm. I suppose 'cause there's lots of room – or you could make room in it – but the reason for a specific Schlumberger vehicle would be because in some areas it wouldn't be noticed."

"You mean because it's common in some areas, like oil fields?"

"Yeah, really anything oil-related. A Schlumberger truck, anywhere in Texas or Oklahoma would not be unusual to anyone. Nowadays that could include Ohio or Pennsylvania."

"That makes sense. Anywhere there's oil activity. Thanks, Daddy."

Camille's mind started wondering – where could that mean?

"You're welcome, Cherie. Anytime."

"I know. Goodbye, Daddy."

"Wait – one more thing, though. Another reason could be if they wanted to smuggle something radioactive."

"What? What do you mean?"

"Well, some logging is done with radioactive tools, so well-logging trucks are identified by signs on the side – warning signs of radioactivity. I suppose if you wanted to smuggle something radioactive, a Schlumberger logging truck would raise no suspicion to a cop with a Geiger counter."

Camille's mind raced, and her heart got anxious. "Oh, that's scary... Gotta go, Daddy. I love you."

"Je t'aime, Darlin'."

Camille, took a deep breath and immediately told Dickerson and Riley. "We gotta look for radiation. Daddy says logging trucks are marked with radioactive signs."

"Whoa, Cammie, slow down. Explain what you mean. What's a logging truck?"

"It carries tools to put down a well to see what's down there. Well-logging trucks are marked with radiation symbols, so if someone were smuggling radioactive material the truck would draw no suspicion."

Riley understood the implication. "Shit. You find out what kind of radioactive material they carry and I'll get some equipment over here to test the area."

A phone call to a Schlumberger office got Camille the answer. "The primary radioactive tool used a combination of Beryllium and Americium-241," she told the men, then added, "I'll call Perez. He can get the FBI's WMD crew over here." However, Perez's response was that Houston's WMD crew was on a training course at Langley.

Riley thought that number sounded suspiciously close to

Uranium-238. He called the DHS headquarters to request the Mobile Radiation Detection Unit but learned it was busy at the docks. Riley ended the call and turned to the others.

"Kirkmeyer says the mobile detection crew is tied up at the port and won't be available for hours. Maybe 4-6 hours."

"Shit," Dickerson blurted. "In that time, they could go anywhere in the city or be all the way to Dallas. Further with their head start."

Riley said, "I'll call the physics department at University of Houston. Maybe they can help. One of you call Rice."

Camille had another idea, "I know a guy at M.D. Anderson who might be able to help. I'll try him."

Dickerson said, "Okay, I'll call Rice."

Camille scrolled through her phone directory to find the number of Monroe Jahns, radiation physicist at M.D. Anderson, Houston's premier cancer hospital. Jahns was a kind and thoughtful man who had comforted Camille when her mother was dying of cancer. He had taken time to sit and talk to Camille and her father during those dreary, dreadful days and nights at the hospital. She remembered that he was a kind of fanatic about radiation.

"Mr. Jahns? This is Camille Richard. We met at M.D. Anderson a few years ago." The fact that she said Mister rather than Doctor did not phase Jahns. Despite the fact that he had a Ph.D. in physics, working for nearly forty years in a large medical center meant you did not use the title 'Doctor' unless you were a physician.

"Ms. Richard," he said in the soft and gentle voice she remembered. "Are you the FBI agent? Yes, I remember you and your dad. But please call me Monroe."

"Fine, Monroe. I hope you are well. I remember that you said you have equipment that can measure different types of radiation."

"Yes, we have to monitor the radiation-exposure levels of our workers in x-rays or MRIs, etc."

"Can it measure exotic radiation? Like what's found in a bomb?"

Monroe sucked in his breath. "You mean like a dirty bomb?"

"Yes, exactly like a dirty bomb."

Monroe hesitated. "It's not what we use every day, but I do have that type of equipment in a storage facility. It's a hobby of mine."

"Is it portable? Can you bring it downtown?"

"Downtown?" Monroe's mind raced. "But I just can't take it down there without permission."

"Look, Monroe. I am with the FBI and I'm here with a DHS agent and a Houston policeman. This is an emergency and we need your help. I'll tell you what I'll do. You go get the equipment while I call the head of the hospital, I'll have him call you directly. But don't wait. Get the equipment now and come to Leeland Street. He will call you sometime before then."

"Ok." Monroe said. Fear of the immense damage that a dirty bomb would do motivated him to get the equipment. At the same time, he doubted the agent would get through to Dr. Rolston. How many times had he tried to get the hospital president's attention about improving radiation safety? He hadn't gotten through once. Not once. Now, he knew the rules about using the equipment outside the hospital, but it sounded like this situation overwhelmed any rule. Monroe knew the major result of a dirty bomb would not be death and destruction but rather terror and panic. Deaths would mostly be from whatever explosive device was used to spread the radiation, and the radiation would be dispersed so much that likely the only direct effects of the radiation itself would be minor. His entire career had shown Monroe several examples of radiation poisoning, but he'd seen the disastrous results of panic for a variety of reasons. Panic was much worse. Americans have an irrational and unhealthy fear of anything radioactive, which had led to the utterly stupid lack of nuclear power. The news of any amount of radiation in the air would cause panic. Hospitals would be overrun by hordes of people imagining radiation sickness – any sniffle or cough would send them screaming to the nearest medical center. Some idiots would even commit suicide in fear of suffering radiation poisoning.

Traffic was strangely difficult for a Sunday morning, then Monroe remembered there was something going on at the Co-Cathedral and the Rockets were playing their first exhibition game of the year at twelve o'clock. And maybe the Astros were at Minute Maid Park today. Still, it seemed early for the basketball crowd. Maybe they were having one of those gather-a-crowd gigs to get people enthused about the upcoming season. Getting close to the Leeland Street address, Monroe found the streets blocked. He called Camille, who had to direct his old Taurus past a checkpoint before he could get into the warehouse with his equipment. He saw two bodies being carried out in bags and placed in ambulances. At least a dozen police were keeping order as a small crowd of onlookers gathered. He unloaded his detector and started looking for traces of cesium or strontium, elements whose isotopes were most likely to be used in a dirty bomb.

CHAPTER FOUR

HOUSTON AND ABDUL'S PRIVATE JET

ABOUT 6 A.M. SUNDAY

This time Abdul answered the phone.

The Consul spoke urgently. "Al-Omari and al-Ghamdi are" – he started to blurt out "dead in the warehouse," but caught himself. Someone might be spying on their conversation. "Our drivers are missing – perhaps they're ill. Our equipment has been misplaced."

Abdul said nothing for a moment. "I don't understand."

Aziz thought quickly. "Our two truck drivers had too much to drink and are so drunk they might as well be dead. The truck they were to drive was not in the parking space."

Abdul responded, "I understand that the drivers are incapacitated. Can you get someone else to drive?"

Aziz grew frustrated but caught his tongue. "The truck can't be found. Neither can the doctor."

Abdul was slow responding again, thinking out his answers. "I understand that the truck is gone. Is the doctor missing too? I cannot turn the plane now. As soon as I get to Denver I'll call you and help you, God willing."

"Bless you, Abdul."

"Who could have hi-jacked it?" Abdul delayed his speaking as if thinking of what to say rather than saying what he'd planned for the occasion. "Perhaps the Zionists…"

"No," Mohammed responded immediately. "There's no way they could have known." Abdul was surprised at both Mohammed's response and his confidence. He'd been expecting Mohammed to grasp quickly onto the old Arab bugaboo. "There's no one in the plan who would go to the Zionists."

"What about spies?"

"No. We kept it so tight – so few people – it's not the Zionists."

Abdul thought of another, "Perhaps the King found out and wants it back."

Mohammed's mind was racing. He decided that it was possible--someone might have told the King. "No, the King would simply have demanded it back."

"Perhaps he wants to use it in his own fashion but blame you and me."

"That's possible, I suppose. He could have waited for us to smuggle it, then taken it for his own uses. Yes, that's one possibility. Who else?" Mohammed was almost pleading.

Abdul responded. "Husain is a possibility – he might have his own place to use it – his reasons differ from yours and mine." Abdul had put Mohammed's and his name together hoping that would take suspicion away from himself.

Mohammed paused, puzzled. "But how could Husain have the connections in America to arrange this?"

Abdul was getting concerned about someone listening to their conversation "Let me think about it. I'll get back to you and we can talk in more subdued tones."

Mohammed realized what Abdul meant, agreed and hung up. He felt more restless and more anxious than ever. It could be Husain or Abdul – or both of them together--or someone else entirely, even the King. Whatever had happened, it was in God's hands now. He tried to submit willingly and ease his anxiety.

How would they be using his bomb?

"Aren't there other Pakistani physicists in America? Maybe old friends of his?"

"Maybe. But unlikely, I think. I suspect it's the King or someone in our group." As he spoke it, Mohammed realized the person with the most connections in America, besides himself, was the man on the other end of the conversation, Abdul. He blurted out, "Did you take it?"

Abdul was taken aback, but not surprised. "No, of course not. I am no martyr. I have no desire to be a martyr. I was glad to be a part in your scheme, to do what I can, but this is your game."

Mohammed was apologetic but suddenly realized he could trust no one, not even Abdul. "Of course. Sorry I'm just mortified with what's happened. I can't tell who my friends are."

Abdul accepted the apology and tried to push the conversation away from himself. "Here's another idea. Perhaps the two Mohammeds were the ones attempting to steal the bomb, but were caught and the others are trying to carry out the mission."

"I thought of that, but why would they not contact me? Why couldn't Husain call me?"

"I don't know. But perhaps Husain is setting it up now."

"No. I've already driven to both bridges. No truck anywhere."

The Consul's plan had formed seven years ago when the King decided to start a nuclear weapons program. God bless the King, thought Mohammed. The King had provided Mohammed with a glimmering possibility, albeit a difficult one. The Consul's vision required several difficult achievements. The first giant requirement was absolute secrecy. Only a very few people could know – only those who involvement was absolutely necessary. Mohammed had to be careful – he could not afford to have someone decide loyalty to the King was more important than the bombing of Houston. Still, he'd need some other men involved due to the complexity of the operation. Second was a means to smuggle the bomb out of Saudi Arabia and into the USA. Abdul Faisal, the CEO of Crescendo Drilling, had said that he could accomplish that feat of smuggling, although Abdul stressed that he had no interest in becoming a martyr himself. Mohammed felt that Abdul was a gift from God and showed that God had provided a blessing on the bombing plot by putting Abdul in his path. He was perfect — Mohammed had known him as a boy. Abdul's oil drilling expertise brought him into common contact with the "fracking research" project, and that served as an introduction to Husain. The third requirement, of course, had been getting Husain to join his cause. Only Husain was capable of exploding a bomb — without his involvement, Mohammed's plan was stillborn. It eventually would take several years of coaxing and convincing to get the physicist Manzur Husain to admit that his plan would provide the revenge that Mohammed reckoned Husain deeply desired. Mohammed reasoned that his personable, intelligent and highly successful nephew might be able to convince Husain to join the group, and that had turned out to be true.

After speaking to Mohammed, Abdul arose and entered the back room of the airplane where a narrow bed promised comfort. Noor was already heating the oils for a massage. They had over an hour before preparation for landing in Denver, plenty of time for her to work out the stress knots in his neck and elsewhere. She'd already lubricated her vagina, knowing that this massage would climax like all the others, with Noor on top of his body, providing a release for the built-up tensions that more and more severely plagued the man she loved with her body and soul. As much as she did for Abdul, she wished she could do more to cure the misery in his heart.

CHAPTER FIVE

AT THE WAREHOUSE IN HOUSTON

AFTER 11 A.M. SUNDAY

Time dragged for Camille. They'd been there for more than a couple of hours, and her anxiety mounted. She checked her watch and thought to herself, exasperated, "God, it's already after 11. Why does stuff like this take so long?" The idea of a dirty bomb being smuggled into Houston nearly made her ill. She wanted answers now. There were just so many different places people could go with such a bomb — what could they do? She imagined they could take it anywhere--a spot where a Schlumberger logging truck would be unnoticed– that would be common on any Houston highway. Today there's a basketball game and tomorrow there's Monday Night Football at NRG Stadium. Her head ached with worry. At least Riley had dropped the Agent bullshit and was calling her Camille. Finally, Dickerson got a phone call and motioned to the Federal Agents. "George says they saw on the tapes a dark limousine going down the street early this morning after the truck had gone and before the police got here. Lights off – could not see a license number."

Riley spoke first. "Limo – could be drug dealers or perhaps a Saudi related to the dead men."

"No shit, Sherlock," Camille blurted, then immediately apologized as Riley glared. "I'm sorry, Riley. I thought the same – I'm just so nervous."

Riley hesitated, then said, "It's okay, Camille. I'm on edge too." Camille's mind raced, and settled on being grateful for wearing flats instead of heels this morning.

Suddenly a loud boom rattled the windows. Everyone in the building heard the explosion and automatically looked toward downtown, where the explosion seemed to come from. "Fuck! They used it!" Riley spoke for all of them. Camille's heart sank. Dickerson turned his scanner on, using the speaker so they could all hear. They listened breathlessly. "Toyota Center!" He spoke, disbelieving their misfortune. "The Rockets have their first preseason game. Shit!" Riley shivered with shock. Camille blessed herself and said a silent prayer.

The many cops in the building looked imploringly at Dickerson. He – they – knew they would be much more useful at the explosion site than standing around in an empty warehouse. Dickerson understood their desire to run to trouble and dismissed the uniforms – telling them to go to the Toyota Center to help. The crowd of cops evaporated as if ordered by angels. He dialed his supervisor but could not get through and left a message with the dispatcher for Chief of Police Canales to call him as soon as possible.

The DHS agent looked stunned. "Riley," Camille's voice was soft as she realized the implications of what had happened. "We're too late to stop them. Now we've got to concentrate on finding who did this."

He looked at her. "You're right, Cammie." Her heart lightened to hear his endearment, a small sunbeam in the horror descending on Houston.

"Oh, Christ, no!" Dickerson yelled. He looked up from his cell at the Federal agents, his face a mixture of anger and surprise. "Another explosion at the Galleria. It's Paris all over again."

Now Callahan looked as if he'd been punched in the gut. Camille grabbed his arm. She blessed herself again and earnestly prayed in her mind, "Sweet Mother of God, help us in our hour of need."

"Let's report in, and see what our next course is," he said, and she murmured agreement. "I imagine they'll want us to head in." But before they did, Jahns called them over. His voice was soft, as if it were walking on eggs. "I don't think that was a dirty bomb at Toyota," he said. "I don't see any evidence of Cesium-137 or Strontium-90, the most common isotopes that might be used for a dirty bomb. I see a lot of Americum-241 but some traces of U-235. That's the stuff in a real bomb. And much too difficult to obtain to use in a dirty bomb, I'd think."

"A real bomb--you mean like an atomic bomb like the one used in Hiroshima?" asked Dickerson.

"Yes, like Hiroshima."

Now everyone was stunned into silence. They looked at Jahns, then at each other as if reaching for comfort. Dickerson was the first to speak. "Are you sure?"

"That's what I see. I'm seeing concentrations of Americium-241 and a little U-235, on one particular area of the floor and on the blade of that big saw. The Americium is used in smoke detectors and some industrial measurements and in well-logging tools in the oil business. The U-235 is only used for atomic reactors and weapons as far as I know. No Strontium-90, and no Cesium-137.

"Mr. Jahns, how would they use this stuff?"

Riley interrupted her," I'll get the Mobile Unit here right now. No need to call the university."

Jahns spoke slowly. "I've scanned three times because I want to be wrong," claimed Jahns. "I'll call some friends at U of H to confirm, but I'm pretty sure. I'm not an expert on what an atomic bomb can do, but I had a roommate at Cal Tech, Bradley Holland, who got his doctorate in nuclear physics and who works at Los Alamos. Well, I suppose he's retired now-he's my age. Anyway, he's an expert on nuclear weapons."

Riley seemed to grow taller. His demeanor changed and his presence suddenly commanded everyone's attention. "No. Not yet. As of this moment, DHS is taking control of this scene. I have got to notify Washington. I'll have to get confirmation from the Mobile Detection

Unit. Right now, each of you has to promise me that you will keep this completely secret. You cannot tell anyone, not your wives or your family. Dickerson, do not tell Canales yet. Jahns, do not tell your boss. Tell no one until I get approval from Washington." All grimly said they understood the need for secrecy.

Dickerson's phone rang and he held up his hand to the others while he listened. "Yes, sir. I'll be right in to report." He paused, listening. "Any details you can share?" Another pause. "Yes, sir, it is definitely related." He looked at the two agents. "The blue paint on his shoes means he was in the building I'm standing in. I'm headed in now." He looked at the two agents – "All that was left of the Toyota bomber was a pair of shoes with blue paint on the bottom."

"Shit," said Riley. The three shook hands. Riley looked Dickerson in the eye. "No matter what the protocol, we three have to stay in touch and share what we know. You will hear from me," he promised.

"Good luck," said Dickerson, and Camille answered. "God be with us."

Camille could barely breathe. A hundred thoughts rushed into her brain. It couldn't be: a nuclear bomber in Houston – all these people – America's fourth largest city. It could destroy half the country's refining capacity in one burst. All that death and destruction wouldn't fit in her head.

"Camille," Riley said. "Call that nuclear guy and learn what you can."

Camille's mind raced, trying to trying together the few pieces of evidence. 'A logging truck? That explains the radiation, but why U-235? And why in this place? If it's a real Schlumberger truck then it'd be painted in a Schlumberger yard. So it's been painted to look like a Schlumberger truck. Why that? Obviously, the conclusion is that they are smuggling something – logging tools? Not hardly. Using logging tools to hide radioactivity?' Her mind took that from probability to possibility to certainty. 'What other reason to use a fake logging truck?'

CHAPTER SIX

POJOAQUE, NEAR LOS ALAMOS, NEW MEXICO

A FEW MINUTES LATER

After Jahn's recommendation, Camille had pulled up on her smart phone the FBI file on Bradley Holland and had had ten minutes to scan it before dialing.

A woman's voice answered, "Hello."

"Hello, Mrs. Holland?"

"This is Mizz Brightwater." The edge in the voice, a little too forceful with the correction and Camille realized she'd offended the woman. She remembered the file – this was Holland's third wife.

"I apologize Ms. Brightwater. Is Dr. Holland available? I need his help. This is Special Agent Camille Richard of the FBI."

The sound became muffled, as if a hand was placed over the speaker, but Camille could hear the voices. "It's the FBI. She says she needs your help. I'll run her off."

"No, gimme the goddamned phone."

Camille remembered the file mentioned his antipathy toward the FBI.

A gruff voice shouted into the phone. "The FBI? You want me to help the fucking FBI? The Fucking Bureau of Investigation? No fucking way!" The phone slammed down.

Camille felt as if she'd been slapped. She forced herself to calm down, told herself that brains and education didn't prevent rudeness, then redialed. The phone rang several times, then went to voice recorder. She left a message saying that he had been recommended by

Monroe Jahns, that she needed his expertise, and would explain why when they talked. Then she dialed again. This time she left a message that she'd keep dialing until they spoke. This time the woman answered.

"He does not want to speak to you. Go away."

"I'm sorry, Ms. Brightwater. This is a national emergency and I need to speak to him."

"A national emergency? What?"

"I'm sorry, Ms. Brightwater. I need speak to him directly. Tell him Monroe Jahns said he was the one person who could help me. Now, please."

Josie hesitated. "Okay, but I'll have to go outside. He went to ride his horse to calm down. Let me warn you, though. Don't mention the FBI. You guys ruined the career of one of our friends, Shih-Hua Wu, and Bradley is very angry about it still, 20 years later."

Camille thanked the woman, then waited many minutes until the gruff voice spoke.

"What sort of national emergency?"

"It relates to your explosives."

"That's vague. I'm retired. Talk to one of those young punks at Los Alamos or Oak Ridge."

"I'm sorry, sir, but I need an expert on outdated technology." As soon as the words came out, she realized she'd blundered again.

"Outdated, am I? Fuck off!"

She dialed again, and the woman answered. "You upset him again! You're going to give him a stroke!"

"I'm so sorry, Ms. Brightwater. But I need him. Please let me try again."

The gruff voice came on again. "What?"

"I apologize again, sir. Not outdated, just out of use. The young guys just aren't familiar with this technology and I have a very short list of names. After you is Amir Tacawy."

The voice erupted in anger again. "Tacawy! Don't you dare call that right-wing meatball son-of-a-bitch! Tell me what you need and I'll see."

"One last thing, Doctor. I need you to get on a secure line. I'm not sure your house line is secure."

"You damn well know it's not secure. You bastards have been tapping my line for years. You can damn well talk on this phone."

"Yes, Dr. Holland, the NSA has been listening on your phone." Camille surprised herself with her boldness. "But so have other countries. It's because you are a national asset. We have to protect you from those other countries!"

Holland's voice softened with the compliment. "I suppose you're right."

"Now, because I'm in a hurry, I've had a secure phone headed to your house. Think of some place where people won't be able to hear. Is there a park or library or church nearby?"

"My backyard covers five acres. That ought to be safe."

"Agreed, the courier will be there shortly. Please go into the backyard alone – far enough away from there that no one can hear. Not your wife or the courier. Understood?"

"Yes…" His voice trailed as if he were going to say "ma'am" or something, but he caught himself – just couldn't be nice to an FBI agent.

"Okay." She gave him her number and told him to call as soon as he could.

An interminable 20 minutes passed before the phone rang. "Richard here."

"This is Holland."

"Ok, Doctor. Please understand that I am totally ignorant of all this stuff but need to know."

"Of course – what's happening?" Camille realized that he meant her ignorance was a matter of course.

"Doctor, we have evidence to suggest uranium-235, perhaps a bomb, has been smuggled into the US by terrorists."

"Are you sure? Not stuff for a dirty bomb?" Holland seemed dumbfounded and disbelieving.

"Radiation sensors in the smuggling area in Houston show uranium-235, that's what Jahns says, in small quantity but no cesium or strontium.

"Is Monroe using a scintillator?"

"Yes. He says it's the latest model."

"Is he there? Let me talk to him," Holland demanded.

"Yes? Brad?" Monroe said in a deferential tone.

"Monroe! Do you remember me?"

"How can I forget the time you rat-fucked me?" He answered, speaking of an incident when Holland and buddies had locked Jahns in the stairwell of their dormitory at Cal Tech and poured a trash can full of water on him.

"That was a good one!" shouted Holland. "But tell me exactly what you're using for detection and what you'd found."

Jahns described the scintillator he had and what he'd measured in physics terms that neither of the agents nor Dickerson could follow. To them, it seemed like the physicists were speaking a completely different language. After a few minutes, he handed the phone back to Camille.

"Richard here," she said.

"Serious business," replied Holland, subdued.

"Yes, there are several areas I wish to explore with you. First, how much damage could a nuclear bomb do?"

"Let's see. Let's assume it's a small bomb. Houston's spread out. Even the smallest bomb would destroy everything and everyone within three miles. If it were dropped from a plane and exploded two thousand feet from the ground, it would cause even more damage. The damage would not be just people – the bomb would destroy all the refineries in Houston. How much is that? Half the country's capacity?"

"Something like that. From a plane?"

"Yes, think of what you can see from the ground, and how far you can see from the top a building. Up to a point, the further the bomb can see, the more damage it can do."

Camille flashed on the bridges over the ship channel. "From a bridge?"

"Well, a bridge doesn't get very far up above the surface of the ground, but yes, from a bridge would cause slightly more damage than from the ground."

"So, we should look for airplanes, for any bridges, or the tops of buildings."

"Anywhere, really. From the ground would be plenty of devastation. But I wouldn't worry too much. Having a bomb isn't enough. It's not easy to explode a nuclear device. It takes sophisticated technology and experience."

"Who?"

"A nuclear scientist," he said in an exasperated tone. "But who? Aren't all the rogue Pakistani physicists dead?"

"Yes, but lots of people have nuclear technology, and we can't track all of them. Think of all the nuclear power stations in France, and their homegrown terrorists."

"Nuclear power stations? Hah!" Camille could tell she'd offended Holland again. "Those guys are engineers, not scientists! All they do is drop the rods into the boiler and pull them out."

Camille tried to change the subject. "What about Iranians?"

"Nah. They have yet to actually detonate a weapon, and experience counts, I promise. I'd be more worried about Koreans."

"We do watch them closely, I'm told. We think the smugglers are tied to the Saudis."

"What? Nonsense. The Saudis need us for protection, and they have no nuclear capability of any kind, just a small nuclear power station."

"Not the Saudi government. But some Saudis are involved. Think 9/11. Think Osama Bin Laden."

"Okay." He corrected the point. "Let's say Saudi extremists, and certainly they have enough money to buy any nuclear scientist."

"Even an American? Do you think that is possible?"

"An American, or even Chinese, you bitch. Wu was a great friend and you destroyed him."

Camille let Holland rant, but she knew from the file that Wu actually had been spying on his American friend, even if he did not want to believe it. She attempted to bring the conversation back.

"What kind of technology is needed to detonate the bomb?"

Holland stopped, gathered his breath, and then spoke slowly. "You have to force the uranium nuclei together — by that I mean the nuclei naturally repel each other with a certain force. You have to overcome that repelling force with even greater force in order to begin fission. The fission is the nuclear explosion. And you have to have just enough uranium or plutonium, that's called critical mass. But it requires just the right amount of force in just the right amount of space and just the right amount of material. It's delicate and forceful simultaneously. That's why it's so difficult and that's why you need experience. It takes a lot of practice to get it right. But we know how. So do the Koreans and Pakistanis and Indians and French and Brits. And Russkies and Chinese."

Camille took a deep breath and spoke softly. "I'm feeling overwhelmed here."

"Look Darlin', I'll help you. Tell me what you need to know."

Camille was surprised at his term of endearment, but understood it was a reaction to her plea. He seemed to really want to help. She recovered and spoke firmly, "How do we find it?"

"Listen, Miss Richard. Here's a dirty little secret. Properly shielded uranium is almost impossible to detect with a scintillator. You'd have to be standing practically on top of it. Even standing on top of it, you wouldn't detect it."

"What do you mean, properly shielded?" asked Camille.

"With a lead shell only 10 centimeters thick, a scintillator would not pick up any radiation if only a half-meter away."

"10 centimeters?" queried Camille. She knew a meter was about a yard.

"God," exclaimed Holland. "Americans and their damned inches and feet! Idiots. Ten centimeters would be four inches. Take a block of uranium and put it inside a sphere whose lead shell is four inches thick. You know what a medicine ball is, don't you?"

"You mean like in phys ed?" winced Camille.

"Goddamn, exactly like phys ed," said Holland. "Or think beach ball."

"Yes, sir. I understand this, you could put a bomb inside a beach ball of lead and we couldn't detect it?"

"Listen! I did not say we could not detect the uranium. I said we could not detect properly shielded uranium with a scintillator. What we have to do is make the uranium fluoresce in order to detect it."

"What do you mean?"

"Think of...say, a Halloween costume that glows, say a skeleton with glowing ribs. You show light on it and when you go outside it glows in the dark. It's fluorescence that makes it glow."

"Yes. My daddy had some fishing lures we'd use at night. He'd shine a flashlight on them and then they'd glow, so the fish could see the lures in the dark water."

"Exactly. That's just what we do. Take a container off a ship. We run it through what we call a nuclear car wash. The container is zapped with gamma rays, and if there's anything radioactive, then it glows, like your fishing lure."

"Even if it is what you call properly shielded?"

"No, not exactly. If properly shielded, the lead medicine ball shows up as a dead spot on the picture, so we know we have to investigate what's in the dead spot. A dead spot is like a neon light that says something is being hidden."

"So do we zap all containers?"

"Of course not! That would take forever! There are too many containers and too few nuclear car washes. Almost 7 million containers enter the US every year – some ships carry 3000. To inspect every single one would be impossible. Anything suspicious gets checked, of course, or everything coming from certain countries. And then they pick some at random, just like going through customs. It's not just containers, either. Every ship that enters any American harbor gets zapped on entry. There are detectors on the ocean bottom at the entrance to every harbor. Every tourist on every cruise ship gets zapped and doesn't know it. Every bag on every ship or airplane entering the country, every person on every airplane. We're all getting zapped because it's too important to ensure no uranium gets in. The control of uranium doesn't start there. It actually starts at every uranium mine. Every ounce is counted. The IAEA knows how much is mined and how much goes where. Detailed tracking across the globe."

"So how could it get out?"

"Come on, you're FBI. You're supposed to know people. There's theft and bribery to start with. Lots of money to pay a guard to look the other way. Don't you know that?"

"Of course. Please. I'm getting the picture."

"Ok, we've got a great plan in place to keep track of nuclear materials and prevent it from entering the US. But there are plenty of disgruntled rich people like Osama bin Laden who will act against their country's best interest because of ideology. Look, in 2013, we shipped 15 pounds of uranium from Indonesia to the US as a test. The uranium was not detected. That illustrates the problem. No matter how much we try, we aren't going to catch it all, even if we didn't have to worry about bribes and treason. And who do we have guarding the posts and manning the scanners? TSA agents, border agents and such. Ever hear of a border agent taking a bribe from a drug cartel? How we gonna keep our nuclear guards from taking bribes?"

"Aren't they military?"

"Some, but not all. Depends on what they are doing. Anyway, the best laid plans of mice and men oft go ugly."

"So where will they take it?"

"You're asking me? You're the FBI! What's your idea?"

"Well, I think Houston would be a great target because of the oil industry. Or they could take it to Washington or New York maybe."

"First they have to carry it to wherever they are going to assemble the bomb. If they were going to use it in Houston, I think they would have assembled it there in the building you're in."

"Perhaps that was the plan. We found two dead Saudi men here. There are lots of questions. Did they take the uranium out of the lead ball? Were they trying to assemble the bomb? What happened? Who killed them and why? Did someone else kill them and steal the bomb?"

"It's not a bomb yet. You'd have to transport the uranium in two separate pieces lest you accidentally get critical mass. So, you'd have two medicine balls. They'd be heavy, but no problem for a hoist, even an engine hoist could do it." Camille focused her eyes at the two hoists near the wall.

Holland continued, "Then uranium needs to be removed from the two medicine balls and put into the bomb framework. Although not balls. They'd be lead cubes to keep from rolling. I suspect it's the Little Boy design, that's the easiest to construct. But still takes a lot of skill. Perhaps some U-235 leaked out when the lead cubes were being opened. No, Monroe would have seen a hell of a lot more uranium if they had been opened. I'd say they are taking it to wherever they are going to use it, cut the cases open, and assemble the bomb there."

"What do you mean by the Little Boy design?"

"There are two basic designs. The Little Boy is a cylinder, like a rifle barrel. The Fat Boy is a sphere. Deadlier, but more difficult to make and use."

"So, if the uranium is in a lead ball here in Houston, how did Monroe detect it?"

"I suspect there's a leak in the shields. Perhaps one got broken during transport." He paused. "Wait! Monroe said he'd gotten signals from the saw blade. They must have begun cutting the lead case open, then stopped before extracting the uranium."

Camille thought she knew the answer, but wanted to be sure, so asked, "What other elements did he find?"

"U-235, U-238, dominated by Americium-241," said Holland. "That's used in smoke detectors and oil-well logging."

"Yes, we know," Camille said. "We think the material is being transported in a well-logging truck."

"Of course! Brilliant plan!" Holland instantly understood the implication while Camille was lost in her ignorance of nuclear physics. Holland continued, "That Americium is a red herring!" His voice rose in recognition and excitement. "With a thin coating of Amercium-241 painted on the lead, the dead spots would not be dead, they'd show up as cubes of Am-241 especially if stamped logging tools. Nobody would take a second look. Anything else will be considered trace contamination. Ingenious! Good thing you had Monroe there."

Camille felt an urgency to tell Riley and Perez and Dickerson. "Thank you, Doctor Holland. I confess that I am overwhelmed here. You have been very helpful and I probably will have more questions. I ask you to please not tell anyone, not even your wife. Call me on the secure line if you have any thoughts you think can help us or I will call you with questions. Tell the courier to return to base but you keep the phone. Don't let anyone use it. I imagine people in Washington will call you to confirm what you've told me." She hesitated. "Perhaps you and Mr. Jahns could talk and think of something."

"That's Dr. Jahns," said Holland indignantly.

Another detective, a short muscular round-faced black man with short black hair speckled with grey, interrupted the three men standing near Camille. "Detective Dickerson, we found a fingerprint on the wall in the bathroom. The people who wiped the place weren't as thorough as they thought."

"Have you submitted it?"

"Yes. It came back as Mohammed al-Omari, who works at the Saudi consulate here in Houston."

"Good! Find the Consul, Jones. Interview him and the others at his compound. Farman, you go as translator."

"Yes, sir," they replied simultaneously.

CHAPTER SEVEN

WASHINGTON AND HOUSTON

SHORTLY AFTER NOON, SUNDAY

Camille rang off and found Riley had called. First, though, she dialed her boss, Robert Perez, who immediately said, "The directors will be on in ten minutes – get ready for a conference call. I'll be in our conference room if you can make it. Otherwise dial in. Ask Heather for the numbers." Then he abruptly hung up. Camille blushed in anger, and dialed Riley, wanting to tell him she felt sick with horror, but he simply said, in a voice firm and powerful, "I had to take the car to get over here for the conference call." She hung up and asked Dickerson for a police detective to drive her to the DHS office in the La Branch Federal Building twenty blocks away.

Camille entered the conference room in a hurry and sat down beside Perez. She gave a brief nod to the other members of her CID team: Larry Mozart, beefy ex-Marine: George Nyguen, a wisp of a man whose parents had escaped Viet Nam during the fall of Saigon and who, like Camille, had gotten into the FBI due to his language skills; and Mercedes Hernandez, with the same name as the small town in the Rio Grande Valley where she'd grown up and the only one of the four who had actually practiced law before joining the FBI. Camille's concentration, though, was on the wide screen, where she recognized sitting around a table the heads of several agencies: the FBI, DHS, NSA, and other people she did not know, but apparently heads of agencies. She wondered where they were seated, in the Situation Room in the White House, or maybe the NSA office. There were a couple of men in uniform. Several other people, mostly younger men and a few women, stood surrounding those seated. Clearly, introductions had already been made. As she sat down, David Bramwell, lanky Secretary of the Department of Homeland Security, was speaking, but was interrupted by heavily mustachioed Luis Ochoa, head of the Houston office of DHS and Riley's boss.

"I'm sorry, Sir, but we don't have time for questions," declared Ochoa. "We are not assembled just because of the suicide bombings in Houston today. We think a nuclear bomb may have been smuggled into Houston. I'm going to turn this over to our man on the ground, Riley Callahan."

Mumblings of surprise and astonishment swept the assembly.

Riley began, "Sirs, let me go through what we know. This morning we found a warehouse with two bodies in it who we believe are Saudis. We found traces of uranium-235 there, the kind used for nuclear bombs, but none of the cesium or strontium expected to be used in dirty bombs."

Ed Rosenberg, the skinny Director of the National Security Agency stood and raised his arms. A grey-haired man with bulky glasses that matched his bulky eyebrows, his intensity created a shiver. "Christ! Today is September 11th!" The implication froze everyone. They stared at him. "Perez, has this been verified by your WMD team?"

"Not yet, sir," replied Perez. "They were on a training mission at Fort Benning but are en route back to Houston now."

"Ochoa, what about your mobile detection unit?'

"They are on the way to the scene now."

"Christ! How do we know this is true?"

Perez replied, "We have a radiation expert from a cancer hospital on the scene who found the U-235."

Rosenberg seemed incredulous. "Christ! You mean all we have is a cancer doctor?"

Riley forcefully responded, "Dr. Jahns is a radiation physicist, sir, an expert in radiation. He knows what he is doing."

Rosenberg sat and slumped, then said, "Let me know when it's confirmed."

Bramwell continued, "The President needs to know this. Ms. Ehni, find him, and let him know we will contact him soon." A slender dark-haired woman dressed in black, nodded her head and headed for the door, punching her phone. "Now, Agent Callahan, you may proceed. "

Riley took a deep breath, then continued. "The two suicide bombers in Houston today were connected to the uranium and the bodies. They had the same paint on their shoes as the two bodies in the warehouse so we think they were all involved together, but fortunately there was no radioactive material in their bombs. We're thinking that perhaps the two in the warehouse decided not to be suicide bombers, but were shot for that. The truck involved in smuggling is an oil-field truck, common in all oil-producing states – that includes Pennsylvania." Some of the people in Washington squirmed, clearly uncomfortable with that knowledge. "Agent Camille Richard of the FBI has just spoken with a nuclear expert in Los Alamos. I'll let her speak."

Before she could begin, one of the older men at the table asked, "Couldn't uranium be used in a dirty bomb?"

"Yes, sir," Camille said, and repeated what Jahns had told her. "But it's so rare and difficult to obtain that it's unlikely to be used in one. So, we think we should assume it's a regular atomic bomb. Now, our expert…"

The first question seemed to open the floor for others to speak, and several eagerly started talking over each other. Bramwell cut them off. "Let Agent Richard finish, then you can ask questions."

Camille began again. "Our expert in Los Alamos, Dr. Bradley Holland, says that a nuclear bomb could destroy all of downtown

Houston and all of its refining capacity, which is nearly half the refineries in America."

A tall, fat, bespectacled man with wild black hair standing in the back of the room interrupted loudly. "That's nonsense!" he shouted. Bramwell and the others turned and looked at him. "Houston has less than 10% of America's refineries. That 50% number is an old wives' tale. It arose because along the Ship Channel is Houston you have a large concentration in one place. You'd have to include all the refineries in the Gulf Coast, from South Texas to Alabama, to reach 50%."

"Thank you, Doctor Zimmerman," said Bramwell, and turned back toward Camille. "He's our infrastructure expert," he explained.

Camille was flustered and thrown off-balance. "Sorry, that's what I was told."

"What else were you told?" asked Bramwell.

"Easily a half-million people dead or injured, and radiation poisoning would continue for years." She was guessing at the number, and hesitated, waiting to be corrected again. She did not want to be caught with incorrect information twice. With no response, she continued. "The real impact would be economic. When Hurricane Ike hit Houston a few years ago, the closure of the harbor cost 400 million dollars of lost business in three days. An atomic bomb would close the harbor for many, many years. The loss of the Ship Channel refineries would affect the entire country. Take away half – 10% of the gasoline in this country – think of the implications. For the most damage, the bomb would be dropped from a plane, but being detonated from the top of a building or a bridge would be very damaging, even from the ground would destroy downtown, the refineries and the harbor."

Zimmerman interrupted again. "Actually, Houston is the terminal for several critical pipelines. Several pipelines come there from offshore and from South Texas. Some of those major pipelines serve the Northeast. That would cause more of an impact than the refineries themselves. Remember, 92% of our transportation fuel in this country comes from oil..."

Bramwell brusquely cut him off. "Dr. Zimmerman, I want a full assessment of what an atomic bomb in Houston would do to our infrastructure. Have it to me in an hour."

Zimmerman seemed abashed but eager. "Yes, sir."

Several men started asking questions again in raised voices now. Bramwell cut them off again. "Gentlemen, clearly we must establish some priorities and chains of command. But right now, I want to hear what Agent Callahan and Agent Richard have to say. "

Riley began to speak but got interrupted by Bramwell again. "Sorry, but I'm ordering the Special Investigative Unit to Houston. We need the very best down there." Camille and Perez shuddered at the news, as they knew the implications of the DHS taking over the investigation and the consequent weakening of the FBI's abilities.

Riley began again, speaking directly to the head of the NSA in Washington. "Mr. Rosenberg, please speak with the President. Let us know your priorities and plan of action as soon as possible. To simplify things, please direct all Houston questions to Robert Perez, the head of the Houston office of the FBI. Mr. Perez and Mr. Ochoa of the Houston DHS are working together." Camille admired Riley's masterful redirection.

Perez took the cue and continued, "After this meeting, we will inform the Mayor, the Governor and the National Guard. Still, due to the potential for panic, this must be top-secret — whatever your highest classification is, Mr. Rosenberg. Houston is in an uproar after the suicide bombings today. And there's Monday Night Football here tomorrow." More questions and murmurs arose from the group.

Again, Bramwell shouted them down. "Gentlemen, now we have no time for questions. I'm turning the meeting back to Mr. Ochoa. Agent Richard and Callahan have much work to do. So do all of you."

"Mr. Perez! Mr. Ochoa!" When Rosenberg spoke in his senatorial tone, everyone became quiet. "I'm not sure we want you to inform the Mayor and Governor now." He looked around the table and the others were nodding in agreement. "We will discuss this with the President and get back to you. Wait until you hear from us before informing anyone of the possibility of an atomic bomb."

"Yes, sir." Perez responded, understanding they must avoid a general panic.

The same conversation transpiring in Camille's mind was being voiced at NSA. "Ideas, people!" shouted the Director of the DHS. "I needed possibilities! Brainstorm! Call out your ideas, and we'll list them, along with your reasons. Then, one by one, we'll discuss each scenario."

"Call Schlumberger and ask them to halt all their trucks. Tell them a cell of terrorists is using an old truck of theirs. Then tell the Highway Patrol in all states to stop and investigate any moving Schlumberger vehicles."

"Worth a try but the Highway Patrol can't check every road."

"Get the Sheriff's departments involved too. We got to get lucky."

"How about a call to radio stations for anyone who sees a moving Schlumberger truck to notify the Highway Patrol? Same excuse – stolen by terrorists."

Perez replied, "We have an alert out for any Schlumberger logging truck in Houston. Any found will be investigated. In fact, Schlumberger told us that all their trucks have a tracking device mounted inside."

"Wouldn't the perps have removed such a device?"

"Yes, if they know it's there. If we find a truck without the tracker, we'll know got them."

"Ok, have you checked out Schlumberger's tracking yet?"

"Sir," Camille interrupted. "It's not a real Schlumberger truck, only painted to look like one. Their tracking devices will be useless."

Perez continued, "Nonetheless, Schlumberger is helping us. We'll have all their trucks accounted for some time today, and if any other is seen we'll know it's the one we seek. But we have to consider that the terrorists may have transferred the bomb to a different vehicle."

"What if they've changed vehicles?"

"I don't know. We have to get lucky."

"We might consider stopping all truck traffic."

"How could you explain that to the public?"

"We would say we are looking for conspirators of the suicide bombers, and we have information that says they are in a truck."

Camille whispered to Perez, who spoke her thoughts out loud to the group, "Maybe it's still in Houston. Maybe they had some difficulty getting it to go off. Maybe they are just waiting for the proper time."

"Good thinking, Perez. Let's blanket Houston looking for the damned thing."

"Already started, sir," replied Perez. But the WMD guys tell me we can't detect a properly shielded U-235 bomb."

Director Bramwell turned to Amir Tacawy, the NSA's expert on atomic weapons. "Is that true?"

A short thin man who looked as weak as his scraggly beard, Tacawy was a physicist who'd had a difficult time gaining acceptance in the United States. Born Egyptian, due to early brilliance he had been provided a full scholarship to the Moscow Institute of Physics and Technology. However, his experiences in Russia had soured him to the country, and he came to America seeking a position. His research work provided him several avenues, but he had eyes only for Princeton, so he could breathe the same air that Einstein had. He had difficulty getting government research grants due to his time in Russia and due to his vociferous denunciations of Russia and arguments for strong American weaponry. The CIA was concerned that attitude was part of an act, and followed him closely for over a decade before deciding he was on America's side. He had finally gained respect and ultimately made it to the NSA. He responded, "Unfortunately, yes, sir.

A properly shielded atomic bomb would not be detected with simple detectors. Probably a reason why they chose this weapon."

"What do you mean by properly shielded, and why can't we detect it?"

"If uranium is put into a lead container four inches thick, it's invisible to a scanner. That is why we use nuclear fluorescence machines at all airports and harbors. When we shower anything with gamma rays, it glows like the sun if it has anything radioactive, unless they are in a lead container. In that case, they show up on the screen as dead spots. Everything else fluoresces slightly, but not the lead. If we see a dead spot, a lack of fluorescence, we know there's something being hidden and we can check it out."

"Okay," said Bramwell. "Now let's consider the possibility it's elsewhere. Driving to its target in another state, or elsewhere in Texas. Let's assume they left the warehouse at five a.m. In that case, where could they be?"

DHS Director Ochoa was ready with the answer. "It's already 1 p.m. Houston time. If they went east on I-10, they could be in New Orleans already setting up the bomb. By six p.m. today, they could be all the way to Tallahassee. If they went north, they could already be in Oklahoma City, and by six p.m. could be in Kansas City. If they went northeast, they could be in Little Rock, and by six p.m. could be in Nashville. If they went west, they could be well past Austin or San Antonio by now, and by six p.m. could be past El Paso. If northwest toward Cheyenne Mountain and Denver, they could be in Wichita Falls by now, and by six p.m., could be past Amarillo. At 6 a.m. tomorrow morning, they could be in virtually any city in the country except perhaps Seattle or Boston.

"Why would they take the bomb to New Orleans when they already had it in Houston? Isn't Houston's port bigger?"

Zimmerman stepped in. "The difference is how the freight is handled. From New Orleans, shipments go up river all over the Midwest, all the way to Pittsburgh or St. Paul. More trains service the New Orleans terminal than any other. Also, don't forget the reputation for debauchery that New Orleans has. Remember the bomber in the gay night club. New Orleans would be a severe economic blow and make a morality statement at the same time."

"Makes sense," agreed Bramwell.

"If you discount the anti-debauchery statement, and the fact that more people would be killed, I think a more severe economic blow would be the Atchafalaya Dam," stated Zimmerman.

"What?"

"Blowing the Atchafalaya Dam would be a death blow to the ports of New Orleans, Baton Rouge, and South Louisiana. Combined, they are bigger than Houston's port, for sure."

"You gotta explain what you are talking about."

"Okay, but I've got to give you a little geology lesson first. The Mississippi River has not always been in its current course. Over thousands of years, it's been like an out-of-control garden hose, spraying all over south Louisiana. It would go down the Atchafalaya or the Bayou Teche, or even the present-day Mississippi, or somewhere else entirely, switching from one place to another, evening out the sediment across the entire southern half of Louisiana. Right now, it wants to go down the Atchafalaya, but human-made dams confine it to the Mississippi's course. If the atomic bomb were used to destroy what is called the Old River Control Structure, most of the water flowing down the Mississippi would divert into the Atchafalaya—that's the course nature wants—and there would not be enough water for ships to go to New Orleans or Baton Rouge. That would be a tremendous economic disaster for the entire country, not just Louisiana. And the bomb might create a big enough hole that it would be impossible to fix."

"Jesus. We have to put this dam on the list of likely targets."

"I think not," Tacawy interjected. "Although blowing the dam would be a tremendous economic blow felt for years, it would kill few people other than a few thousand living in the Atchafalaya flood plain. To date, the terrorists have always struck where they would kill people, and with an atomic bomb they'd want to kill hundreds of thousands. My point was that economically speaking you'd want to take out the dam, but the terrorists have other goals than economic. They want to kill people, too."

"At the least, let's beef up security at the dam," said Rosenberg. "General Marietta, will you contact the Corps of Engineers and take care of that?"

"Yes, sir."

"Note that the bombers could already be there," stated Zimmerman.

The General glared at Zimmerman, his clenched jaw pulsing. "Noted."

"What are the possible targets?" asked Bramwell. The ideas came: New York City, DC, Philadelphia, Fort Knox, New Orleans, Atlanta, Chicago, San Francisco, Los Angeles, Omaha, Las Vegas.

Riley spoke, "Sir, to date all the targets have been symbolic, the World Trade Center twice to strike at our financial heart, the White House to get the President and the Pentagon to hit the head of the military."

Someone interrupted, "The Pentagon and the White House were military targets in their minds. Cut the head off the snake."

"Ok, ok," Riley spoke louder. "The point is I think we have to consider a symbolic target. The White House is one, maybe the most likely."

Bramwell looked directly at Rosenberg, his eyes narrowing, as if they were communicating silently. Rosenberg nodded. Bramwell spoke, "We must get the President to Cheyenne Mountain. Is Molly Ehni back?"

The President's aide stepped forward from the back of the room. "Yes, sir, I've been listening. Are you ordering the President to Cheyenne Mountain?" The question was crucial for Presidential protocol. After last month's Executive Order, the Secretary of the DHS or the head of the NSA were the only ones who could order the President anywhere, and that was only in a time of national crisis. A positive answer would inform the President that the country was facing an imminent serious threat.

Bramwell hesitated and took a deep breath. He looked around the room. "Can anyone here argue that I should not give the order?" He looked at each person, waiting for a reply. In time, each person said, "No, sir."

Bramwell looked directly at Rosenberg, who nodded. "Yes, Ms. Ehni," he said gravely, with a lump in his throat. "Mr. Rosenberg and I are ordering the President to Cheyenne Mountain."

The President's aide rushed from the room, already speaking into her phone.

"Gentlemen," Bramwell spoke with authority but without acknowledging the women in the room. "We have failed in our first mission to keep nuclear weapons out of the United States. Now we must do everything we can to stop its use."

Several men started speaking at once. Bramwell held up his hand and spoke, "Director Ochoa, what you doing?"

Ochoa replied, "I'll let my Houston people respond."

Riley looked at Perez and Camille, then stated, "We have stopped all private flights beginning in Houston area airports. We have delayed all outbound public flights. We have shut down the bridges that we consider the most likely places to explode the bomb, in our way of thinking, citing security after the two suicide bombings. However, remember they have a three-hour head start. So the weapon could have been flown out of Houston before we were aware."

Bramwell interrupted, "What do we know about them, the suicide bombers?"

Camille spoke, "We know nothing about them except that they

were in the building where the truck was painted and the two bodies were found. One of them worked for the Saudi consulate. We don't know about the other. That's all we know at the moment. As we speak, HPD is headed to the consulate to meet with the consul. We will let everyone know what we find."

Bramwell whispered to an aide, "Who is she?"

"FBI, sir." Bramwell nodded.

Bramwell turned to the Director of the FBI, a rotund man on the opposite side of the desk. "Mason, was that in your brief this morning?" The tone, the timing, and the implication in the question demonstrated that these two men strongly disliked each other. Camille was astounded that they would let their personal animosity interfere at a time like this.

"Of course, Director." The tone was level but insinuating. "If you had taken the time to read it."

"Thank you. I must have been busy. Perez, what else can you tell me?"

"The WMD crew, when it arrives, will work with DHS's mobile unit to sweep the city, but as stated before, it's unlikely that we'll find anything if they know what they're doing. We have not told the governor nor the mayor yet as we wanted to clear it with you. We are worried about panic if word gets out. Besides, they have their hands full with the suicide bombers."

"Rightfully so. What are you doing outside Houston?

"As stated before, we have an alert out to stop all Schlumberger trucks. But it's been hours now. They could be all the way to Oklahoma now, or in Louisiana."

"Then let's think ahead now. What targets do we have to protect?"

"Disney World," Riley blurted out.

"Holy shit. All those children," muttered Bramwell. "Do you really think they would?" As he spoke, he realized he already knew the answer.

"Of course," Riley said. "They haven't hesitated to kill children in Syria, in Nigeria, anywhere. If you wanted to create terror, or to bring on the final war with the West, what better way?" Not just symbolism, but a strike that this President could not ignore."

"CIA, have you heard any chatter about such a thing?"

The rotund black man, who had gone from a simple music degree to military intelligence to law school and had worked his way up the ladder to the top of the CIA through obsessive drive, pushed his large-rimmed glasses back and wiped his glistening forehead. "No sir, but with that idea we will reassess. However, if 9-11 is significant to these folks, the bomb will go off today. We need to focus on Houston."

"Yes, yes," responded Bramwell defensively. But we must check out other possibilities, and other potential targets, including Disney World. Ochoa, double your efforts to check vehicles traveling near Orlando."

Camille inserted, "There's lots of oil activity in the western panhandle, so the logging truck would be able to get that far without suspicion. There is little oil activity in Florida other than in the western part of the panhandle. Past there, they'd want to transfer vehicles, and they could be there soon." She felt sick as she realized what that might mean.

Ochoa spoke, "We will concentrate on logging trucks in western Florida, starting now." He whispered to an aide, who swiftly left the room.

Someone spoke, "Will somebody explain what this logging truck is? Obviously, you are not talking about what I think a logging truck is."

Camille spoke, proud to show her knowledge. "It's a big truck that carries tools that are lowered into a well to log it, that is, to measure the rocks in the hole to see if there's oil in there."

"So it's big enough to carry a bomb?"

"Yes sir. About the size of a large garbage truck."

"Christ, what do we look for next? A school bus with a bomb?" The problem looked insurmountable, and all were depressed about the prospects of locating the bomb.

Bramwell interrupted, "Targets, folks. What other targets? So far we've got Houston, NYC, Disney World, the White House."

Mason spoke, "We could go on all day talking about targets. Those are four great ones; there may be a dozen more. Unless we can get inside the heads of the terrorists, who knows what they are thinking. I say, concentrate on those four until the eavesdroppers find something concrete. Now, what about informing the governors?"

Bramwell went stiff at the challenge to his authority. He had to force control over the urge to shout at that fat pig Mason. He calmed down, then said, "It's my opinion that we not tell the governors about the weapon. If word leaks, there will be panic. Let's just tell them that other terrorists are on the loose and we are looking for them. Anyone disagree?"

Again, he went around the room and got "No, sir."

"Okay," he said. "Let's end this meeting, learn more, do more. When you find something let me know. Be available to reconvene in 20 minutes notice."

Ochoa interrupted. "Excuse me, sir. We have found the well-logging truck abandoned at a truck stop. Whatever it was carrying has been transferred to another vehicle, a different truck we expect, one probably not a well-logging truck."

"Shit," murmured Bramwell. "Was that before or after you sent out the APB?"

"After." He wondered why Bramwell thought that was significant. "I just got the message that an alert patrolman spotted it and investigated."

"So, it could have been transferred when someone heard we were looking for a Schlumberger truck. We must have a leak."

Mason interrupted. "Not necessarily. That could have been the plan all along, especially since it appears it was stolen. More important, it could be in any kind of truck now."

Camille began to speak, but Tacawy interrupted. "Worse, sir," said the physicist. "The bomb could be assembled and be in the vehicle with the detonator."

"Oh, God! " exclaimed Bramwell, exasperated. "What do we do now?"

Tacawy shouted down the others. "Sir, if the bomb has been assembled, then that means it lacks the thick lead cover. That means we could detect it with just a scintillator. We should mobilize all available detection units."

"What's a scintillator?"

"Like a Geiger counter, sir. It counts the amount of radiation given off by anything."

"Who handles the disposition of the detection equipment?"

"Several agencies, sir," said Ochoa. "The DHS has some at every port and airport. The Border Patrol has some. The military has lots."

"General Ujifusa?" Bramwell turned toward the Air Force representative on the Joint Chiefs of Staff. The man, whose family had been forcibly moved from Oregon and confined to a 'relocation camp' during the second world war 'for their own protection', had driven himself furiously with a desire to prove his loyalty to America all the way to the Joint Chiefs, responded, "Yes, sir, we have airplanes with radiation detectors at every air base."

"The Geiger counter kind or the nuclear car wash kind?"

"The scintillator type. As Tacawy says, we cannot detect through a heavy shield, but once the uranium is taken out of the shield, we should be able to detect it."

"That's true," said Tacawy. "But once it's assembled, we might have only minutes before it is detonated. So, we must be able to move quickly. Let me suggest we order all radiation detection planes to the major cities immediately. They are scattered all over the country right now, especially at the borders."

The Chairman of the Joint Chiefs, Admiral Schmidt, spoke for the first time. "I agree with Professor Tacawy. I will order all military aircraft with scintillators to cover the major cities. Bramwell, you do the same with DHS aircraft. Send your equipment guy to see General Ujifusa immediately so we can coordinate. We will need the National Guard mobilized in all the cities to aid the police in apprehension if the device is located. For that, you are going to need to inform the governors."

Bramwell felt both agitated and relieved that someone else was taking command.

"Okay, everyone," announced Bramwell. "Let's all take a deep breath and put our thinking caps on. Let's reconvene in 30 minutes with ideas. A brainstorming session."

Camille was pleased they were pausing. It felt like they were covering the same ground over and over, and making no progress. Her training had taught her to think things through carefully, then move on, building upon one's conclusions. The confusion and the bumbling at the meeting irritated her. Camille thought Riley had been masterful. His handling of his part of the conference, his differential manner while controlling the meeting when he had the floor, the tone of his voice. She glowed in feelings of admiration and love, then forced her mind back to the horrific monster staring at them. Simultaneously, Camille felt frustrated and angry. She knew what the SIU meant: that the head of the DHS did not trust the FBI to do its job properly. Was that because of the animosity between Bramwell and Mason? It meant that the FBI would be shoved aside, and the DHS would handle everything. She'd be fetching coffee or something. She's the one who had called their attention to radiation, thanks to her geologist father; she's the one who got an early reading of radiation, and now she would be shut out by the bureaucracy, thanks to her clumsy mistake in the conference. She felt sure Riley would keep her informed, if she ever got to talk to him again. She forced herself to get away from these negative thoughts, and get back to the question of where and who. Have they left Houston? The lack of any trace of radiation seemed to imply so. If not Houston, then where? Everyone had that same problem staring at them: where could it be? D.C. seemed most attractive to her mind, as it was the center of the government. The plane on 9/11 that went down in Pennsylvania was headed that way, so why not finish that job? If not the political and symbolic impact of D.C., what other reason than to hit an economic target? That's why Houston seemed so obvious. A 20% drop in oil supply back in the 70's during the oil embargo caused a leap in gasoline prices. What would a 50% reduction in gasoline supply create? Okay, not 50%, 10%. Just growing food and delivering it by trucks probably claims more than 10% of gasoline supply. There would not be enough gasoline to supply basic needs to others. And it would take years to replace those refineries. It would be chaos. New York City is the financial center of the West, not just the US, what could possibly be worse? Was there a place where half the electrical supply could be destroyed? She thought not. Hitting D.C. would be a terrific blow psychologically but Camille thought that somehow the country would get along just fine without a formal government. People would cooperate in a crisis. She'd seen that during 9/11 in New York City and during Hurricane Ike and the Tax Day and Memorial Day floods last year. If she were the boss, she'd concentrate on Houston, Washington, or NYC, as they were the most likely, and she'd forget anything else. Hard to contemplate, but in this situation, we might be forced to sacrifice a city in order to concentrate on saving the most critical places. It might mean losing a whole city like Chicago or St. Louis, but they wouldn't cripple the country like a loss of the oil capabilities of Houston. That was difficult to contemplate. Her mind raced.

CHAPTER EIGHT

ON THE ROAD

SAME SUNDAY MORNING

Dolecek could not recall driving a truck so old and out of date. The fact that the truck did not have digital log monitors meant it was at least 10 years old, but he was sure the two-ton GMC was more like 25 or 30. "Whatever they've got back there must be really heavy," he thought. He knew that they were smuggling something – you don't get this amount of cash up front each day unless there was something illegal going on. He'd never met his fellow driver before. Kern and he had each received verbal instructions on their cell phones. They were instructed where to meet, at Truckers Paradise on Loop 610, what kind of truck to seek - a white GMC with a box bed, and provided not only their first day's destination but even what roads to take. A dark blue Chevy Suburban passed and settled in front of them, and soon it became clear the vehicle was acting as a sort of buffer with traffic. Then Dolecek noticed a red Corvette behind them, following their every movement. "Wow," he thought, "Lots of cover." After Dallas, the three vehicles went off the Interstate highway and were restricted to back roads. No stops except for fuel and rest rooms. Fast food only. But absolutely no tickets, so that meant driving the speed limit always. Easy to do when money got your attention. $2,000 deposited upon acceptance of the job. $2,000 deposited every night. They were even given permission to check their bank accounts each morning. Then another $2,000 upon completion. Three days driving they'd been told. $12,000 for three days work; they'd be able to afford a plane ticket home.

The road rolled on and on. Every small town meant traffic lights and slow movement. Dolocek grew irritated with that, as they knew the interstate was a short distance away, with the speed that implies. But they plodded along. Every two hours they switched drivers, noticing that the Suburban and the Corvette did the same. Clearly their client wanted drivers fresh, and no messing with cops. Instructions said no more than 3 mph over the posted speed limit — and the Suburban was watching. What was the purpose of the Suburban anyway? "Why didn't those guys just drive the truck?" thought Dolecek and Kern. Eventually he noticed the men in the Suburban looked Middle Eastern or maybe Indian, and they realized their clients wanted Americans behind the wheel if the truck got stopped by police. Less suspicious. And he and Kern were ignorant of the cargo, too.

Clearly this age of vehicle meant they wanted no digital record of their trail nor of the hours they were driving. That's why they were told to bring paper logs. Kern had had to search in his attic to find some old ones.

The truck was well-worn, with cracked seats and a broken dashboard. Still, it drove fine, as if the engine had been overhauled for this trip. But why had a radio and cell phone been prohibited? All they had was a walkie-talkie with which to communicate with the foreigners in the Suburban and the Corvette.

FBI OFFICE, HOUSTON

TWO P.M., SUNDAY

Stunned by the introduction of the SIU into the case, Camille felt as if she'd been pushed aside by all the big boys, as if she were back in Lafayette with her brothers. They'd play with their little sister up to a point, then when things got exciting, a chance to play football or snag an alligator; they'd leave her and run off. She'd yell at them and complain to her parents, but the fact was, she was smaller, and younger, and a girl. That was then, though. Now she was a Special Agent for the FBI. She was an adult in great physical condition, had passed all the same physical and mental exams as the male agents, and she could shoot better than most. Rationally, she understood rank was the only deciding factor in this situation, but that understanding did not preclude ancient emotions from boiling up. She sighed, knowing that Riley would keep her in the loop, and concentrated on the task she'd been given, learning about the two murder victims and how they related to the smuggling. She called Detective Dickerson.

"Detective, what do you know now?"

"Hello, Special Agent Richard. How are you, Camille?" There was a special welcome in his voice. Camille realized Dickerson seemed to prefer working with female officers. He appeared more joyous around them. She thought he must have been quite a womanizer in his youth; and indeed that was true. Dickerson loved women, loved being around them, loved the joy they brought him. He simply felt more alive around women. He could not understand how age had made him invisible to young women, especially considering the way they made him feel.

"I'm fine, Detective. Sorry for forgetting my Cajun heritage. How are you?"

"Great, Camille, I suppose you want details?"

"Yes, sir." She could not see Dickerson wince when she said "sir".

"Both were popped off by a 9 mm, two bullets each; the second one to the head. We've gotten a fingerprint hit on one Mohammad Al-Omari, works for the Saudi consulate."

"I heard that. Have you heard back from Detective Jones at the consulate?"

"No. I've been overwhelmed by the bombings."

"Do you mind if I join him?"

"Please do. Just let me know what you find."

Camille rang the consulate and was initially told politely to call back tomorrow, but when she stated that an employee of the consulate had been murdered, the person stated that the consul was at home on Sunday, that he would call the FBI agent immediately. And in just a few minutes, her cell rang.

"Hello, Special Agent Richard."

"Hello," said a voice with a formal British accent. "This is Prince Mohammed Aziz, Saudi Consul in Houston. What about a murder?"

"Sir, an employee of yours, Mohammad al-Omari, was found shot to death this morning."

"No!" gushed Aziz. He hoped his practiced response sounded natural. "How?"

"Sir, I'll give you details, but I wish to meet with you in person. Some policemen are on their way to your house now. Have they not arrived yet?"

"Of course I will help you. No police have arrived. I'm at 27 Lazy Lane in River Oaks. Please come here. Or would you rather me go there?"

"I'll come there. Be there in 15 minutes or so." She was wrong about the time. The mess of emergency vehicles and street blockages forced Camille to find a way around downtown, and it took nearly 40 minutes. She reckoned that must have delayed Detective Jones, too. Twenty-seven Lazy Lane was a River Oaks mansion, of course. The Saudis did not mind flaunting their wealth, gained by selling oil to the West. Walking up the sidewalk to the front door she noted plastic pink flamingoes amongst the landscaping. "Do they know how bad plastic looks in a mansion? Do they know that flamingoes don't live in Texas?" She shrugged. Lots of money does not mean lots of elegance.

Detective Marion Jones was already there with Farman Yousif and had been questioning the people who worked at the Consulate. Camille approached him, re-introduced herself and asked, "What's your line of questioning?"

"We're trying to find out the basics, like their living arrangements, what mosque they attend, how they interacted with the suicide bombers and the dead men, that sort of thing."

"What do you think, Detective?"

"The Consul seemed genuinely distressed when we told him that al-Omari was murdered. He said he could not believe the man was involved in suicide bombing or smuggling or whatever. Said that he had been a model employee, was a reliable driver and mechanic. Said that al-Omari went to the mosque on Eastside Street. That's the one Olajuwon built."

Camille reflected on that. The mosque was known city-wide as peaceful and inclusive. Akeem Olajuwon was the face of Islam to many Houstonians. He continued to be extremely popular, maybe the most popular athlete in the city, although in that regard he might be in danger of being overtaken by J.J. Watt. She remembered that Olajuwon won a vote as Houston's favorite number 34, beating out local son Nolan Ryan and the legendary Earl Campbell. Quite an achievement, but the basketball player had brought Houston two championships. Above that, he was a model of kindness and generosity. From numerous charities to teaching the Rockets' young center how to play well,

Olajuwon generated warmth and affection from Houstonians, and had done a great deal to make Islam acceptable. Muslims were common in Houston, thanks to the oil business. They came from any Muslim country that Americans drilled wells in, from Indonesia to Nigeria, from Pakistan to Malaysia, as well as the Middle East. Houstonians had lived, worked, shopped, become friends with Muslims. Today's bombings would be a terrific shock to the city. She wondered how it would react. Not well, she imagined, from what she'd seen of humanity. "Have you sent anyone to the mosque yet?"

Jones smiled. "Not yet, Agent Richard. We just learned that fact."

"Sorry," Camille said. "Of course."

"We will soon," he replied with a smile. "I promise."

WASHINGTON, D.C.

THE BRAINSTORMING SESSION

Director Bramwell opened the session gruffly and without introduction. "Okay, let's see if we can identify the source of the uranium. Maybe that will give us a clue. Let's go through the list of nuclear powers: Us, Russia, China, Britain, France, India, Pakistan, Israel, North Korea. Let's eliminate the easy ones. I say North Korea is so self-absorbed that they would not be inclined. Anyone think otherwise?"

"It's possible," replied Director Rush of the CIA. Chairman Kim wants to yank on our chain any way he can. If he could smuggle a bomb in to our country and set it off, it would increase his status among his people and strengthen his hold on power."

"Do you think that likely?"

""No. And I don't think the North Koreans are well enough connected to pull it off."

"Next, Israel. The rancor with President O'Brien over the Iran nuclear deal is a short term spat, in my opinion. Anyone think they might do this?" There was a general response of "No".

"Okay, let's move on. Pakistan. My immediate reaction is that Pakistan is most likely. Not the government itself, but there are lots of Jihadists there inside and outside government, and it is well-connected to Saudi Arabia. It could recruit more Jihadists there. Let's suppose the Houston agent--what's her name?"

He turned and looked at his assistant, who said "Camille Richard."

"Let's suppose Richard is right and the Saudi's are involved in the smuggling. Director Ochoa, check recent shipments out of Pakistan on Saudi ships."

He turned to the head of the CIA. "Director Rush, I thought we'd nailed all the rogue nuclear physicists from Pakistan."

"Yes, we have, Mr. Secretary. All we've known of are accounted for. Of course, another could go bad and we not know about it until too late. But we are confident of our intelligence."

"Don't we monitor their arsenal?"

"Both us and the IAEA. But in a place as corrupt as Pakistan, there are ways to fool us if so inclined."

"Okay. I think we must move Pakistan to the top of our list. Anyone disagree?" No one disagreed.

"Next, India. Mr. Rush, what is your assessment?"

"India keeps its nukes ready due to frictions with Pakistan and China. We do not consider them likely. We know of no rogues there—they seem to be totally defensive minded."

"Fine. Let's move on. France?. "

"We have been concerned here due to the number of Jihadists in France and the fact that the number keeps growing. But we have seen no evidence of Jihadists in the nuclear power industry, of which they have the largest in the world- France gets 80% of its electricity from nuclear. And we have no concerns so far in weaponry-closely watched by both NATO and the IAEA."

"Great Britain?"

The CIA Director responded half-heartedly, as if he could not believe Bramwell might actually believe that Britain would do such a thing. "We have some of the same concerns we have with France, but no evidence of infiltration. Britain is a rock-solid ally."

"Russia?"

The CIA Director seemed more intensely interested in this possibility, leaned forward and furrowed his large black eyebrows. Despite a career in intelligence, his emotions showed openly in his face.

"Prime Minister Rasputin is a concern. Ukraine is just one example of how he is probing our weaknesses, and his psychology is such that he might try anything as long as the evidence does not point back to Russia. So, he would be a good candidate to try something like this. He has the ability to hire Saudi and Pakistani mercenaries to carry it out. Indeed, the only real question I have is how deep their connections are to Saudi Arabia and Pakistan. Russia has a big enough arsenal to do this. In addition, they are buying more uranium sources, including 20% of American's uranium resources with the purchase of the Canadian company Uranium One. Moreover, the 2011 assessment by the National Intelligence Agency indicated that when the Soviet Union collapsed, a significant amount of nuclear material went missing. Eventually the US worked with Russia to retrieve it, but since the records were so poor we don't' know how much was lost. We don't know who has it or where it is."

"Enough to make a bomb?"

"Easily. It takes only nine kilograms to build a Nagasaki-type bomb. And the Soviets had 45,000 nuclear warheads. Still, with all that, we rate Pakistan as being riskier than Russia."

"Okay, so let's put Russia and Pakistan at the top of our list right now."

"China?"

The CIA Director lowered his intensity. "Our opinion is, despite the rhetoric and grandstanding, China's economy is so dependent upon American trade that we think it highly unlikely they'd try anything like this, although they certainly have the capability."

"Finally, what about us, the U S of A?"

NSA Director Rosenberg said that the proper person to respond would be Director Ochoa of the DHS. Ochoa began, "The US has the best monitoring system of its nuclear arsenal of any country in the world. Still, things can happen. In 1979, nine kilograms of weapons grade U-235 was stolen from our facility in Tennessee. That is plenty enough to make a bomb, and it's never been recovered. The point is that it's possible that some material could be stolen from us, probably through bribery or blackmail, however unlikely, but still one would have to construct a bomb for the material, and that is a very difficult task and requires an expert. If that's what you were doing, though, why go through the rigmarole to do this smuggling? We are convinced this came from outside the country."

"What about nuclear submarines? Several have sunk over the years."

The Director of Naval Intelligence responded, "We can exclude those. The ships with unrecovered nuclear devices, whether ours or Russian, are in very deep water. To recover them would require an incredible effort, one that would not go unnoticed. We monitor those sites by satellite, but if the nukes were obtainable, we'd have them already."

"Okay," said Bramwell. "I conclude our most likely case is that this material was smuggled here from Pakistan or Russia, using Saudi agents. Even if that theory is true, it would still require a nuclear physicist to set off the bomb, wouldn't it?" When someone agreed, he continued, "The most likely candidate would be a Pakistani, as they are closest to Jihadists, but we can't rule out a Russian."

"Let's not forget the possibility of a rogue American physicist, through ideology or bribery." This thought brought more gray faces and tightened jaws.

"God," he said out loud while his mind roiled with possibilities. "Let's concentrate on Pakistani or Russian. Does anyone think ISIL is involved?" He almost said ISIS but remembered the President preferred the use of ISIL.

"Sir," said CIA Director Rush. "ISIL was quick to claim responsibility for the suicide bombings but we think not. Each time ISIL has been involved in the past ten years, there has been chatter on the internet beforehand. Bragging about becoming martyr, watch me in the news, et cetera. We had absolutely zero chatter before today. For that reason, we think this group is acting on its own."

"Where will they explode the bomb? What targets do we need to concentrate our efforts on?"

CHAPTER TEN

HOUSTON FBI OFFICE

THREE P.M.

Perez and Camille huddled in his office. He put his hand on her shoulder. "Camille, think it out. It has nothing to do with you or the fact that you are a woman. This is standard protocol and you know the procedure. In such a situation, the DHS calls in the Special Investigative Unit, the so-called experts. It doesn't matter that it will cost time and they won't use what we already know. They know what is best for all of us. After all, they are from Washington."

He smiled ruefully and she weakly responded, "But, Boss, we already have identified the major evidence and they are just going to take up precious time retracing our steps."

Perez tried to cheer her, "Camille, they have all those experts at their beck and call, and it'll only take 12 hours or so for them to catch up to us."

Camille relaxed and smiled a little more, but still protested, "But I'm the one who got us on track!"

"Now, Special Agent Richard," his voice growing more serious. "I know you're upset. Think back a few months ago when that Houston police detective complained that you failed to inform him of new evidence."

"Well, sir, that was different. I'm an FBI Special Agent, and he's just a police detective who could not act on the evidence."

"And right this minute those guys in SIU are saying, 'We're the very best and she's just a regular agent'."

"It's not the same"

"Think, Camille. To his mind, the situation was exactly how you are seeing the SIU."

Camille paused and tried to consider how the detective had seen the situation. She closed her eyes and moaned to herself. She hated the possibility that he might have felt the same way she did this minute, but Perez was right.

"I'm sorry, boss. I get your point."

"Okay, Agent Richard, let's get on with our job here. Bring the rest of your CID team in."

Camille rose and opened the door, and let Mozart, Nguyen and Hernandez into Perez' office.

"Let's separate what we know and what we think," Perez began. "Just what do we know now?"

Camille iterated, "First, we know some rogue Saudis are involved in the smuggling."

"Apparently involved in the smuggling, he corrected."

"Right. We know the two Saudis were drivers for the Consulate." She paused, then gasped, "Christ! That's obvious! Why did I not catch that before? They were to be the drivers for the truck."

"That's my girl," said Perez. "Think it through. But let's not get too hasty. It's possible that they were to assist the suicide bombers but decided against it and were killed for that reason. But because they are drivers, we can assume it had something to do with their driving the truck. It's possible that the two were going to hijack the truck, but were stopped and killed."

Hernandez flashed her eyes at Camille, then looked directly at Perez, irritated that Richard was dominating the time with their boss. "It seems to me the more likely case is that they were killed trying to stop the theft of the bomb."

"Whoa, Mercedes. We don't know that the bomb was stolen. This may have been part of the plan."

"I can't see any other reason to kill two drivers," she replied.

"Perhaps," said Perez, "but let's keep the other possibility in mind."

"Whoever stole the bomb, if it was stolen, had to know the details of the smuggling, had to be intimately involved in the operation."

"I agree with that, too," said Perez. "Someone had to know exactly what was going on. You wouldn't just stumble onto the theft of an atomic bomb. On second thought, maybe they did and decided to sell the bomb on the open market."

"God, Chief," said Camille. "I had not thought of that."

"If it's true, though," suggested Perez, "then the Intelligence ears ought to pick up chatter on that. The CIA says no chatter."

"That's another thing," said Ngyuen. "That's something amazing about this. The lack of chatter. The smart ones think that means ISIL is not involved. I just think it means the plot is very tightly confined to just a few people."

"And at least one of those few people has to be a nuclear scientist," said Perez. "Who is he and where's he from?"

No one answered. After a pause, Camille said, "The two suicide bombers were involved in the plot. If they were going to set off an atomic explosion, why use simple explosives like those strapped to their chests? I submit that the suicide bombings might have been just a distraction."

"Perhaps," responded Perez, "but it would seem to me that the suicide bombings drew the attention of the entire law enforcement branches of the US government into investigating. That would seem counterproductive."

"But they don't know that we know that uranium is involved," pleaded Camille. "That's very important. To them, the suicides would draw our attention away from their real intent. In fact, they may be thinking that this investigation is just a Houston Police investigation, not knowing we found the trace of uranium."

Perez paused in thought, then said, "I'll buy that."

Hernandez interjected, "We know there's radiation including

weapons-grade uranium of some amount and they were using a well-logging truck as a way to get past radiation detectors. But we really don't know how much U-235 they have. Enough to make a bomb?"

Perez replied, "Due to the implications, I think we must assume they have enough for a bomb and intend to use it. If it were just a small amount, they'd have used it in the suicide bombs—make them dirty."

Camille responded, "The smugglers probably brought it in by ship, and there have been several shipments of Saudi Arabian oil lately, and one shipment of drilling equipment by a Saudi outfit."

"Camille," Perez cautioned. "Although Saudis were involved in the smuggling does not mean it was brought in by a Saudi ship."

"Yes, Chief," she agreed. "But I'm looking for the most likely scenario right now."

"Understood, but let's keep alternatives in mind."

"Chief, I really don't think we have time to mutter about alternatives. I think we must work out what's most likely and move on that." Camille thought a few seconds, then said, "If the plot was so tightly held that there's been no chatter, I conclude that only a few trusted people were involved. And if some of them are Saudi, I think most or all of them are Saudi."

"I like your logic, Camille. What's next?"

"The fact that they dumped the logging truck means they no longer feel the need to hide the radiation. That means either the bomb is already in place in Houston, or in another vehicle on the move somewhere else. It could be anywhere. Where is it and what is the target?" She said in a despairing tone. "Okay, chief. I'm taking a leap of faith that everyone involved is Saudi, like 9/11. I say a Saudi ship was involved in smuggling. Perhaps not the company owning the ship or the equipment, but someone on board, some of the crew or passengers, if any."

"Okay," said Perez," but keep in mind that's a hunch without confirmation."

"Yes, Chief. But I feel we are short on time and we must do something. If you can think of something better, let me know. You're the boss."

Perez thought for a moment. "How big are these containers?"

Camille answered, "Minimum size would have to be about 12" to 16" cubes, if I remember what Holland told me."

"Then I don't think they could have gotten them through security and onto a public airline. Do FedEx and UPS have radiation detection gear for packages going onto their aircraft?"

Mozart replied, "Yes, sir. Standard protocol."

"Ok, Mozart, you check FedEx and the other bulk carriers. Find out whether they have the equipment and whether they shipped any heavy lead boxes greater than 12" cubes anywhere this morning. Nyguen, find out how many private planes left this morning after 5 AM and where they were going and whether they were big enough to carry such weight."

"That's a lot of planes, sir," interjected Hernandez. "And it might have left out of some of the other small airports, like Beaumont's."

"Right," said Perez. "You two work it out. Richard, you check every shipment that's come into the port for the last four weeks. Check whether any tankers off-loaded anything but oil. Get the list of equipment from the Saudi ship."

"Thanks, Chief." I've already got Fiongos working on it."

"Very well," said Perez, shaking his head. "Listen, guys. Everyone in this office has been told that you have total command of all resources. Get with it. Let me know what you find as soon as you find anything."

Perez realized the most practical matter was to determine the target and stop the bomb from exploding. But another question bugged him, who would do this and why?

CHAPTER ELEVEN

RIYADH, SAUDI ARABIA

THE KING CHANGES POLICY
JUNE, 2009

The Saudi King and the new American President had just completed their meeting where President O'Brien had laid out his vision for Iran becoming a new regional power, and how he hoped his negotiations would transpire. The King was incredulous. Indeed, the King was so shocked at the idea of America helping Iran eventually become a nuclear power that he hardly spoke a word at the formal dinner for the President. On the second day, he had voiced several objections that were vital to Saudi Arabia but the President had swatted them aside as he would an irritating fly.

The President had explained that his primary concern was that he wanted no more American soldiers to die in wars in the Middle East. He wanted a regional power to keep the peace, and Iran was his choice to be that regional power. He laid out his plan to entice Iran into being the moderate country that kept the peace in the region. The King was aghast. He objected to the concept. Iran would throw its weight around, in his opinion, not bring peace. The King had never been able to comprehend the short-sightedness of American Presidents — they seemed to be able to think only four years into the future, so what appeared to be a success for O'Brien was a tragedy for the King. The President seemed to think that making Iran wait 15 years before starting on a bomb was a successful strategy. A nuclear Iran, regional powerhouse, in only 15 years! The King knew he would most likely not live that long but he needed to leave his people a way to defend themselves from a nuclear Persian lion.

And 15 years was if Iran didn't cheat! Amazingly, the President was voicing Iran's cheating on the current agreement as an excuse to make this deal — but the King understood that the President deeply desired no more Middle East wars for his people. Ok, so be it, although Turkey would have been a better choice for a regional power, in the King's opinion. More stable. Closer in temperament to the West. Last, the President did not comprehend the King's objection that a nuclear Iran would destabilize the Middle East.

The King had to act in his beloved country's best interest. So, before Air Force One had begun taxiing, the King called for an emergency session of his top advisors. Although he appeared to all to possess his normally serene demeanor, inside the King was disturbed and roiling, anxious and upset. During the meeting, he laid out the President's plans to a stunned and incredulous audience. The King asked for contingency options to be brought forth in one week's time. However, before the meeting adjourned, a consensus already had arisen: Saudi Arabia must obtain nuclear weaponry. The only question was whether to do it themselves or buy from a friendly power like Pakistan.

CHAPTER TWELVE
SAUDI ARABIA

ABDUL'S HISTORY

From the time he was a small boy, Abdul had been unusually curious. He had always wanted to know what was on the other side of the mountain, how a machine worked, what had caused the strange shapes on the ground or the colors in the sky. School had inflamed his curiosity as teachers generally didn't satisfy him, and discouraged his consistent questioning. He read book after book, then found one person who shared his love of learning, his cousin Noor. She also loved to read and their first connection was talking about books. She also was a whiz at math. When Abdul would brag about some mechanical problem he'd solved, she'd stump him with a math problem and bring his ego back down. She taught him how to approach math, but he was not close to her understanding--he needed something concrete to hold and had difficulty with abstract concepts. They studied together and read together and helped each other and stimulated each other until one week when she acquired a different aroma, and suddenly she began wearing a veil and they were no longer allowed to study together or even to be together alone. As a result, he stopped studying math and concentrated on mechanics, but missed their interactions, especially her curiosity about everything. He found another place where people seemed to welcome his questions: in the Arabian oil fields where his father would take him occasionally. His father was a prince who had been given responsibility of a large oil sector. Naturally, he was merely a figurehead while the foreigners did all the work. All the foreign workers were employed by Saudi Aramco, a company comprised of the Saudi government and several oil companies who had found and developed the oil fields before they were nationalized. Many of the foreigners were Americans, and most of them seemed boisterous and brash. Abdul was uncomfortable around them at first but eventually realized they were fun-loving and safe, and usually hailed from Texas, Oklahoma, or Louisiana. The workers, though, took a shine to the little boy who asked all the questions about how machines worked and why certain things were done. One man in particular showed interest in the boy, a Venezuelan named Saul Rodriguez. Their connection began one day when the boy, walking around a gas separation facility, came upon Rodriguez using a grease gun to lubricate a joint. "What are you doing, Mr. Rodriguez?" the young Abdul asked.

"I'm greasing this joint so it moves better."

"Why does it move better when you do that?"

Rodriguez looked at the inquisitive boy. The question seemed more complex than the usual "why" question, so he decided it needed a more complex answer. He looked around and spotted a piece of rebar in the shade of the plant building. He grabbed it and told Abdul to scratch the concrete sidewalk with it. Abdul did so, and wondered what was the point. Rodriguez then squirted a bit of purple grease onto the ground and stuck the end of the rebar into it. Then he told Abdul to scratch the concrete again. Abdul did so, and Rodriguez thought he noticed a widening of Abdul's eyes, and asked, "Did it feel different?"

"Yes." said Abdul. "It moved easier."

Rodriguez showed Abdul the grease gun, and asked, "How does this work?" Without waiting for an answer, he began taking it apart. He unscrewed the base of the gun and extracted the plunger, covered in a smear of purple grease. He unscrewed the nozzle and laid it down, and continued with the rest of the gun. Abdul was intrigued and watched the man gently lay each part on the concrete. Rodriguez explained how each piece fit with the others, and how they worked together to push the grease out of the gun into the zerk and the joint. Abdul was fascinated. Then the man told Abdul to put the gun back together. His eyes widened, and he was pleased the man thought he might be able to do so. Rodriguez gently helped Abdul, and they reassembled the grease gun.

Over the next several years, whenever Abdul got the chance, he would plead with his father to go to the plant site or the drilling rigs and would seek out Rodriguez for more lessons. The childless Rodriguez got tremendous personal satisfaction teaching the inquisitive boy about mechanical equipment. Any teacher with a willing student becomes motivated—that's why they teach, to spread knowledge; a teacher with a brilliant student becomes inspired, knowing that he is passing his knowledge to generations, a form of immortality. The boy was eager and persistent. Rodriguez would select a piece of equipment and explain its purpose. Then he would take it apart and lay out all the individual pieces, down to rods and springs and joints. He'd illustrate what each piece did and how it interacted with others to help the machine achieve its goal. He demonstrated that there were no extraneous parts, nothing that wasn't dedicated to that goal. He'd ask Abdul questions--why was this arm longer than that, why was this spring exactly this size, why was this part lubricated but not that one. At the end of each lesson they would reassemble the equipment, then Rodriguez would ask Abdul to go home and draw the pieces and explain each part. Naturally at first Abdul made lots of mistakes, particularly omissions. Rodriguez would patiently explain what was wrong and thereby taught Abdul how to think about how things interacted. Eventually Abdul learned to reason through each piece of equipment. He learned about leverage, about tension and strength, about action and reaction. In a few years, Rodriguez could lay down a piece of equipment and ask Abdul to draw its inner working from his imagination. Abdul could, if he knew the piece's purpose. Rodriguez moved from individual pieces of equipment to the separation plant itself, then on to a drilling rig, and Abdul learned how each part related to the goal of drilling a hole sufficient to produce oil. He saw how not only each piece of equipment but also how each person on the rig meshed together to drill a well and how here were no extraneous people or machines on the rig. Abdul thereby learned how organizations worked efficiently. He gained tremendous confidence in himself through his knowledge of equipment. His time in the oil fields provided a framework that made the information in school pertinent and motivated him to study harder. He understood why he had to learn math, for example, to make machines work.

Consequently, in school he leapt far ahead of his brothers and cousins who were motived to learn only by the fact they were ordered by their parents. By the time he was ready for college, Abdul was able to disassemble an engine and put it back together. Abdul had plenty of options for college, as money was no object, of course. The King encouraged members of the royal family to go to capital cities. Boys he knew were going to places like Paris, Tokyo, Copenhagen, Moscow. Abdul, though, saw English as the most important language for business and engineering and so decided on Imperial College in London for that reason and also because London had a large Muslim population with a variety of mosques available for worship. Suddenly he was sent off to Imperial College and came face-to-face with the licentiousness of the West.

Abdul was amazed by the West. People seemed to think humans were basically good, despite the fact that the Holy Book said otherwise. The followers of the Prophet Moses had their Torah, the followers of the Prophet Jesus had their Gospels, and the followers of the Prophet Mohammad had the Koran. Each book taught that humans were corrupt and fallen creatures. Despite that, the West seemed to think people would be good if treated nicely. Abdul wondered if it had always been that way- he remembered one of the American Presidents had said "walk softly and carry a big stick." Abdul thought that made a better foreign policy than what was happening in the West now. One of his relatives (his grandfather?) had once proclaimed "Americans are honest, but stupid!" Never had that been more in evidence than in the current foreign policy of the USA.

Despite the warnings his older brothers and cousins had given him, Abdul had been unprepared for the debauchery he found in London. He'd thought college would be for learning – a place where he'd find others as curious as he, people eager to search for understanding. His expectations were as high as his disappointments were low. What he found was that the students were interested only in the next hook-up or party. Studying was merely an incidental necessity to staying at the glorious party. The women did not value themselves. Every single woman who went on a date with him, except one, expected sex on the first date. That exception would have opened up on the second or third date, no doubt. It was all pleasurable physically but hugely disappointing spiritually. Abdul had sampled drugs, too, but he disliked how they made him feel when he couldn't control his body. He became eager to leave London and hoped a graduate school would finally provide the educational experience he desired – a group of people all searching together for learning, to satisfy the curiosity that drove him incessantly.

While Abdul was in London, Noor was married to his brother Hamza, and they saw each other only infrequently at family gatherings. Abdul loved looking at her oval face with soft brown eyes and lovely black hair, but had to avoid being seen staring at her. He noticed her eyes seemed sad but her skin looked exceptionally smooth, as it had in their times together years ago. They said nothing more than normal words of greeting and farewell, although one time several years later she congratulated him on his success and a few times he caught her looking at him and smiling.

By the time he left Imperial College, Abdul knew he wanted to learn more about petroleum engineering and geology. The earth fascinated him and he felt drawn to the field where Saul Rodriguez had worked. It would make him better suited to replace his father one day, he thought. His father wanted him to follow his brothers and go to Harvard or Cambridge, although if Abdul insisted on a technical education then Cal Tech or MIT. Abdul respectfully declined. He told his old friend Saul Rodriguez of his desire to get a master's degree in petroleum engineering. Himself a product of the University of Tulsa's petroleum engineering program, Rodriguez said that there were many excellent petroleum engineering programs in states where oil production occurred, particularly in Texas, Oklahoma, Louisiana and Mississippi. At Saudi Aramco he'd met drilling engineers from all over the world but most seemed to come out of several universities in those states, yet most of the bosses seemed to come from Texas A&M University so that's where he recommended and Abdul went.

Again, however, Abdul did not find the group of like-minded learners he had sought, a coterie of searchers sitting around discussing approaches to difficult problems. Only once did that occur, at a seminar on a particular drilling problem with flexible pipe in the high-pressure environment of the deep ocean. How could the joints of the flexible pipe be sealed in such high pressures? The seminar had brought technical experts from major companies around the globe. One afternoon session had consisted of a few presentations by different engineers of their proposed solutions, followed by a discussion. It became clear that this was a problem that these people had been wrestling with passionately, and the questions were difficult and pointed. Proposals were shot down with stern admonitions of terrible consequences if that particular path were followed. Abdul was astonished as people leapt to the white board and from the top of their heads wrote down (what were to Abdul long-forgotten) equations with explanations of how they applied. Abdul was fascinated by these world experts wrestling passionately with a difficult problem and realized this seminar was the educational experience he'd long sought. These people wanted nothing but to learn the answer. Nothing else mattered – certainly not the feelings of their colleagues. The lone female engineer in the room teared up when her research results were brutally questioned. The discussion continued long after the scheduled close of the session, past the time of the dinner supplied in the next room. Finally, the caterers closed the seminar by stating they were going to start removing the now-cold food. The thrill of that experience buoyed Abdul for years.

After graduation from A&M, Abdul declined to return to Saudi Arabia and instead took a job as a roughneck in the oil fields in Oklahoma. He wanted to learn the basics of drilling, so he did not disclose his degree. No one knew he was a prince of Saudi Arabia. The other roughnecks called him "college" or "raghead" and teased him mercilessly for months, until Abdul proved he would and could do any job they asked. And they were amazed at his knowledge of how equipment works. Eventually, he earned some respect, and after those several months, the workers finally adopted him as a kind of mascot.

One day, Abdul got a message that his old friend Saul Rodriguez had been killed in an accident on a drilling rig. Despite his understanding of the risks of working there, Abdul was shocked by the idea that someone he loved could die that way. The next day on the rig floor, Abdul lost concentration while thinking of Rodriguez. His fingers got caught in the chain that wrapped around the pipe. He might have lost all his fingers if not for the quick reaction of a fellow roughneck, and all he lost were the tips of two fingers. That he was back trying to work the next day with a heavily bandaged hand provided "College" with great respect from the other roughnecks, many of whom had the red badge of courage that oil field workers wore – a missing finger or two. Rodriguez's death and his own accident deeply motivated Abdul's mechanical mind with a problem to be solved. After a couple of years, at age 27, Abdul returned home to the welcoming embrace of his father and to the first bride his father had found for him. Two more brides and two children would follow in the next two years. The only thing important to Abdul, though, was his idea for improving drilling safety. After Abdul made a detailed proposal on his concept, his father agreed to fund a drilling equipment company to be run by Abdul. Despite initial reluctance, the final argument was that George H. W. Bush, whom his father greatly admired, had started a drilling company after his college and military service. His father invested, and Abdul's company grew far beyond his father's original expectations. His father expected that Abdul would tire of his business venture and join the life of luxury and indolence that his brothers and cousins enjoyed, but Abdul persisted. Faisal indeed became quite proud of his son and planned to turn his oil sector over to Abdul when retirement loomed. His older brothers would not care, Faisal was certain.

Abdul's first idea was for a machine that would replace the dangerous hard work with the chain. Initially he was going to name his company Crescent Drilling Company, but realizing that might be detrimental for an international company during a time when people were hesitant about Muslims, he decided on a clever variation: Crescendo Drilling. He obtained a few Saudi Aramco contracts. The foreigners seemed amused by the grown-up lad who'd bugged them with questions years ago. He would offer cut-rate deals to get business, then demonstrate that his company was reliable and excellent. Crescendo Drilling grew outside Arabia to North Africa and finally to North America, just in time for the horizontal drilling boom. The company's growth exploded as drillers across the globe paid for the extra safety. Abdul would have become a multimillionaire at age 30 solely from the success of his tool machine company even if he had not already had family wealth. Seeing his idea change drilling habits, he was motivated to solve other problems and he soon built a drilling robot, a complete mechanical device that needed humans only to oversee drilling progress and push some buttons. By the time Abdul turned thirty-five, Crescendo's name was synonymous with drilling efficiency and safety. Crescendo Drilling became a household name in the oil business, and the money poured in.

He traveled in his private jets to every oil capital: Houston, Aberdeen, Stavanger, Kuala Lumpur, and many more. His three wives had produced six children, all girls, giggling, happy, excitable, rambunctious girls. More children would arrive, some boys, but the eldest six girls enchanted him especially. He adored them, doted on them, took them places, provided the best tutors he could find. He desired to protect them from all evil, God willing.

As they grew and he traveled through different cultures, he became more acutely aware of the degrading effects of Western culture on women. He became more protective of his daughters and more disgusted with the West. The more he saw, the more bewildered he felt. How could a father teach his daughter that pleasure is the most important part of life? How could a father miss teaching the lesson that there exist spiritual things more important than pleasure? How could an entire society not realize it? He finally understood why Islam demanded isolation and protection of women. Not all Muslim countries followed the restrictions of the Koran. In Bursa, Turkey, for example, with women in bikinis, he disgustingly reflected that he might have been in Brazil. Eventually he preferred strict adherence to Sharia, especially as his oldest approached the time that she'd start wearing the veil. He'd enjoyed the sluts in London and Texas and Oklahoma himself, but could not fathom how fathers could allow their daughters such behavior, not if they really loved their girls. You could see the effects of that behavior everywhere in the West, from any television show to any grocery store. It seemed all ads were about sex, no matter what was being sold. But that was the way of the West. Sex was everything—sex and money.

Abdul's disgust grew inside until he wanted to explode whenever he had to work in the Western society and imagined the effects on his daughters. He'd began to withdraw, then his uncle Mohammed, the Saudi Consul in Houston, asked for his help in his strike against the Great Satan. Abdul quickly agreed. His role was simply to facilitate the smuggling of something into the USA. With all the commerce his companies did, shipping thousands of tons of equipment in and out of Houston and New Orleans, that was an easy task.

CHAPTER THIRTEEN
HOUSTON FBI OFFICE

3 PM SUNDAY

"Chief. I've been thinking about the oil field truck again. Killing the President of the US with an atomic bomb would be a tremendous political statement for the terrorists."

"Of course, but how?"

"Well, here's an idea. As we all know, he goes duck hunting on the opening day of duck season in mid-November."

"Of course. I remember the uproar among the pundits when O'Brien said it was good thing opening day was after the election because he said he was going hunting no matter what his campaign manager said. He was keeping his tradition with his buddies and they were going to go shoot ducks. The pundits went crazy and the Party thought that would cost him the election, but it had the opposite effect. In the end, he picked up a lot of Republican voters—hunters who thought he was one of them."

"Yes. O'Brien, a man of the people," said Perez with some disgust.

"People love him, chief. You can't deny that even if you don't like his policies."

"That's what defines a populist, Camille. Let's get back to work. How could the bombers locate him? No one knows exactly where they go except his inner circle and the Secret Service. They could be anywhere in South Louisiana. One year they went to Arkansas. Assuming there was no leak of the camp location, how could one find out?'

Camille already had an idea. "Don't they disallow planes from flying over the President's air space?"

"Yes. You know that."

"Even to 35,000'?"

"Yes, even to 35,000' there is a no-fly zone monitored by fighter jets."

"Could someone with access to flight patterns or rerouted aircraft figure out the no-fly zone?"

"Hmmm. Perhaps. Let's check on that."

"Well, if they did, could a suicide bomber come in kamikaze-style and ignite the bomb before being shot down by the jets?"

"Good question," remarked Perez. "Let's ask the Secret Service to check into it."

"Here's the connection with the well-logging truck," said Camille. "I'll bet there's not a duck camp anywhere in South Louisiana that does not have an oil field nearby. They could be driving the truck to an old oil field, store it there with other old equipment for the next two months, and wait for hunting season. If the field is close enough to the camp, they could wait until the President is there, then explode the bomb and wipe out the camp."

"How close?"

"Dr. Holland said within three miles."

"No way they could get close. The area would be crawling with Secret Service."

"No, remember the President has pissed off the Secret Service before with his insistence that they keep far enough away not to interfere with the hunting. One year he blamed poor hunting on the Service, and they won't make that mistake again. So there would be no helicopters flying around or black Suburbans roaring down the roads, or airboats in the marsh."

"Okay, we must consider that. But what if the chosen duck camp is far from the stored bomb truck?"

"Then they drive it to a private airfield and fly it in. The physicists can tell us how big the private plane would need to be to carry the bomb. The plane ignores the warning of the fighter jets and before they have time to react, POW!"

"Quite a devious mind there, Camille. I'll alert the Secret Service but I imagine it won't take much to adapt their plans for such."

"You know, since there will be no more elections for him, I'd bet that they will go this year to the place where they used to go every year before his first term. If I wanted to find out, I'd go hang around DeRidder and talk to old folks and people he went to school with. I bet I could find out exactly which camp."

"Okay, okay. I'll have Director Mason talk to the Secret Service."

CHAPTER FOURTEEN

ON THE ROAD

SUNDAY

After initial reticence, Kern opened up and became friendly, was jovially opinionated like most truck drivers, so it seemed like it'd be an easy trip if they didn't get caught smuggling whatever was in the back. By noon they had crossed the Red River into Oklahoma. The road rolled on through red hills, past farms and ranches and small towns. In the late afternoon, while Kern was driving north toward the Kansas border, Dolecek was silent for a while as if thinking, then said, "I'm feeling kind of exposed here."

Kern looked directly at Dolecek and mouthed, "Later." Dolecek nodded and began talking about Texas Aggie football.

In Dodge City, while the truck and the other vehicles were refueled, Dolecek and Kern went into the Men's Room at the truck stop. Kern said, "I know what you're feeling. I'm glad I brought along my little friend." From behind his back he pulled out a 9 mm pistol.

Dolecek laughed, and said, "I knew there was a reason why I liked you."

When they returned to the truck, the four men from the Suburban were standing at the front of the truck, obviously waiting for Kern and Dolecek. Kern tensed. One man, apparently the leaded, stepped forward. A man of average height, he had a thin face with a complexion common to almost anywhere in the Mediterranean, from Greece to Lebanon. He was wearing a blue t-shirt with Astros in orange, with a light windbreaker with the same colors. Kern and Dolecek suspected the windbreaker in the heat was to cover a concealed weapon.

The leader spoke in and English accent, "It's been a long day. Let's sit down to eat. How about a steak?"

Wary, Kern said, "The steak house where I used to eat here is gone. Seems everything is Mexican now."

"Yeah, that's the way of the west these days," said the leader. "Everyone okay with Mexican food?"

All nodded, and Kern said, "I know a good one on the west side of town. Come on, I'll lead y'all there."

While the six men were seated at the table, after their meal orders had been given, the leader said, "Here are your phones. You may check your accounts and call your wives. Just don't tell them where you are, and turn off location services first."

Both Dolecek and Kern were lightened by the gesture, and made their phone calls. After doing so, they visibly relaxed.

The leader said, "We have rooms for tonight in Garden City. Do you think you can make that?"

"Piece of cake," said Kern. "Are we continuing west? Should be able to make it to the Colorado line. Maybe even Lamar, but might want to make a reservation in Syracuse just in case."

Dolecek added, "Syracuse is easy. The stench of the stockyards will keep us awake." The two truck drivers laughed heartily and the others, not quite sure what they meant, joined in.

"Okay," said the leader. As soon as the sun gets below the horizon, we'll head out. Don't want to be looking directly into the setting sun."

Back in the truck, Dolecek said, "I feel much better now." But they both doubly locked their hotel room doors that night.

CHAPTER FIFTEEN

SAUDI ARABIA

THE LAST STRAW: ABDUL CHANGES

"I took you to Zurich and Geneva," said Abdul to Yasmeen, his eldest. Her name meant "Flower" and he thought it was a perfect match for a perfect child, his favorite. "Did you not see the vulgarity of the women? And Switzerland is nothing compared to France, London or America."

"Is Bursa the West? Is Istanbul? The women there dressed the same. They drive cars. They are independent."

"Turkey is different, and it's moving back to traditional values."

"And we are going forward. The King has said women will soon be allowed to drive. That's just the beginning. Someday Saudi women will be independent, too."

"God forbid!" exclaimed Abdul. "That would be a disaster. Our lives would be destroyed. Our country would collapse."

"Has Switzerland collapsed? Has the Great Satan collapsed? Independence is what made them great!"

Abdul was enraged. He could not believe his daughter, his precious Yasmeen, could speak such filth. He raised his hand and slapped her across the face. "No," he cried. "I will not hear my daughter speak like this!"

Yasmeen was stunned. Shocked. Her father had never struck her. He had never been angry with her. Her face stung but the emotion she felt at the rage of her father against her was stronger than the pain. She ran to her room, confused, bewildered, hurting, crying.

Abdul felt like he would explode with anger and guilt. Fatima rushed to him. He slapped her face with full strength. She cried out in pain and shock and fell back onto the floor several feet away. "You did this to her," he shouted at Fatima crying. "You allowed this to happen." He stormed to his room, and it sunk into his consciousness, no it was not Fatima's fault. It was his. He'd introduced his Yasmeen to the West. He thought he'd given her strength to withstand the instincts. But she'd succumbed to the lure of the West. It was his fault. Abdul knew as husband and father he had the absolute right to strike his daughter and wife and the violence did not disturb him. But the apparent loss of his daughter to the West's insidious moral corruption was unbearable. His heart ached. It was unmanly, but he lay across his bed and wept, the tears flowing openly, the ache in his heart burning. His life was crumbling.

The next morning, he was in the breakfast room when Fatima and Yasmeen meekly walked in. Fatima was wearing her veil, most likely to cover her bruised and swollen face. Yasmeen just stood, quietly, face down. "I'm sorry, Father." Abdul closed his eyes and took a deep breath. He desperately wanted yesterday's incident to disappear, to never have happened.

Abdul's mind raced. He wanted to hug his daughter close, to kneel on the floor, to kiss her feet and apologize. But he knew he had to play the role of the stern father.

"Yasmeen, do you know not to speak that way to your father?"
"Yes, father."
"Do you reject the attitude you spoke last night?"
"Yes, father."
"Will you be the obedient daughter of a proud Muslim?"
"Yes, father."
"Very well, you may have breakfast."
"No, thank you, father. I am not hungry."
"Very well," he responded. "You may return to your room."
"Yes, Father." She left meekly. Fatima remained standing. "Have

breakfast with me," he ordered. Fatima sat but did not eat or speak during the meal and kept her head down.

One day, just after Yasmeen's eighteenth birthday, Fatima broke the rules by interrupting Abdul at work. Frightened, she uttered nervously, "Yasmeen is missing."

That statement did not make sense to Abdul. "What do you mean?"

"She did not come to breakfast. I checked with her friends-no one knows anything," she said, shaking.

Immediately alarmed, Abdul demanded, "How could it happen?" It did not make sense. "A girl can't just walk out of her house and disappear." His voice grew louder as he became more concerned.

"I'm afraid she's with Moteb bin Saud," dropping the name of Abdul's cousin with disgust and fear. Abdul realized that Moteb was related closely that it would be acceptable in a religious sense, but he was an immoral beast, so it was not acceptable in his family.

"How could that happen?" He demanded again. She shrank from the shouting but did not let it break her determination.

"Abdul!" She screamed, shaking with fear for her daughter. "Find Yasmeen!"

That shocked Abdul. A woman in Saudi Arabia could not just walk onto an airplane and leave. She could not have obtained a passport and visa without his permission, but Yasmeen could have left with Moteb bin Said, unfortunately. He was anti-Saudi to the extent that he might have listened to the pleas of Yasmeen and agreed to smuggle her out of the country. Moteb had the money to bribe her way out and was evil enough to do it. Fatima was right. But where? And for what purpose? Abdul sickened with the grim possibilities of Yasmeen becoming one of Said's licentious women. That thought almost made him vomit. Yasmeen! His Flower!

Abdul fought his tears and called Moteb, who answered on the first ring. "Abdul, I know why you are calling."

"Of course you do, you filthy bastard."

"Abdul, I will tell you just one thing: Yasmeen is safe and well taken care of." He hung up before Abdul could sputter a response. Abdul threw his phone against the wall angrily, desperately. Abdul called Moteb several times a day for weeks, but Mohammed never answered.

Then, three weeks later, Moteb surprised Abdul by phoning. "Abdul, I want you to know that Yasmeen is safe and happy."

"You spawn of evil!" Abdul shouted. "Bring her home!"

"No, Abdul," he said softly but directly. "It is her choice to live here, not mine. She wants to see what the world is like. She's a teenager. She wants to drive a car. She wants to walk without a chaperone. She wants to meet people not in her family. She wants to live free."

"Bring her home!"

"No, I will not," said Moteb. "If she returns to you it will be because she wants to." He hung up the phone.

Eventually, in despair, Abdul realized that he'd lost his eldest daughter, his favorite daughter, to the West. He cursed the West with every ounce of agony in his soul. He swore he'd kill Moteb. Abdul sent spies to Los Angeles to watch Moteb, hoping they might find Yasmeen, but Moteb had expected such, so had first set up Yasmeen with some friends in Toronto, where she could sharpen her English and learn to live in the West before coming to California to his compound. Abdul began wondering how he could make his cousin and the West pay for despoiling his daughter. Helping the atomic bomb explode in Houston would cause injury to America, but now Abdul wanted to destroy it completely, and his mind sought a way.

From that day on, the change overtaking Abdul accelerated swiftly. He would not spend a moment in a room with his first wife. He spent more and more time away from home, and started thinking of ways he could retaliate against the West for what it had done to his beloved eldest daughter Yasmeen, his special flower, who had been contaminated by its evil influence.

Abdul brooded over the incident, and when in the West grew more offended by the constant bombardment of licentiousness. He felt more and more isolated and alone. Then a tragedy occurred--a lucky tragedy for Abdul. Hamza was killed in an unusual accident, and Abdul found himself honor-bound to marry Noor, the widow of his brother. On their wedding night, they did not speak. When Noor began to prepare herself for Abdul, he stopped her and led her to bed. They simply laid together for hours without speaking, Noor nestled in his arms, reveling in the simple pleasure of being together after so many years, breathing together with skin touching, silently saying prayers of thanks and gratitude for this miracle. Abdul was also grateful for the miracle, and grateful for the opportunity he had had to assist its occurrence.

Abdul from that time onward spent little time with his other wives. Noor began traveling with him everywhere. He got a larger private plane so a bed could be installed. His Chief Operating Officer and constant companion, Hassan bin Hassan, said nothing, figuring the natural reason, although the main reason was actually the massages Noor gave the increasingly driven and anxiety-ridden Abdul. She began attending business meetings and was given the title of Chief Financial Advisor. At first, she said little but simply tried to understand the business and the pressures on Abdul so she could help him cope. Her mathematical mind adapted quickly, and she began asking pertinent questions and offering solutions and became part of the business machine. Abdul had expected such, and admired her for it, but still mainly needed his soul-mate for comfort and peace.

CHAPTER SIXTEEN

BACK IN HOUSTON

FOUR P.M., THE DAY OF THE SUICIDE BOMBINGS

"I'm sorry, Riley, I know you're busy, but I just had to hear your voice. I feel so helpless. Somewhere there's a bomb out there, and a million people could die. I just can't seem to find a clue. And all we know is that there are some Saudis involved. Maybe the bomb is in Houston or maybe somewhere else. But any moment a million people could die."

"I hear you, Cammie. It's scary. It's frustrating. We just have to keep working. There's a clue out there somewhere. Keep looking for it. You're good at what you do. You figured out it was radioactive before anyone else. Focus. Concentrate."

"I wish you were here. I wish I could curl up in a ball."

"So do I, Cammie. But you won't, because you're a good agent and you'll work this through to the end."

"Yes, yes," she said.

"Take a ten-minute break. Clear your head. Then get back to it. I'm with you. I love you, darlin'."

"I love you too, Riley."

"How do I clean my head of this mess?" she thought, deciding to go for a run. She absent-mindedly turned on the TV. It was all about the stupid election in two months to replace O'Brien after his two terms. Pundits yelling at each other. She could not stomach that. She wished the election was over, just so she wouldn't have to listen to all the crap. She flipped to another channel and saw the image of the plane going into the World Trade Center on another 9/11. Her gut wrenched. She'd seen that video many times in a seminar at Langley on the mind of a terrorist, but she still did not understand them. She found the Discovery Channel, hoping it might take her mind to a far-away place. The scene looked like a National Park. She stripped and put on her running clothes, was lacing up her shoes when, suddenly, her mind jumped to the thought, "What if the smugglers do not know we know about the radiation? If so, what did the evidence mean?" She tried to look at the warehouse scene in a fresh way. "Why had the fingertips been cut off? How did only one fingerprint survive the cleansing?" The conclusion came thundering through her brain, as if it had been cavalry waiting for the bugle call. "If I were from somewhere else and wanted to make people think the smugglers were from Saudi Arabia, what would I do? I'd leave dead Saudis and use their cut-off fingers to plant a fingerprint. Then law enforcement would think we were from Saudi Arabia and not look elsewhere." Camille felt totally crushed. "Oh, no! They fooled us!" Suddenly she realized that she and Riley and Dickerson and everyone else knew nothing, absolute-ly nothing. The two Saudis could have been lured there, or maybe killed elsewhere and just dumped in the warehouse. She realized the implication. "The smugglers could be from anywhere: Russia, North Korea, Iran, China, God knows." An immense cloud of darkening desperation smothered Camille, and she slid down the side of the bed and slumped on the floor, her head on her knees. She felt alone. She felt tiny. She felt insignificant.

After several minutes, she rallied and called Perez. He answered, "Robert Perez."

"Chief, I just had a horrible thought. What if the fingerprint was a plant?"

"What do you mean?"

"The question of why to cut off the fingers bothered me, and I tried to look at the scene differently."

"Go on."

"Suppose I was from Iran or Russia or somewhere but I wanted to throw people off my scent by making them think I was from Saudi Arabia. On September 11th, I'd kill two Saudis and dump their bodies, but take their fingers and plant fingerprints. Why else cut the fingers off? That way they didn't have to drag the bodies into the rest room, just the fingers."

"But why leave only one fingerprint?"

"Because they wanted us to think we got a lucky break and are solving the case. They want us to think it was Saudis, but it could be anybody! Even ISIL!"

Perez thought a minute, then responded, "Yes, that fits the facts we know. That means either they completely fooled us and made us think it's Saudis, or it really is Saudis and we really did get lucky. Two completely different paths."

"We're back to square one."

"Unfortunately, yes. I will call Washington and inform them. Have you heard back from the Port? Have you found if any radioactive materials came into the Port in the last month?

"Haven't got an answer yet, but I'm working on it," she said, stretching the truth.

As she got ready to dial Fiongos at the port, the sound from the television penetrated her funk. The word "Saudi" caught her attention. Looking up at the TV, she saw a drilling rig surrounded by pine trees with a mountainside for a backdrop. A reporter was speaking to a strong-looking Middle-Eastern man who spoke with assurance bordering on arrogance.

"My success in business allows me to indulge my interest in science," the man said. "I've loved science since I was a little boy and this question about a fault here in Yellowstone intrigues me. I funded this effort myself because I want to know the answer now. It would take 5 years, maybe 10, to get a permit to drill on federal land. Thanks to the Healy's we can drill on private land now and I am paying for the drilling because I want to do it my way and do it now."

"What exactly are you doing?"

"The geologists in the Park want to know the amount of stress in the ground caused by the fault. My company is an expert on that and we are going to install underground some new measuring devices we've developed in Saudi Arabia in our research on hydraulic fracking for oil production.

The reporter winced, as if the man had cursed. She hoped the editors could cut that out.

"Thank you, Mr. Faisal," she said and turned to a thin, red-haired woman with streaks of gray. Camille recognized her from television.

The reporter spoke, "We have our own expert on faults right here, the famous hostess of "Quakin' & Shakin'", Dr. Laura Bigley-Puzio." The reporter was careful to pronounce the last part as the French 'Peugeot,' as she knew of the professor's snappiness at people who pronounced it as if Italian.

"Hello," said the professor, smiling brightly. The sun made the silver streak in her reddish hair glisten.

"The geologic community is grateful for Mr. Faisal's generosity in paying for this test well," she spoke on, but Camille was no longer paying attention, but dialing Fiongos.

The phone rang several times and went to voicemail. "Joe, this is Camille Richard." Before she could finish, her phone buzzed—someone was trying to call her.

"Camille, what's up?"

"Sorry, Joe, but in those shipments, was there any radioactive material listed?"

"Yes."

"What company, do you remember?"

"Yeah, I'll check but I'm pretty sure one of them was Crescendo, the big Saudi drilling company. Another was a medical company."

"Does it say what exactly or where it was going."

"Oh, there's a long list somewhere of the equipment, but I did not look at that. As for where, it probably went to their pipe yard in Houston. They have a big one somewhere west of town."

"Can you find out?"

"Yeah, all paperwork has to list the destination address."

"Please check, and call me." After she spoke, she realized that a fake address could have been written down, so the destination listed might mean nothing.

"Okay," he said. "Anything else?"

"Anything Saudi. There seems to be a connection somehow. Might be a coincidence but I want to know."

"Hold on," he said. "I can check online for the documents covering radioactive material. Here's one: M.D. Anderson received a shipment of Molybdenum-99 from New York three weeks ago."

"Sorry," said Camille. "Forget everything except Americium-241."

"Okay, let's see." He hesitated, browsing through his list. "Last week some Americium-241 was imported from Sudan by Crescendo Drilling. It says the destination is Cody, Wyoming."

Camille realized that was going to the site that she'd just seen on television. A science project. "Okay, not that one. What else have you got?"

Another shipment of Americium-241 was brought in from China last week for an industrial supplier in Houston. They are a distributor, I believe. It says the equipment is smoke detectors."

The word 'China' brought more interest from Camille. "That's it," she thought.

"Good. Text me the company name and the destination address. Any more?'

"Halliburton brought in some well equipment from Nigeria, with Americium-241 listed. That's going to their yard in west Houston."

Camille called Perez and relayed what she'd seen and heard, and said all three companies needed to be investigated.

"Camille," he said. "I think you're grasping there. Those three companies probably have shipments in and out of Houston every week. Crescendo is one of the biggest drilling companies in the world. And who cares about some science equipment in Yellowstone Park when we're looking for an atomic bomb?"

"Yes, chief," she said. "The Park seems farfetched but the fact that they are constantly bringing equipment into the country might provide a good opportunity for smuggling."

"True. But they have a lot to lose if they get caught smuggling something. I don't believe it. If it's being smuggled, don't you think that the destination listed might mean nothing? Also, we don't know if Holland was right thinking the container holding the uranium is salted with Americium. That was speculation based on a weak signal of uranium. The smugglers could have been counting on the fact that they could sneak it in without proper paperwork, through bribery, for instance, so the paperwork could be meaningless. Finally, don't forget that the uranium might have been some stolen from US sources, and not come through the Port at all. Forget the pipe yard and those companies for now. Concentrate on the individuals we know about. See if Dickerson has learned anything new. Meanwhile, I will get some people digging into the Chinese company. That seems most likely."

Camille rubbed her forehead. "Saudi, Saudi, Saudi," she thought. She ignored her boss and instead called Fiongos and requested the Bill of Lading for the drilling equipment. Then she was gripped by the notion that she had to get more out of the Consul. She started to dial the Saudi Consul but decided to go to the River Oaks mansion to see him in person. She looked down and realized she was still wearing her running clothes. She began changing and called the Consul's home to inform him that she was coming over.

"I'm sorry, Agent Richard. The Consul is not here. He's gone to Washington."

"Hmm" thought Camille. "Must be due to the bombings."

She felt frustrated. Out of the leads from Fiongos, China seemed the most likely yet somehow the drilling project near Yellowstone Park kept bugging her. She wanted to know more about the Saudi drilling magnate and what he was doing. If someone in his company was smuggling a bomb, where did it come from? Who in his company smuggled it? Where would they use it? Houston seemed quite likely, but, if so, why no explosion yet? Her thoughts tumbled over and over. Saudi consulate, Saudi workers, Saudi ship, Saudi drilling equipment, Saudi businessman. Her mind could not turn loose of the coincidences and focus on the murders. Saudi, Saudi, Saudi kept throbbing in her brain. The image of Osama bin Laden popped up, and the horrific images of people jumping from the Trade Towers. She snapped. It was all connected, she thought, and the focus seemed to be Abdul Faisal, the head of Crescendo Drilling. She looked up the list of Resident Agents near Yellowstone Park. Finding one in Billings Montana and another in Cody Wyoming, she checked a map to see which was closer to Yellowstone and determined Cody was. She checked the location of the drill site of Crescendo's science project and reckoned it was about halfway between the two towns. She picked Cody and called Perez, asking if he knew the FBI agent in Cody, Leland Joffe.

Perez said that he did not, but continued, "Camille, you can call him and ask him to get information, but don't you get off target. I want you to investigate working on the Chinese here."

"Listen, Chief. We have only one set of clues. They may be a classic red herring deception that has fooled us. If that case we have no idea who's done this or where they will take the bomb. On the other hand, if we did get lucky in finding out that Saudis were involved, then we need to follow this path to its conclusion. Maybe it's nothing, but I'd like to ask Agent Joffe to check out the head of the company and what he's doing."

"Okay, but you get back to your job. If we want to get his attention, then I should call him."

"You, or Director Mr. Mason"

Perez smiled, "No, let's get this done now." He called Joffe, who was glued to the television reports about the suicide bombings in Houston.

CHAPTER SEVENTEEN

RIYADH, SAUDI ARABIA, AND THE RED SEA

FEBRUARY, 2010

The King's visceral distaste for the female American Secretary of State disturbed him. Quite simply, he did not like her. He did not understand his emotions, but reckoned it was due to the unfortunate news she brought. He had not been bothered so much by the other two females who had held the office, although the first had been a bit of an adjustment due to her sex. Still, he was aware of the West's strange obsession with sexual equality. Eventually he'd gotten used to both of them and almost enjoyed working with them. They made him think that perhaps modernization could be good for Saudi Arabia, given a cautious and slow entry. This Secretary of State, though, carried more bad news on the Iran front. She reported that the negotiations with Iran had not gone as smoothly as planned, although what she called progress was being made. The King feared the longer the negotiations lasted the more the U.S. would give, and it was bad enough the way the President had laid it out for him. When the unfortunate one-sided deal was finally made, the joke amongst Arabs became that O'Brien was lucky that he'd had been negotiating with merely a Persian, that an Arab would have ended up with the keys to the White House and both O'Brien daughters.

The King used his country's helplessness as a ploy in his presentation to the Secretary of State, as she made several promises of American aid and protection. But promises were not enough for him. Eventually an invitation to her husband to speak in Riyadh along with a large contribution to the Hilliard Foundation moved the Secretary to agree to supply Saudi Arabia with more military hardware. The specific Boeing F-15 aircraft she approved, the F-15SA, would have more "payload capacity," in airplane jargon and he knew what that meant for his nuclear weapons program.

Shortly after the Secretary's visit, Saudi Arabia announced a new research facility, the King Abdulaziz Center for Oil Recovery Research, claiming they needed to catch up to the new fracking capabilities being utilized by the Americans in their oil shales. The new facility would be located outside Riyadh next to the facilities of the Atomic Energy Research Institute, part of the King Abdulaziz City for Atomic and Renewable Energy. That atomic energy effort had been started many years before, with the goal of providing 20% of Saudi growing electricity needs by 2020. They were short of that goal but did have one small nuclear reactor providing some electricity.

The king's own brother was installed as Director of the oil recovery facility, a signal to the world of the serious nature of the Saudi goal to protect its stature as the world's premier oil producer. One man who held a low title, Assistant Technology Officer, seemed to have a lot of stroke, a slightly stooped man who had been raised in Pakistan by Saudi parents, Saleh Tawfiq Saleh. Advisor to the Director was the drilling magnate and head of Crescendo Drilling, Abdul Faisal.

Naturally, the King needed a source of uranium for his nuclear weapons. He could buy all that was needed for the Saudi nuclear power plant through normal channels monitored by the IAEA. The international agency knew how much uranium the power plant required and closely monitored shipments to ensure that no more entered the country than exactly that amount. When he had voiced the source problem, the always surprising Abdul Faisal volunteered that he knew where to obtain the uranium and how to bring it into the country. The King did not ask details, and neither did anyone else.

Another major problem facing the King was how to obtain the

centrifuges needed to enrich the uranium for the bomb. Enrichment of U-238 to fuel-grade U-235 for his small nuclear power station was closely shepherded by the IAEA. Its agents didn't even have to travel to Saudi Arabia to check. The centrifuges were monitored by Siemens engineers in Munich, who knew how often and how much the centrifuges were used. From that they could calculate how much fuel-grade or weapons grade U-235 had been created, and that was shared with the IAEA, whose inspectors could verify no weapons-grade uranium had been made by their centrifuges in Riyadh. By those centrifuges, anyway.

The king needed a source for secret centrifuges. There was a growing black market in uranium centrifuges, but no one in that business could be trusted to be discreet. Any of the European companies/countries would blab to the Americans. So would the Koreans and Japanese. The Chinese or the Russians would drive a perilous bargain. Pakistan was so loaded with spies it was a miracle the Husain conspiracy had not been discovered. The King decided his best bet for reliability and discretion was his sworn enemy, Israel. The King could not expect an immediate reception from the Prime Minister of Israel, but President O'Brien had during his June visit publicly lectured him and the other Arab countries on the need to make peace with Israel. The King used that public lecture as an excuse to make a public overture to the Prime Minister. Naturally the Prime Minister rebuffed the King, so O'Brien used a speech to Congress to lecture Israel, and the Prime Minister reluctantly agreed to meet the King. O'Brien beamed at his next press conference, looking forward to his second Nobel Peace Prize.

The Southern tip of Israel is only 30km from the northwest corner of Saudi Arabia, about 20 miles. The resort city, Elait, sits on the top of the Gulf of Aqaba. Lots of Israeli's go there to stay at the Queen of Sheba Hotel, or the King Solomon, or the Royal Garden, relax and enjoy the water-themed pleasures of the beach or scuba-diving the reefs. Consequently, no one took much notice of the impressive motorcade from the airport, or even the large yacht with the Greek flag in the harbor. Just another wealthy American or European, they thought.

On the other hand, in the small town of Haql, in northwest Saudi Arabia, where the only attraction is diving the pristine reefs in the Gulf and few people visit other than scuba divers and eco-tourists, the arrival of several helicopters and a visit by the King was a major event. It was the first time any King had visited Haql, and the Jordanian news broadcast his tour of the town and his stepping onto a yacht for a joy ride in the beautiful waters of the Gulf. He spent several hours at sea.

THE SEDUCTION OF MANZUR HUSAIN

SAUDI ARABIA
BEGINNING AUGUST 2009

Manzur Husain, the older man with the slight stoop who'd seen his death staged from a rooftop, was welcomed into Saudi Arabia by the King and his government. Through the Saudi spy program in the USA and throughout the Middle East, the Saudi government had been able to create the illusion of a renegade nuclear scientist, and help the Americans "kill" him. Husain had been the perfect candidate. Not only one of Pakistan's top scientists, he had no family. His wife and children had been killed in an unfortunate mistake by the Americans during a missile strike against a Taliban village when Husain's family was there visiting relatives. It did not matter to him that the Americans apologized for the "mistake." It did not matter what it was, just that his family was gone, suddenly gone. He missed his rambunctious children. But he missed his gentle and loving wife the most. Her wit made him laugh and think at the same time. Her cleverness was a stimulus to his own mind. He loved her terrifically and was devastated by her death. So, he was fine to leave his home in Pakistan to get away from the pain. Plus, it gave him a small way to get back at the Americans. The Saudis had lured him with a magnificent budget – actually anything he asked for – and were building the facilities he'd designed himself. They had even provided him with a Saudi wife and, of course, a new identity. He suspected that she was a spy for the King, but due to the large invest-ment in his project, that was to be expected. His Saudi wife was polite and generous, and provided him with two children. Due to his accent, the government did not try to pass him off as a Saudi native but as a Pakistani born to Saudi parents. The people around him accepted that story, as he was clearly a man well-respected by the royal family.

Mohammed Aziz, the Saudi consul in Houston, began his plan to destroy Houston by trying to become friends with Husain. He spent weeks in Riyadh just to get the physicist to know him and, hopefully, to like him. Having no success, Mohammed reckoned that Husain's scientific mind might relate better to Abdul's, so he convinced Abdul to become friendly with the physicist and suggest their plan. That would be delicate, of course, as Husain might just turn around and tell the King. So, Abdul began his friendship with Husain by showing him where his precious uranium came from.

During a walk in the coolness of an evening, Abdul explained, "The King gave us a terrific problem when he said he wanted to begin a nuclear weapons program. The first was where to get uranium. We were buying uranium on the open market for the power plant, but realized that ears would perk up when they heard we suddenly started buying more. Unfortunately, buying seemed to be the only way. Then, one day God inspired me to fly from Cairo to Khartoum where I could from the air see several ring complexes on the ground."

"Ring complexes?"

"Many millions of years ago several volcanoes erupted in a line across northern Sudan, just like the volcanoes that formed Hawaii. They left several volcanic cones in a line, like round pyramids, but the wind and sand of the Sahara blew away the cones and eroded the cores right down to the ground. Now when you walk through the desert, they don't stand out, but when you fly over them, they are obvious to anyone's eye. They are round, that's why they are called rings. Below the ground they are actually volcanic pipes, long cylinders of hardened lava that go deep into the earth. Ancient volcanic plugs. They are like pipes bringing lava to the surface. They were extremely hot and melted the surrounding rocks. Minerals differentiated out, sometimes pure elements. The diamonds in South Africa are found in similar pipes. Sometimes uranium is found in pipes, and so I investigated these in Sudan at a place called Ras ed Dom."

"Did you find any?"

"Turns out the Soviets already had. They were here in the '50's, did some analysis and found some uranium. Their research results were in the Energy Department of Sudan, although in Russian, but translation was easy. The French also followed and studied the area. Unfortunately, there's not much uranium and it's a long way from anywhere. It's terrifically expensive to exploit. All the water for the entire operation has to be piped from somewhere far away. The Soviets decided it would be too costly even during the Cold War and left. I thought it might work with today's technology. The most important thing is that minerals differentiate in these pipes. Sometimes you get diamonds like in the pipes in South Africa, sometimes you get molybdenum and manganese and uranium, like at Ras ed Dom. It's our guaranteed uranium source. We report half of the uranium we mine to the IAEA, so they can keep track of what goes to our nuclear power generation through normal avenues. We don't report what goes through Halaib to our other nuclear project, your bombs. The IAEA thinks we're fully in compliance."

"Halaib?"

"You will understand when we go there."

A few weeks later, Husain, as Saleh Tawfiq Saleh, boarded Abdul's private jet and flew with him to Port Sudan. When they landed, Husain asked, "Why are we in Sudan?"

Abdul was pleased to reply. "Two reasons, my friend. First, while it is easy to get you into America, it is not so easy to get your equipment there. Fortunately, I have an operation in Sudan which gives me a cover for the radioactivity of your equipment. Second, you will gain your new identity here."

"Is my equipment here in Sudan?" Abdul was surprised that

Husain's first question was not about his false identity, but realized that the nuclear bomb was all that mattered to the man.

"Not yet. But tonight we shall welcome it into the country, God willing."

"Through Port Sudan?"

"No, you shall see." Abdul smiled.

Later, at the appointed time, the men got into a car that took them to the airport and to a small helicopter.

"No Crescendo logo on the side?" Husain asked.

Abdul was relieved – he took the light-hearted question about his company's logo as a sign Husain was loosening up. "Not for this trip, unfortunately for my ego." He laughed, and Husain actually smiled.

The helicopter followed the Red Sea coast north. Under the copter, Husain could see dry yellowish-brown ground, with the rocky Red Sea Hills to his left. On the right was the gorgeous blue water of the Red Sea. Often a reef appeared near the shore. Occasionally he saw a sailboat near shore or a commercial ship off shore. After a couple of hours, the helicopter landed in an open area near the shore. A Toyota Land Cruiser was waiting there, with a canopy set up and chairs set out nearby. "Are we still in Sudan?" asked Husain.

"Depends upon whether you ask a Sudanese or an Egyptian. This is the Hala'ib Triangle. On Sudanese maps it's marked as part of Sudan, on Egyptian maps as part of Egypt. Sudan claims it has administrative power of the area, but just over that hill is an Egyptian army base. So, do you, Manzur Husain, wish to claim control, too?" Husain smiled, shrugged, shook his head.

The driver of the Toyota, a thin bespeckled sunburned man with wild black hair, greeted them, and shook hands. "Abdul, Greetings."

"Nigel. Saleh, I'd like you to meet Nigel Wheelwright, our driver, mechanic, caterer and all-around handyman. Nigel, I'd like you to meet Saleh Tawfiq Saleh, a senior scientist of ours at the fracking research facility."

"A pleasure to meet you, sir."

"And you, too, Nigel. I must admit that the first names and informality make you two sound like Americans."

Abdul laughed. "Ha! Nigel's done so much for me over our years in Sudan that he's earned a first-name basis."

"Thank you, Abdul. Let's get comfortable, gentlemen." He pointed to the chairs under the canopy. The helicopter pilot joined them, and Nigel set out the tea. He opened a box filled with bubble wrap and extracted cups of fine china.

"Nigel," inquired Saleh. "Are you English?"

"Yes, sir," said Nigel as he poured the dark tea into cups.

"It seems no matter what remote area of the world I've traveled, there's always a solitary Englishman there. Why is that?"

Nigel laughed. "Some would say it is because Britannia ruled the world for so long that Englishmen are comfortable everywhere. But I can't speak for others, just my own story."

"It's a good story," interjected Abdul. "Please tell it."

"I was working in London as a cinematographer, thinking everything was right with the world, when my girlfriend of five years suddenly threw me overboard. I was crushed. So, a grieving lover must do something romantic, mustn't he? I quit my job, sold everything I owned, and bought a Triumph motorcycle. I took it apart and put it back together so I would be able to fix it, then set off across Europe. I rode it through Turkey but was stopped when I got to Lebanon. I wasn't allowed to cross the country. So, I took a ship to Alexandria and started up the Nile. I drove farm roads all the way to Aswan and then by paths to Khartoum. That was my romantic adventure."

"Fascinating journey. So why have you stayed here?"

"Oh, I feel like I fit in. I like the Sudanese people. And I have talents that are useful. My main job has been catering to operations like the mines at Ras ed Dom or the oil operations in South Sudan. I once catered a seismic crew right here in the Halaib Triangle. Sudan has been good to me."

"Quite interesting. That must have been an amazing journey up the Nile."

"Absolutely amazing, yes."

"Now we must wait until dark," Abdul said. "Then we'll have our meal."

Just after sunset, Abdul and the pilot laid out their prayer rugs for the evening prayer. Husain remained standing. Abdul was astonished but said nothing. Instead, after the prayer he explained the situation. "Halaib is a tiny village near the Army base that guards the southern border of Egypt. It is a nothing town most of the time. It gets only three centimeters of rain a year, so nothing grows there. The village and the base get their water from wells. Most of the month all the town does is supply the army base with things, especially those things that are not mentioned in Islamic society but which army men have been demanding since Adam and Eve were kicked out of the Garden of Eden. However, for several days every month for some strange reason the best truck mechanics from Egypt and Sudan live here."

"You are about to tell me why, I expect," said Husain.

"Yes. During the three days surrounding the full moon, Halaib is a bee hive. Two days before the full moon trucks begin arriving in town. Thirty years ago, all the work was done on just the night of the full moon, like tonight. Now the demand is so great that the nights before and after the full moon are also used. "

"For what?"

"There is an old concrete pier at Halaib that is no longer used except on these full-moon nights. When the full moon comes up, the lights of the Army base will go out, a ship will pull up to the pier, and the trucks will be loaded with goods. In two days, there will be no trucks in Halaib."

"Will I be able to watch?" asked Husain.

"Yes, when the ship appears on the horizon, Nigel will take us to the offloading."

It happened just as Abdul has described. When the full moon rose over the calm Red Sea, the lights on the Army base went out. There were no vehicle lights around the town, no lights on the ancient pier. The Toyota went over the hill and stopped on the edge of town, about half a kilometer from the pier.

Abdul continued. "On these nights, Halaib becomes an import-export haven for both Sudan and Egypt for certain things. The area just outside the pier is littered with pinnacle reefs. The water depth is generally about 40 meters, but the pinnacle reefs are like needles raising up to the water's surface. Think of sailing along in 40 meters of water, when suddenly there is a reef at the surface staring at you. Some are only 30-50 meters across, but they're at the surface of the water and can easily punch a hole in a ship. Before GPS, the only ships that would approach the pier were those with pilots intimately familiar with the area—remember they'd be arriving at night and must deal with all those reefs. The number of trained pilots were deliberately kept low. Now, though, any ship with GPS and Google Earth can make it and many more ships use the Halaib pier. It's a secret that can't last, because now too many people know about it. Activity has gotten so great that you have to have a pass to get a truck close to the pier. After a couple of accidents, the town decided that trucks would be driven onto the pier only by local experts. You can see how narrow it is."

Husain nodded and said, "Yes."

"A driver pulls his truck up to the pier, gets out and the local pilot backs the truck down to the end of the pier, and off-loading or on-loading occurs."

Husain was fascinated. As Abdul had described, movement was like clockwork, with trucks backing down, loading handled by cranes on the ship and then trucks driving off the pier. No time was wasted. The next truck already had a local driver ready to go as soon as the first truck got off the pier. Everything was done by the light of the moon. The scene was eerie.

Abdul hesitated, then spoke to Husain. "Doctor, we have things to do. The helicopter can take us to Port Sudan. The truck is going to the mining site. In the morning, we will fly there, God willing."

They spent the night at the Red Sea Hotel in Port Sudan, and after prayers and breakfast headed in the airplane to the ring complex at Ras ed Dom. As described, from the air Husain could identify several large circles in the ground darker than the surrounding rocks and sand. Abdul pointed them out, and the mining operation.

"Yesterday I told you about our uranium supply from the ring complex in northern Sudan. What I did not tell you was that it makes no economic sense to get it from here. Every drop of water for the operation, for the workers, has to be transported. We had to build a 700-kilometer (500-mile) pipeline from the Nile at Abu Hamad for the water. See it down there? We had to build a 700-km road along the pipeline and another 700-km road from the ring complex through the Red Sea Hills to Port Sudan. No economic sense, but if you need a uranium supply that's what you do. The Russians first discovered the uranium there in the 50's but even at the height of the Cold War they thought uranium extraction there was not worth it. The French looked at the situation, for their nuclear programs, but came to the same conclusion as the Russians. For us, though, it was critical in our secret effort to supply you with uranium. To the King, the cost did not matter. The amount of uranium was all that mattered. Consequently, your uranium is the most expensive on earth." He laughed and slapped Husain on the back.

Husain smiled sheepishly. "Are we going to land?"

"Another time," answered Abdul. "I know you'd like to see it, but I must return now." On the return journey, he continued talking about the effort. "Then there was the question of centrifuges. We felt it unwise to go to Siemens, as the first thing Germany would do is alert the IAEA, and the whole world would know. We'd do that if we have to, but we thought it best to have the bomb in hand before word got out. Consequently, our King went groveling before the Israelis.

Think about what it took for our King to beg Israel for help, a country he'd sworn to destroy. But there was no choice, he thought. Think of how skeptical the Israeli's were – how the people in that country would have objected if they had known."

"I can imagine."

Abdul continued, "When the King began making conciliatory statements about the Zionist state – you know how badly our people reacted. The King truly feared a coup."

"Actually, I was not here yet and was unaware," said Husain.

"Oh, of course," said Abdul. "But things settled down. The King decided if news about our atomic bomb got to the Iranians it wouldn't be a complete loss – at least they'd know we were working on defense. The Israelis did understand how fearful we are of Iran with a nuclear weapon, and came to believe that they might need an ally against Iran, even a Saudi ally. Thankfully, they decided to provide us with centrifuges, but they did not trust us, and agreed only with very strict oversight. That was why the King lifted the ban on Israeli citizens coming to Saudi Arabia. It seemed to the West a big conciliation, no one really expected a tourist trade to develop – but we had to provide for their inspectors to come at any time."

"Yes, that was a shock to hear, even in Pakistan."

"It's worked out, hasn't it? You've got your a-bomb production facilities. How many do you have now?"

"We are completing our seventh."

"Would you care to destroy the Zionist state?"

"No," replied Husain. "They have done nothing to me."

"How about Iran? How about sending your bomb to Tehran on one of the new airplanes the Americans provided as compensation for their Iran deal?"

"That's why I'm here."

"Would you not prefer to drop your bomb on the USA?"

Husain was shocked at the question, but said nothing.

The seduction had begun.

CHAPTER NINETEEN
SAUDI ARABIA AND SUDAN

2010

Over the next few months, Abdul talked to Husain many times, each time upping the ante with the possibilities. He planted the seed by discussing what would be the result of an atomic bomb in America. They talked about the best place to explode a bomb. At first, Washington DC seemed most attractive, being the center of government, the head of the snake that had killed Husain's family. But Abdul kept bringing up economic targets, and finally mentioned the critical importance of America's fourth largest city, Houston, and its port, the country's third largest. He discussed the far-reaching effects the atomic bomb would have on American society. The pipelines which supply most of the oil and gasoline to the northeastern states would be destroyed. "Just consider one thing: with not enough fuel how would food get transported into cities? What little that did would be sold for exorbitant prices, there'd be accusations of price-gouging, then theft and murders, then no more food would make it into the center of cities and there would be riots, then roving gangs looting stores and breaking into homes looking for food. The big cities, New York, Los Angeles, Chicago would be the worse, but even the smallest towns would suffer in the same way. It would be chaos: violent, convulsive chaos."

The descriptions of the damage the bomb would cause in Houston, along with the difficulty in moving it close to the center of Washington, finally convinced Husain that Houston was the most practical target. Still, Husain took almost eight weeks mulling it over before committing his talent to the group. He explained that a critical piece of his thinking was whether his best students were capable of exploding a device after he was gone, as he felt committed to providing Saudi Arabia a means to defend itself against Iran.

With that commitment, Abdul decided it was time to get Saleh Tawfiq Saleh, nee Manzur Husain, a new identity, a Sudanese identity. When Abdul told Husain, the physicist objected, "Why a different identity? I've already established a Saudi identity, thanks to the King. I'll never pass for Sudanese."

"Oh, you'll be surprised, I believe you will pass for Sudanese, God willing. More important, when the time comes, we need to be able to move you out of Saudi Arabia without the King's permission. A Sudanese passport will enable us to do so."

Abdul asked the Saudi ambassador to Sudan for some suggestions for an expediter, a person who could weave them through the Sudanese bureaucracy through friendship or bribery, and was surprised by the name that the Ambassador gave him. After gaining permission from the King to take Husain to visit the actual uranium mines in Ras ed Dom, Sudan, the two men flew first to Khartoum, where a taxi picked them up. Abdul was almost silly with amusement over the little joke he was to play. After a half-hour driving through the city, the taxi drove down a dirt road lined with modest homes built from mud. Abdul questioned the driver whether this could possibly be the address, but it was confirmed by the Ambassador's handwritten note. The two men had to step across the dirt equivalent of a gutter. No grass grew along the ditch. They approached a head-high light-green wall that extended the entire block, and they could see similar mud walls separated the houses and yards. A simple wrought-iron gate opened into a dirt yard. Abdul knew how much money he was paying the Sudanese man who lived in this humble house, and imagined the man must make many multiples of that in a year and should be able to afford a much better house. A man about fifty appeared at the gate with a broad smile on his round brown face, heightened by a brushy moustache. His black hair had turned grey at the temples. He wearing not the traditional Sudanese robe-like jalabiya, but tan slacks and a loose-fitting embroidered shirt similar to a guayabera, what Texans call a Mexican Wedding shirt.

Abdul grinned with giddiness, amused by the joke he was about to play on the men. He grabbed the arm of his bearded companion, and said, "Saleh Tawfiq Saleh, please meet the Sudanese Saleh Tawfiq Saleh." Startled, both men gazed at each other, then broke into laughter.

"Welcome, namesake!" said the Sudanese warmly as they grasped hands. Husain seemed pleased. Later, Abdul would explain to Husain that his Saudi same had been suggested to the King due to his admiration for the Sudanese expediter, but the Sudanese was not to know the Pakistani's real name.

The family entered the courtyard. The Sudanese man glowed as he introduced his son and three daughters to the two men. The oldest girl was about 10, long and lean with an eager smile. The boy, about 8, was thin and handsome. The youngest was about four, ready to play. The third child, about six, had the face of a person wise beyond her years, said nothing, but gazed intently with large dark eyes at the strangers, as if a judge. Abdul could sense the joy the man felt in his children, and that sense brought back his own difficulties with his family and disturbed him. Yasmeen's image flashed in his brain. Suddenly his mouth turned sour. He wanted to leave immediately, but Saleh's wife joined them, offering tea and coffee, delighted to meet another man with her husband's name. As much as Abdul wished to leave, he felt compelled to honor the family, so stayed in the unpretentious household, sitting on simple chairs. He let the others do the talking.

The taxi then took the three men north across the White Nile Bridge to Omdurman. When the British ruled Sudan, they called the small suburb 'The Arab Quarter', but after the Mahdi drove the British out, he made Omdurman his capital, so it grew and eventually became the cultural center of Khartoum. Omdurman was renowned for its markets, and the taxi went to the central souk, a huge plaza of two large city blocks full of tents where owners hawked their wares. The three men exited the taxi, and the Saudi and Pakistani-pretend-Saudi began following the Sudanese through the market. They passed people sitting on tarps displaying large delicious fruit and vegetables, the best from El Gezira, the land between the two Niles. Spices and herbs, piled in cones on table, provided a delicious aroma. Cloths and clothes and household goods, even suitcases, were being sold. The men got plenty of time to examine the offerings, as it seemed Saleh knew almost every other person. And when Saleh saw someone he knew, he would yell in delight, warmly grasp the hand and arm of the man, and talk engagingly, as if to a long-lost friend. They were not short exchanges. At first, Abdul was bothered by this waste of time, but reckoned this is what made Saleh a good expediter. He knew lots of people and they liked him. It would be easy for him to get things done because people would go out of their way to do things for some-one they liked. But by the time they got across the souk nearly an hour later, Abdul realized that this Sudanese Saleh genuinely liked hu-mans. He got a joy out of them-that's why he greeted people like that. Indeed, he received such joy out of his family and friends that he had no need for a pretentious house or material trappings. Abdul realized this was why the Ambassador liked the man and had honored him by suggesting that name to the King.

Saleh led them out of the market into a narrow passageway. Along the walls were some small shops, mostly silversmiths it seemed. He ducked into one and familiarly greeted the salesman in front. The room held two showcases of silver jewelry with barely enough room for the three men to stand. Saleh motioned for the Pakistani-Saudi to go with another man behind a curtain in the back of the shop. He did, and Saleh and Abdul talked about the jewelry. Abdul saw an intricately constructed bracelet, imagined how it would sit on Noor's wrist, and began to negotiate. It had been years since he had done so, and it took several minutes to get into the rhythm of showing disinterest and disgust, and threatening to walk out. The salesman knew the game well, and kept referring to the majesty of the piece and how it would help Abdul express his love. He let Abdul show his fake emotions, slowly reeling the customer into the purchase. Abdul enjoyed the game, and bought the piece just before Saleh emerged from behind the curtain with a new passport, this one Sudanese.

The Sudanese host said he had planned an experience for the two men, and in the late afternoon took them to a white-walled mosque with turquoise-colored onion domes sitting on dusty ground outside of town. They went up the stairs of a nearby building to the roof where they could easily see the mosque. Nearby was cemetery mostly covered by sand and dust. Below them, a group of people were gathered in a large area outside the mosque, waiting for the action. Several hundred meters away, a drum was beating, promoting the movement of a crowd of colorfully dressed men.

"What is going on?" asked Husain.

The Sudanese replied, "This is the mosque of Hamed al Nil, a leader of one of the local groups of Sufis 150 years ago. What you are about to see are the whirling dervishes. They are a Sufi sect. These dervishes provided the soldiers who fought for Muhammed Ahmad, the man who proclaimed himself the Mahdi, the messiah of Islam, the prophet who would drive out from Sudan the Turks, Egyptians and British who ruled the country. In the 1880's he did so, even though his men were armed primarily with spears and swords."

"I've heard of them," said Husain, and Abdul nodded. "Why the whirling?"

"You will see how they get caught up in the music and dancing, and the twirling takes them to a religious ecstasy and prepared them for battle."

The people standing in the area spread into a large ring, forming an arena with men in front and women to the rear, and the dervishes walked into the center, bobbing along with the drumbeat. Some were dressed in the traditional white Sudanese robes, but some wore bright green robes with red collars and hems, and a couple wore patchwork robes that looked like an American quilt, made from many pieces of different colored cloths. Saleh pointed out one piece that looked like an advertisement for a motorcycle. The drums were joined by cymbals, and the bobbing of the dancers increased in time with the music. Some onlookers joined them. The drums became more insistent, and drowned out the cymbals trying desperately to be heard. Men started chanting, many were bobbing to the beat of the music. Suddenly, one man in a green robe and a high-peaked green hat began spinning slowly, then starting moving across the open area, arms out. A man in a patchwork robe with a many-medaled skullcap began twirling in another part of the arena, then one in white did also. Several others copied them, each man lost in his own experience, feeling the music, spinning faster and faster, their brains reaching for ecstasy. The experience went on for over half an hour, and the three men on the rooftop watched intently. Finally, the music started to calm down, and a black-clad man circled the arena scattering incense on the participants and the crowd. It was time for the prayers of remembrance.

"Amazing," said Husain as they began to leave.

"Can you see how the British soldiers might be cowed by the sound and sight of the whirling dervishes before a battle?' asked Saleh.

Husain gruffly responded, "I don't understand why a man would need to do that to get motivated to drive the invader from his country, or to kill those who had murdered one's family."

Abdul smiled inwardly, noting how the performance had affected Husain.

"Ah, but it wasn't just to expel the invaders," replied Saleh. "They were fighting for who they believed was the Mahdi, the new prophet of Islam. It wasn't just a battle, it was a religious experience."

Abdul interjected, "When I was in London, I read Winston Churchill's account of the Battle of Omdurman in 1899, where he almost got killed in the last cavalry charge of the British Empire. He claimed the dervishes did their ritual to get ready to commit suicide against the much more powerful British army."

"Ah, yes," said Saleh. "He denigrated the dervishes for going into battle against overwhelming odds, but glorified the Light Brigade for doing the same in the Crimean War. There's even a popular British poem, 'The Charge of the Light Brigade.'"

Husain laughed. "He's got you there, Abdul."

Abdul smiled, "Yes, I believe our Sudanese friend has won the day."

"When I read history, I like to read both sides," said Saleh. "I've read both Churchill's *The River War* and also *Karari*, the Muslim version of the battle by a local historian."

"That's truly uncommon even-handedness in these times," remarked Abdul, profoundly impressed by the man: quiet, likeable, knowledgeable.

"One thing I've learned," said the Sudanese, "is that if someone is willing to die for his cause, he can find others to join him."

"Truly," replied Abdul.

CHAPTER TWENTY

BACK IN RIYADH

"**M**ajesty, I think the trip to Sudan was a success. Husain visited our mines. He saw the high costs in mining and shipping. He saw how the clandestine shipments are made. I believe he now understands how important his nuclear project is to Saudi Arabia. He appreciates the huge investment you've made in him. I'm sure his attitude's gone from 'working on a science project' to 'working on a State defense project critical to Saudi Arabia's survival.' He's always been dedicated to science. Now he is dedicated to something more important."

"I'm grateful for your assistance in that, Abdul."

"I also want you to know I took him to the market in Omdurman so he could buy silver jewelry for his wife. I think he appreciated that gesture, too. While there, the Sudanese guide took us to the tomb of Hamed al Nil to see the whirling dervishes. I'd never seen them—quite a marvelous experience to prepare for the prayers of remembrance."

"Sound like a worthwhile experience."

"Even for Husain, I believe."

"What do you mean?"

"Majesty, please do not get upset with Husain over this, but this is just the way he is."

"Please be straightforward, Abdul."

"Husain does not believe God exists."

The King was silent for several moments, and Abdul knew to let him absorb that news. The King had heard from Saleh's wife that he did not practice prayers faithfully, but still was amazed. Finally, he said, "Tell me more."

"That is just part of him. His whole world is science, is physics. He does not have room for God. Or rather, he says science can explain everything and he does not need God."

"Astonishing. It's difficult for me to imagine how anyone can live without faith, especially a scientist when he sees all the incredible wonders of the universe."

"Me, too. But remember that Husain does love the science of what he's doing here in Saudi Arabia. He likes the wife that you found for him and the family she's provided."

"Thank you for the report, Abdul."

"You are welcome, Majesty. Just one more remark, if I may. Our guide was the Sudanese, Saleh Tawfiq Saleh. I now understand why the Ambassador recommended the name. The man is a remarkable person, one who puts family and simplicity and happiness above money. I offered him a job at many times what he makes, and he declined rather than be separated from family and friends. He is truly a religious man. His name is a good omen for Saudi Arabia, and the Ambassador is to be commended."

"Thank you, Abdul."

CHAPTER TWENTY-ONE

AT THE CANYON VISITOR EDUCATION CENTER,

YELLOWSTONE NATIONAL PARK, WYOMING
SUMMER, 2014

The Center had several large rooms explaining the geology of the Park to visitors, how the Park had formed during the last three eruptions of a super volcano. One display was a comparison of the sizes of the eruptions of those three eruptions with that of Mount St. Helens, the 1980 eruption in Washington that most Americans were familiar with. The most recent Yellowstone eruption had put 1000 times the amount of ash into the air that Mount St. Helens had. The eruption two million years ago had put 2500 times that amount of ash. The most striking display was a large relief map sitting on a table about twelve feet square. The relief map illustrated the major features of the park, and with various lights outlined the extent of the calderas of the three eruptions. Abdul studied it for nearly an hour, and began looking for someone to ask questions of. He noticed a group of a couple dozen young people, perhaps high school students, being instructed by a Park Ranger. Abdul thought the low voice and the stocky body meant the Ranger was a male, but upon turning, her ponderous breasts bulging from the uniform made the opposite clear. While she waited for the students to answer her latest question, Abdul interrupted, "Ma'am, could I talk to you when you are finished?" She seemed relieved, as if the students had disappointed her, and turned to another Ranger, a short black-bearded man with a narrow face and sparkling eyes. "Steve, would you take over?" He seemed pleased with the charge, and went into his speech.

The woman turned to Abdul. She had the weathered face of someone who'd spent a lot of time in the sun, with brown hair showing streaks of grey. She appeared to be quite fit, as if she could carry her bulk easily across the mountains. Then he noticed her name tag that identified her as Mary Rainey, Ph.D., Chief Geologist, Yellowstone National Park.

"Sorry. I see I should address you as Doctor," apologized Abdul.

"Oh, never mind about that," she said, waving her arm to dismiss the apology. "How may I help you?"

"My name is Abdul Faisal, and this Park fascinates me. I'm trying to understand what's happening and have a question. Why do you say the volcano could erupt any time in the next twenty thousand years?"

She smiled. "Oh, that's a geology joke, really. The last eruption was 640,000 years ago, and the one before was 660,000 years before that. The difference is 20,000, so that is why we say anytime in the next 20,000 years. Actually, we have no way to know. The eruption before that was 800,000 years previous, but the one before that was about a million years. The geologist led him to the poster labeled 'Tracks of the Hotspot,' and said, "The hotspot is a plume of magma coming up from the mantle." She lifted her fist like a boxer, keeping her upper arm level. "My fist is the magma chamber, with the magma flowing up my arm." She floated her other hand over the fist. "My hand is the North American continent, which has been moving over the plume. In doing so, it's been creating this line of volcanos through Idaho to Yellowstone."

"Oh, I've seen this," said Abdul. "I got this off the internet." He showed her a map highlighting the track of the hot spot through Idaho into Yellowstone. "It's like the one on the wall."

She glanced at his map, nodded, then pointed at the wall poster. "The dates of eruptions are listed here, some 640,000 years apart, some 3 million years apart. However, the further back in time we go, the more imprecise we are in timing. This one, for example, says 6.5-4.3 million years ago. That could have been one 6.5 and another 4.3, and maybe there was one in between. If so, then our time frame changes to a half-million to three million-year intervals. We have no way to predict."

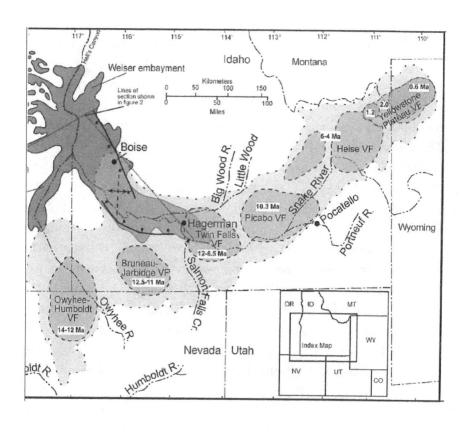

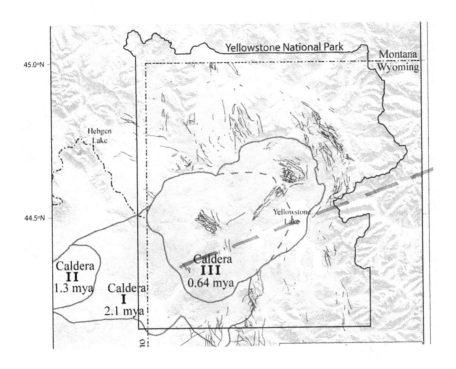

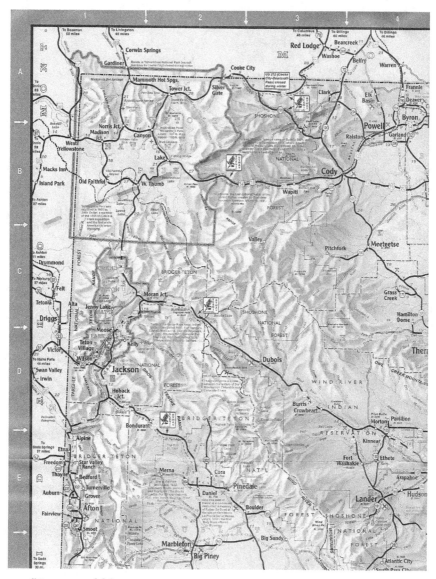

"So, it could happen any time, tomorrow to a million years from now?"

"We are constantly monitoring activity, hoping to be able to predict if an eruption is close."

"Activity?"

"Yellowstone is continually breathing. You can see in this poster an area that has been moving up and down about three feet since the 1920s. Now the west end of Yellowstone Lake is rising, and we have seen movement in this other area called Resurgent Dome. But we really don't know how much movement would indicate an imminent eruption."

"What causes the breathing?"

"It's related to the magma. It's bubbling up, and causes the ground to move, sort of like how your chest moves when your lungs inhale and exhale. I picture the magma as bubbling, turning over, as if cooked by something deeper. All the time it's building pressure and releasing pressure. At some point the pressure will get too much for the rocks to hold and the volcano will explode."

"Okay, any time in the next twenty thousand years. Where will it explode?"

"Good question, and the answer is we don't know. Take another look at the Track of the Hotspot. Notice it was in a straight line northeasterly for about 11 million years, then jumped suddenly due east. Then look back 15 million years and there was another change in direction from due east to northeast. So, will this next eruption be east of the last caldera or northeast? We don't know and we don't know how to tell. We just monitor the activity, the breathing, the small earthquakes, the gases that come out of the ground."

"What gases do you mean?"

"You've been to the mud volcano? You've seen the mud boiling?"

"Yes."

"We sample those gases to determine whether the composition changes over time. We are sampling a lot of the vents and geysers, too."

"Why?"

"There have been some examples where concentrations of certain gases increased just before an eruption. For example, just before El

Hierro erupted in the Canary Islands in 2011, there was a tremendous increase in Helium-4."

"Are you seeing that increase in Yellowstone?"

"Yes, but we don't know whether the amount of increase is significant."

"My God," thought Abdul to himself. "Would an atomic explosion in Yellowstone be a more devastating blow than in Houston? Was God putting this idea in his path as a temptation or as a sign?" He had to learn more. He turned back to the Track of the Hotspot, and asked Rainey, "I have another question. You said that the hotspot moved through Idaho in a straight line, but the last eruption appears displaced from the line." Then he walked to the east side of the large colorful relief map laid out before them, occupying the center of the room. He pointed at the map and said, "If you stand here, you can imagine a line running along the north side of Yellowstone Lake, and along the top of the Absarokas." Abdul then lifted his tablet and a map popped up. Rainey recognized it as the University of Utah's map of Yellowstone faulting. Abdul continued, "I looked at this map on the internet and this group of Yellowstone faults appear to terminate along that same straight line, the one I drew on this map." Rainey noticed he had drawn a large dashed line indicating where he meant. "Does this mean anything," he asked.

Rainey wanted to encourage the man despite having to shoot down his notion. "That is an interesting question, Mr. Faisal, but lots of apparent straight lines can be drawn in such a complicated and complex area. It probably is coincidental and means nothing important."

"But the straight line continues." He pulled out another map. Rainey recognized it as the northwestern corner of the highway map the State of Wyoming gave tourists. Abdul had continued his dashed line outside Yellowstone Park through the Absaroka Mountains and down Sunlight Creek to the Clarks Fork Canyon. He continued, "If you go east outside Yellowstone Park the line seems to travel right down this stream, and the stream seems to follow the straight line to where it joins the Clarks Fork River and they go into the canyon. Is that coincidence?"

Momentarily shocked, Rainey leaned closer and studied the map. She immediately saw the connection from Yellowstone Lake through Sunlight Basin to the canyon was indeed a straight line. It might truly be evidence of a strike-slip fault. Wrinkling her forehead, she tried to hold her thoughts in check. She could not believe it. Hundreds of geologists had worked that area, including herself. No one had ever mentioned the possibility of a strike-slip fault there, as far as she knew, and here was an amateur asking a simple question that had been missed by all those geologists. It just could not be, but once you married the geology inside the Park to that outside the Park, as Abdul had done, it seemed to fit. She straightened and took a deep breath, then spoke. "Mr. Faisal, let me check into that in more detail, and I will get back to you. No one that I know of has investigated the straight line you pointed out, but I may have missed that research. My expertise is the Park and honestly stops at the Park boundary. I'm embarrassed to say that, but it's true." Rainey realized that she wouldn't be the first geologist to miss what was happening across a boundary. The story was legendary how Texas geologists seemed to work as if geology stopped at the Rio Grande River until one day a Texas rancher named Sanchez noticed wells pumping oil in Mexico just across the river from his ranch. That led to the formation of a Texas independent oil company which found the oil on the Texas side of the river several years after the Mexican oil company Pemex had begun producing. "You have me intrigued. I promise to find the answer and let you know."

"Okay," said Abdul. "I would very much appreciate it."

"I promise to get back to you on it. Now, where was I? We monitor earthquakes and the breathing and the gases. One thing we'd like to have but can't is to measure the stress on the rocks underneath the surface. But that would require the drilling of a well and the Park

Service would never allow it."

"Would not Secretary Mathis approve it if you could show her the reasons?"

"Well, by the time we convinced her, we'll have a new Secretary of Interior. It would take ten years to get permission, I imagine. If ever."

"Could we drill a well on private property outside the Park?"

"I must say that's a delicious possibility, if we could get funding. Research money is so tight right now."

"Dr. Rainey, you know I am a wealthy man, and science is my hobby. Perhaps I could fund it personally."

Rainey was taken aback. "Really?"

"It's within my budget limit," he said, smiling.

"Thank you for the offer, Mr. Faisal. I truly appreciate it. However, let's not get ahead of ourselves. First let me evaluate the geology with some colleagues and determine whether we can verify the presence of a fault and justify the drilling of a well."

"Of course," said Faisal. "But the offer remains on the table. Let me know the results of your research, please."

"Definitely," she said, amazed and delighted. "I will get right on it." She hurried to her office and squinted at the official Geological Map of Wyoming, amazed to see a straight line suddenly pop out, one she had never noticed. She pulled up Google Earth and examined the area from Sunlight Basin through the canyon and beyond. She imagined she could see the straight line lining up with landforms past the town of Clark, past the bluff that demarked the end of arable land, and even into the badlands until it crossed into Montana. She took a deep breath and closed her eyes, wondering.

CHAPTER TWENTY-TWO
ABDUL MEETS SOME GEOLOGISTS

THAT SAME SUMMER TRIP TO YELLOWSTONE, 2014

"Let's stop for a snack and admire the view," said Noor. They had just seen Osprey Falls after a hike taking over two hours, and were starting their return, back up the steep hillside, following narrow switchbacks. They marveled at the magnificent canyon, with its steep sides and emerald green water below. Perhaps not as glorious as Yellowstone Canyon, but still breathtaking. It was called Sheepeater Canyon, after the aboriginal tribes that had lived in the area. "Look," said Noor. "Rock climbers." She pointed toward three people huddled along a cliff face.

Abdul gazed for a moment, then said, "No. They are studying the rocks. Must be geologists." He jumped to his feet and scrambled along the slope toward the three. All wore khaki outfits and carried large backpacks. Two had large-brimmed hats, but one blonde man had a bandana wrapped around his head. The nearest person appeared to be a woman, with hair bound in a large net at the back of her head. She was drilling a small hole in the rock, concentrating on her task, when Abdul neared. He stopped, but dirt from his boots settled on the spot she was drilling. She turned in exasperation. Most of her face was covered by absurdly large round sunglasses.

"Oh, no!" she shouted. "You've contaminated my site!" The other two, both men, stood up and watched.

"Oh. I'm so sorry," pleaded Abdul.

"You've wasted my morning! Go away!" She wailed.

The two men walked quickly toward the woman. One was blonde, the other appeared Latino. "Anna, are you all right?" asked the blonde, taking off his bandana. He stepped between the woman and Abdul, and aggressively leaned toward the Arab. Abdul instantly recognized the trait of a cocky rooster defending his hen, and knew the two were sleeping together. Abdul also realized the man was seeking any provocation that would justify his striking the intruder.

Abdul lowered his head and said, "I sincerely apologize," turned and walked away. The two men waited until he had gotten to Noor before returning to their work.

After a brief conversation, Noor walked to where the woman was working, got down on her knees in supplication, and said, "My husband sincerely apologizes and wonders if there is a way to make it up to you." The other two men glanced over, but stayed where they were.

The woman looked at her intruder, studied the tan oval face, instantly recognizing the scarf being worn meant she was Muslin. "Just go away. He contaminated my site. He cost me a day."

"Look," said Noor. "My husband is not just a tourist. He is a wealthy man who runs the largest private drilling company in the world. He is a mechanical engineer with several patents. But he is like a little boy when it comes to science, and especially Yellowstone. He knows he got carried away and would like to do something to make it up to you. Could he pay you for the lost day?"

The woman softened a bit. "I cannot take any money."

"Perhaps a grant to your university?"

"That's between him and Arizona State. I just want to be left alone to work."

"How about dinner tonight or tomorrow? We are camping at Mammoth tonight and Canyon Village tomorrow."

"Oh, I don't know."

"Bring your friends along. I'm sure my husband will have a hundred questions about your geology research."

"I'll talk it over with the guys."

"Okay, please do. Here is my card and my husband's card. Either night. His pleasure is to grill, so be prepared for a delicious meal."

"I'll think about it."

"Do come. It will mean that you accept his apology."

"I'll think about it."

"Okay, thank you for listening." She rose and returned to Abdul. The geologists watched the pair head up the trail.

The sun had set and the area glowed in twilight when the phone call came, informing that the three geologists were coming for dinner. Abdul added more charcoal to the fire, and Hassan seasoned more lamb chops. When they saw the three walking down the roadway between all the campers, Abdul tossed the meat on the grill with peppers and onions. The geologists were wearing the same clothes as earlier, but had added jackets for the growing chill. Abdul reckoned they had worked late and simply washed up before coming over. The blonde man was carrying a small ice chest.

Noor walked up to the woman and put out her hand. "I'm so pleased you came. I am Noor Faisal."

The woman shook the offered hand, and said, "Anna Shalala. This is Derek Compton and Ricardo Gonzalez."

Noor shook their hands, then introduced them to Abdul, and to Hassan, and to Sam Jackson, their driver. The newcomers were struck by the size the driver, a large darkly-hued man who looked strong enough to lift the RV. Derek glared at Abdul and shook his hand strongly, but Abdul did not try to match the rooster's effort. Noor said, "please make yourselves comfortable," and the group arranged itself around the picnic table that sat beside the large RV.

Abdul spoke, "Hassan is what you'd call my right-hand man. We have been together from the very first wells we drilled and we have developed our grilling technique over many years. I hope you like it. It's a traditional Saudi meal. May I offer you something to drink? We usually drink coffee or tea with our meal."

Derek slapped his ice chest on the table and said, "I'll have a beer."

"Derek," pleaded Anna. "We are their guests."

"I'm in America and I'll drink what I want."

"That's fine," said Abdul. "Sam loves beer, too. Just because three of us don't drink alcohol doesn't mean the rest of you can't. Enjoy."

Sam reached out his hand toward Derek, who reluctantly handed him a beer.

"Ricardo, what would you like?"

"I'll have a beer, too."

"I only brought four," complained Derek.

"That's okay," said Sam, and rolled out a cooler from beneath his bench. "I think we're covered." The others chuckled, except a blushing Derek.

"Ricardo," asked Noor, "where are you from?"

"Venezuela."

"Oh, we've drilled many wells in Venezuela," interjected Abdul. "I know the head of the national oil company, PDVSA."

Ricardo did not reply, and Anna spoke, "Ricardo has to be careful of what he says. The wrong word could mean his scholarship is revoked and he's sent home."

"I understand. We were working there when a bunch of PDVSA employees signed a petition protesting Chavez's rule. A purge followed, and every person who'd signed that petition lost his job and livelihood. PDVSA was gutted—so many great geologists and engineers gone—that it's taken years to recover. It's still not fully recovered. But don't worry, Ricardo. If your name comes up, I'll say you had nothing but high praise for Maduro."

"Oh, no!" Ricardo immediately responded. "Don't say that. That would make them suspicious." All laughed, even Derek. "Simply say I expressed no dissatisfaction with the government."

"Got it, Ricardo," said Abdul, smiling. "Here comes Hassan with the food: lamb chops, chicken, grilled vegetables, tabbouleh, and a yoghurt dip, along with bread like what you call pita. Dig in. Enjoy."

Noor noticed Anna picking only chicken. "Try some lamb, too," she encouraged.

"Oh, I don't like lamb."

Hassan broke in, "Anna, I will make you a bet. I'll bet that if you eat one of my lamb chops, you'll eat a second. What's that commercial, 'I bet you can't eat just one'."

Ricardo said, "They're really good. Try one."

Anna sheepishly selected one with two fingers, as if she did not want to touch the lamb chop. But after chewing a bite, she agreed. "Yes, really good."

Derek, gazing at the massive RV, asked, "Is this one of those million-dollar RVs?"

"Derek." Anna put her hand on his arm.

"As a matter of fact, it is," said Abdul.

"What a waste of money," Derek said disgustedly.

"Not so, Derek," responded Abdul. "As an engineer, I focus on safety and reliability and this is the safest and most reliable RV I could find—well, that Sam could find. Plus, its capabilities include a worldwide command center. Crescendo is drilling wells all over the world. This satellite capability allows us to communicate with anyone anywhere. We may be on vacation but we still look at business stuff every day. Sam, why don't you show Derek the inside so he can see what I mean."

Sam stood, but Derek didn't move, not wanting to be shown up again. "Come on," said Sam. "I'll show you what other beers I have inside."

Ricardo jumped up. "I want to see." Reluctantly Derek joined them.

"I'm sorry," said Anna. "Derek can be such an ass sometimes. We had a little campfire romance the first night out and now he thinks he owns me."

Her words 'campfire romance' struck Abdul like a whip. "Western women," he thought. "So loose. So licentious." Now he was disgusted. He realized that Anna was probably somewhere close in age to Yasmeen, and his heart sank. Yasmeen was somewhere he did not know, and doing God knows what. Noor saw his demeanor drop and tried to think quickly of some way to bring him back. Fortunately, a cheerful sound interrupted them.

"Oh, Sammy," two voices musically sang out from the darkness outside the campfire light. Anna could not see them well, just two female figures flickering as the light flickered.

"Don't worry, ladies," yelled Hassan. "He'll be right out." He turned to Anna. "Talk about campfire romance. Those two were on Sam almost as soon as he parked the RV. They're sisters or cousins or something, and they spotted our strong virile driver immediately and made off with him last night. Looks like a repeat performance tonight."

Anna smiled.

Abdul, trying to recover, leaned toward her and spoke in a more serious tone. "Please tell me about your research."

"Okay. This is my second summer gathering data here in Yellowstone. Normally I'd be done this year, but the results so far are so revolutionary, so upsetting to what's thought about the volcano... Sorry, do you know about the Yellowstone super volcano?"

Sam, Derek and Ricardo stepped down from the RV. Hassan mentioned the two women, so Sam grabbed three beers from his cooler and walked into the darkness toward the giggling women.

"Don't ask," said Abdul to Derek and Ricardo. "Anna is telling us about your research." He turned to Anna and said, "Yes, I've read a lot about the volcano."

Anna continued, "The rocks where we were today is one of the outcrops of what is called the Lava Creek Tuff. The tuff is a layer of volcanic ash. The Lava Creek eruption was Yellowstone's last big one, about 640,000 years ago. We think this tuff provides the key to understanding how rapidly the volcano could explode."

"What do you mean?"

"There is this huge chamber below Yellowstone full of magma, that's hot molten rock. This same magma chamber is what exploded 640,000 years ago. Right now, we think the magma in the upper part of the chamber is too cool to erupt. For an eruption to occur, the upper layer has to heat up significantly or somehow the hot magma below has to move up and displace the cooler magma in the upper part."

"Like in a lava lamp?"

"Exactly like a lava lamp. That's what geologists have thought would occur if the lower layer got hot enough—it would bubble up and displace the cooler magma and then you'd have conditions ripe for eruption."

"I understand. Why is your research so revolutionary?"

"We are talking about massive volumes of magma that would have to move up the chamber, so geologists have expected that it would take thousands of years for the movement to occur."

"I understand that."

"But our measurements from last year indicate that in the last eruption the movement occurred on a scale of ten to thirty years."

"Really?"

"Yes. I don't believe it. Nobody in our group believes it. That's why we are here. We are going to every outcrop of the Lava Creek Tuff and taking new measurements, to see if what we saw last year is repeatable."

"Is it?"

"So far, yes. I still don't believe it. That is why we are trying to be extremely careful about contamination, about everything. I'm trying to prove myself wrong, but it keeps coming back with same answer."

"Why is that so awful? I mean, why do you want it to be wrong?"

"Because, if the data are true, and our understanding is correct, then the super volcano could erupt in ten-thirty years from now. That's crazy. How could so much magma move so quickly up the chamber? I can't comprehend it."

Abdul sat back and stretched. "Wow," he said quietly. "That changes a lot."

"Everything," said Derek.

"This is fascinating. Would you tell me the name of your thesis advisor? I'd like to communicate with him."

"It's Dr. Cornelia Buck, a woman."

"Sorry. Again. I seem to keep stumbling."

Noor noticed that Abdul's demeanor, which had been buoyed by the research conversation, seemed to slump. She stood, and the men stood in response. "We wish to thank you for honoring us with dinner and conversation. It's been quite fascinating. We wish you the best of luck in your research. Now get a good night's sleep."

Abdul spoke, "Yes, I hope we see you again someday and learn more. Ricardo, I will remember our pact."

Ricardo laughed, and the three left.

"Fascinating," Abdul repeated softly, shaking his head.

CHAPTER TWENTY-THREE

ABDUL EXPLAINS TO HUSAIN
THE SMUGGLING OPERATION

2014

On another of their evening walks, Abdul explained to the physicist, "My biggest problem was how to smuggle your equipment into America because of the radiation. No matter how we tried to disguise the radiation, there would be some leakage. The Americans count on that. They have a vast network of radiation detectors at all the ports and around the country. So, I figured that the best way to get past that would be to put it with other radioactive equipment. Crescendo is a partner in the Customs Trade Partnership Against Terrorism, so we have credibility with the American government. With our good name, based on hundreds of containers that have passed inspection every year, we have gained the trust of the Crusaders. Crescendo also cooperates by paying for the American radiation inspectors to come to our sites to check out containers as they are being loaded, as at Ras ed Dom. Alas, those inspectors don't seem to work real hard when it's 52 degrees Celsius (125 Fahrenheit). So, I made sure all the mining equipment was exposed to as much low-level radiation of other materials as was possible at the site. Then I got the American government itself and the IAEA to check the equipment and certify that the equipment, despite the radiation afterglow, was okay to enter the USA. The Americans themselves certified the mining equipment! All I had to do was to mix the nuclear bomb in with the certified equipment! Brilliant. Thanks be to God."

One day, in Abdul's office in the "fracking research" facility in

Riyadh, Husain questioned Abdul about the framework of the bomb. "I understand now how you are going to get the uranium into the country, but what about the bomb framework?"

Abdul replied. "Oh, originally I planned just to put in with some drilling equipment. It could be listed as just extra well instrumentation. Nobody would know unless the inspector had years of experience drilling wells. I don't see that as a problem."

"Good," said Husain.

"But then I had a better idea," Abdul smiled. He reached into his pocket and pulled out a USB drive. It looked like one of the billions of USB drives in the world. "Here's your framework, Doctor."

Husain was puzzled. "What do you mean?"

"3-D printing. This contains the code for the framework. All I have to do is to take it to any 3-D printer that handles the heavy plastics, and I can print it out."

Husain was taken aback. "Will that work? Will it be strong enough?"

Abdul responded, "Well, now there is a Swiss company in Houston that incorporates metal into the 3D printing to improve the strength. But we probably don't need that. Let me show you something." He pulled some pictures from his desk. "See this office building? It's in Abu Dhabi. The entire building was made by 3-D printing."

"You're kidding."

"No. Each wall piece, each section of floor and ceiling, all the window frames, everything was made by a 3D printer, and assembled in place."

"Astonishing," said Husain. He was even more astonished when Abdul took him to the 3D printing facility and showed him the exact replica of the framework Husain had been constructing himself. Husain began to wonder if there was anything Abdul could not do.

"But don't worry," said Abdul. "We will ship one of yours in some drilling equipment, too. The printer version is merely our back-up."

Husain smiled, amazed.

CHAPTER TWENTY-FOUR

YELLOWSTONE NATIONAL PARK, WYOMING

SPRING, 2015

"**M**r. Faisal, this is Mary Rainey at Yellowstone Park."

"Hello, Dr. Rainey. How are you?"

"Fine, thanks, Mr. Faisal. I hope you are well. I have news for you." Her deep voice seemed happy.

"Yes, what is it?"

"You may have indeed identified a strike-slip fault along the straight line you pointed out. Let me explain what that is."

"Oh, no need for that, Dr. Rainey. I've been studying some geology. Let me see if I understand. A normal fault drops rocks down, a reverse fault pushes rocks up, and a strike-slip fault moves rocks sideways, like the San Andreas Fault in California."

"Very good, Mr. Faisal. I'm delighted that you are interested enough to study. The implication of a strike-slip fault in Yellowstone is what's significant. The fault, which we are calling the Sunlight Basin Fault thanks to you, is a zone of weakness in the earth. Worse, it might extend into the magma chamber under the Park. If true, it severely complicates our understanding of the potential for eruption. Pressures in the magma seek zones of weakness—that's where the next eruption is likely to be. We geologists need to study this fault. It's possible that it's tied to the Absaroka volcanism, which led to the Heart Mountain detachment."

"I'm sorry, Dr. Rainey. You lost me there."

"Oh, sorry, Mr. Faisal. I forgot for a second that you aren't a geologist. Suffice it to say the Sunlight Basin Fault might put the final touches on a geologic mystery that's fascinated geologists for a hundred years."

"Go back to it being tied to the magma chamber, please."

"Of course. If this Sunlight Basin Fault reaches from the chamber all the way to the Clarks Fork River, it might provide a weak spot near the surface. Build up enough pressure and you've got an eruption. That changes the way we look at predicting the next eruption."

Abdul thought he understood the implication. "So, what do you mean you wish to study the fault?"

"Remember I told you about measuring the breathing in the Park and the gases and so forth?"

"Yes."

"Well, we need to extend those measurements east of the Park along this Sunlight Basin Fault. But I'm getting ahead of myself. I've asked several experts in faulting to come to Yellowstone this summer to study the fault. I'm planning a conference in August for the participants to present their results. I am hoping that you could attend and the see the fruits of your question."

"Oh, this is marvelous, Dr. Rainey. I promise I will attend, God willing."

"Meanwhile, I will speak to my colleagues about the possibility of drilling a well to measure stresses. I cannot speak for the others, but hope they will welcome such a well."

"Thank you, Dr. Rainey. I will chip in any way I can. My deepest regards."

"You are welcome, Mr. Faisal. I look forward to seeing you in the Fall."

"Likewise, Dr. Rainey," he said, and hung up, feeling that God had a hand in this, that God was preparing a path for him in some way for some purpose with this well and the fault. Could the atomic bomb set off the super volcano? If so, that would be much more devastating than exploding it in Houston. He had to study the possibility.

CHAPTER TWENTY-FIVE

THE SECOND SEDUCTION
OF MANZUR HUSAIN

SUMMER 2015

"**M**ajesty," said Abdul to the King, "I would like your permission to take Dr. Saleh to the United States to see Yellowstone Park, a place I love."

The King seemed curious, "Tell me why."

Abdul continued, "I get excited every time I think about going there. It is a fascinating place: more geysers in one place than all the geysers in the rest of the world combined. A place of unusual topography and mountain peaks. And unusual wildlife: bison, bear, elk, deer, wolves and mountain sheep. I've been twice and I'm going again in August, and taking part of my family, God willing. I'd like to take Saleh and his wife and children." Abdul figured that Husain's wife was a spy for the King, but wanted to make his request seem reasonable as otherwise approval would be impossible. "I am always inspired each time I go there. I think it will refresh and inspire Saleh, too."

"Does he need refreshment and inspiration?" asked the King.

"Oh, I expect he'd say not, but I think we all would be inspired by this magical place. Even you, Majesty. I'd invite you to join us if it were possible. You'd love it, I promise. It's truly a special place. Look, I've become Saleh's friend, although I must say Saleh could not become really close to anyone not a physicist. He simply thinks differently about things than the rest of us do. Of course, he still misses his first wife and family. He hates America for that. He says he doesn't miss Pakistan, although I think that is because he is so absorbed in his project. It consumes him, like a small boy with his favorite toy. However, it's gone past the setup and research stage into production, and I think it's become a little boring for him. That's why I think he could use a trip like Yellowstone. He loves science and Yellowstone is a scientific wonder. It's magical for anyone, but the more science you know the more fascinating it becomes. Because of his brain, I think he will be entranced, and be inspired."

"Has he indicated he'd like to go?"

"No. He is a national treasure and I would not think of asking him without your permission."

"You are a national treasure, too, Abdul."

"Thank you for the compliment, Majesty, but I am simply a successful businessman. My companies would go on without me. Husain is so critical to our nuclear program that he is irreplaceable. I know that. I will protect him. I just want to share with him a wondrous place I love."

"Would not the American's face recognition software identify him when he enters the country?"

"Do not worry about that, Majesty. Doing what I do has made me aware of ways to get him in without revealing his real name. If his face is scanned, it will come up on the screen as Saleh Tawfiq Saleh, not Manzur Husain."

"Okay, Abdul. I will consider your request and let you know."

"Thank you, Majesty."

A few weeks later, after talking to Saleh's wife and his Council and hearing their enthusiasm for anything Abdul suggested, the King gave his approval. Abdul asked Husain, but he seemed reluctant at first. After discussing it with the King, though, he agreed to go.

Abdul called his American friend Homer Knost, Secretary of Commerce, who introduced him to the Secretary of Interior, Theresa Mathis. Abdul suggested a large donation to the Park's funding if the trip could be arranged on short notice and kept secret from the media.

Mathis immediately arranged for the luxury suites reserved for government officials at Old Faithful Inn be set aside for the Abdul entourage, one room for Abdul and his family, one for the Saleh family and one for Homer Knost and his wife, Dottie. The Head Ranger and the Chief Geologist for the Park were ordered to be guides for the VIPs. The Senators from Illinois and Indiana who were displaced were upset about losing their vacation plans and threatened to cut funding, but Mathis dared them to try. Wouldn't their constituents like to know that they did not pay for their rooms when they came to the Park?

Timing was absolutely critical. Abdul had to time the group's visit so that Husain could attend the meeting of geologists where they would report their findings on the Sunlight Basin Fault. Abdul knew that only the geologists, using purely scientific evidence, could convince Husain that the fault was present. Abdul would then have to explain how the atomic bomb would release the fault and cause the Yellowstone super volcano to explode. And Abdul had to work the geologists' meeting into the tour schedule. Fortunately, Chief Geologist Rainey was able to arrange the geology conference in Cody, in the building that housed the Whitney Gallery of Western Art and the Plains Indian Museum and Buffalo Bill Museum. Abdul knew the treasures there would fascinate the others in the families and keep them occupied during the geology meeting. That would make the timing and maneuvering easy.

If the geologists could not make it all real to Husain, and he did not see the possibilities of the volcanic eruption, then the bomb would be exploded in Houston. So be it. If Abdul could get Husain into the meeting of the geologists, the rest would be in God's hands. Everything was anyway, in the end. The fact that every piece had fit together so smoothly so far made Abdul feel certain God was with him, helping.

"I don't want to hear your religious reasons — they mean nothing to me," Husain stated gruffly, with a growl in his voice. "If I am going to join you, it will only be for sound scientific reasons."

Abdul was quiet for a moment, then said, "I understand. There is a strong scientific reason. Let's talk geology. Have you ever heard of Yellowstone Park?"

"No – well, maybe. Tell me."

"Yellowstone Park is a famous area in the Rocky Mountains – in the state of Wyoming. It's an area of a multitude of geysers – more geysers than anywhere in the world. Nowadays geologists have figured out that underneath Yellowstone is the world's largest volcano. You know about Mount Tambora in the Pacific – that when it exploded in 1815 it caused a year without a summer around the world."

"Yes, I've read about it."

"Well, the last time Yellowstone erupted 640,000 years ago, it was a thousand times bigger than Tambora. A thousand times bigger! The ash fall covered the USA from Chicago to Houston. It goes off every 640,000 years, and we are within striking distance of another eruption."

"So what?"

"Pressure is building in Yellowstone Park now. It could go any time in the next 20,000 years, say the geologists. Your bomb will create a crack in the shell, and the volcano will erupt. Even if the ash fall doesn't get all the way to Houston, it will definitely blanket the wheat fields and corn fields of the Midwest, the breadbasket of America. It would destroy all of America's grain harvest, all of it.

"Sounds like a fantasy."

"Don't worry, Husain. I will show you all the numbers – you will see I'm right. For now, just picture the difficulty facing America when that happens. No wheat. No corn. You think shortages of gasoline will cause riots? Think shortages of food."

"The picture is intriguing but I don't believe it's possible."

"Oh, it is, but only with your bomb. Let's retire to my cabin where I have maps and information."

In the luxurious cabin, Abdul laid out several maps and charts, details of geology and details of volcanic eruptions. He took Husain on a video tour of Yellowstone Park's volcano. He compared three known Yellowstone blasts to ones Husain was familiar with. Krakatoa, Pinatubo and Mount Tambora. He showed the ash patterns of those Yellowstone eruptions overlain onto agricultural maps. He showed Husain how Yellowstone Lake was already "breathing," that is, the West Thumb area had been rising and falling for decades, getting stronger over the years. The floor of the park has risen 9 inches in just the past 3 years – that's 23 cm! The amount of Helium-4 rising above the volcano is hundreds of times bigger than usual – that was a signal that the El Hierro volcano in the Canary Islands was about to explode.

"Think about the Mt. Tambora eruption in 1815. That happened in Indonesia in the Southern hemisphere." He spun the globe until he found the spot, then pointed to it.

"Yet, all the way on the opposite side of the earth in the Northern hemisphere," he spun the globe and stopped it with his finger in Europe, "the ash caused 1816 to be the 'Year without a Summer.' Famine occurred due to crop failures in Britain, Ireland, Germany and India." With the word "India," he spun the globe further and pointed to it. "It was the worst famine in a century – we've seen nothing like it since, not for 200 years. Now, the last Yellowstone eruption was at least 20 times larger than Tambora. Twenty times! And it would be right in the heart of America. The heaviest ash, meters thick, would fall on the American breadbasket, Kansas, Nebraska, the Dakotas, and wipe out the entire grain harvest. That area would never recover, not for a hundred years. If Tambora caused one year without summer, how many years without summer would another Yellowstone cause? Think of what happens: no bread, no corn, none. Forever gone. America would be destroyed. The West would be destroyed. Only hardy people would survive. Hardy people like the Arabs."

Abdul looked at Husain. The physicist seemed stunned.

Husain studied Abdul's face for a moment, wondering if the man was serious or mad. He needed to know more. "Are all these numbers true?"

"Easily verifiable."

"But Arabs are also dependent upon outside sources for food. What about Saudi Arabia?"

"Think of El Gezira." He was referring to the large area south of Khartoum between the White Nile and the Blue Nile and irrigated by both rivers. "El Gezira used to supply much of Saudi Arabia's food and cotton. It was called the breadbasket of the Arab world before the socialists took over and collectivized the farms. It's taken a long time to recover from that calamity, but things are moving well now. Exports are increasing. Most important, it's all irrigation from those rivers and does not require rain.

"You may have heard that Saudi Arabia has been investing a lot in Sudanese agriculture lately. That's a coincidence, but will benefit our country in this case. More areas of cultivation mean more food for Arabs."

"What about people in Pakistan?"

"Ah, you probably know more than I do, but I see where Pakistan is becoming one of the fastest growing food producers in the world. Millions of hectares of food production coming on line in just the past few years. Pakistan will survive. Not so the West, whose main food production will be wiped out. Think: no bread, no corn, no pasta, no pizza. All the wheat fields and corn fields gone. Just the start. No sorghum to feed the cattle and pigs. No grass for them to graze on. No sunlight for years due to the ash cloud circling the globe. Now think of New York City. Ten million people crammed into a very small area. What's going to happen when the food stops being transported in? First the sparkling grocery stores will be looted. But that won't last long. What'll people do then? They'll steal from each other, and kill each other. Gangs will form for protection and turf, and fight each other. Still there won't be enough food. Pets will become food. Eventually people will face a choice: starve or eat each other. It'll happen. Think of those soccer players in the Andes – those people on the wagon trail that got stuck in a blizzard. When people have eaten pets and their pets' food, where are they going to turn next? With hunger craving at their bellies, when they can't think of anything but food, they will look at their neighbor differently."

"Gruesome."

"Gangs will move out of the city and roam the country. Only the most brutal and best-armed will survive."

"New York is just an example. All the American cities will face the same. Next will come London and then Paris and all the European cities will face the same famine. The West will die, and along with it will be those Muslims who've chosen to enjoy the pleasure and debauchery of Western civilization. The famine will lead to a collapse of the energy sector across the globe. People will lose their dependence upon air conditioning and electricity. They will have to go back to the basics of life."

"Appalling, but you have not proven to me that the bomb would set off the super volcano eruption."

"No, but for that you need to understand the geology of the park, and I'll let the geologists there explain it. For now, let's look at it from a business point of view. It's a matter of reward to risk. Let's say that the explosion in Houston has a 90% chance of succeeding, meaning the bomb goes off and destroys the refineries and pipelines and the city center. We know the amount of damage it would cause, say $100 billion. So, in that case, we have a 90% chance of $100 billion destruction, or an expected value of $90 billion. Do you follow?"

"I know probabilities, Abdul," said Husain in an irritated voice.

"Okay, let's look at the Yellowstone case," continued Abdul. "We're talking about destroying Western Civilization. The Gross

World Product is about 75 trillion dollars. If exploding the bomb at Yellowstone has a 1% chance of succeeding, but the reward is $75 trillion in destruction, the expected value is $750 billion. That's just for one year, and science indicates the destruction would last many, many years, decades. In that case, Yellowstone is a better bet."

"I understand, Abdul," said Husain. "But I'm sticking with Houston unless you can convince me of the exactness of the risks in each case and the true amounts of destruction. And the convincing will have to be done by the geologists, not you."

"I will do my best, Saleh," said Abdul. "But the biggest question mark is the value of the destruction of Western Civilization."

CHAPTER TWENTY-SIX

THE GEOLOGISTS MEET TO DISCUSS RESULTS

CODY
AUTUMN, 2015

Mary Rainey, Chief Geologist at Yellowstone stood at the podium and addressed the group of geologists. "Good Morning, everyone. Continue to enjoy your breakfast. I'm pleased all of you have responded to my invitation and decided to see for yourselves something most intriguing. First, I'd like to thank the Buffalo Bill Center of the West (she was careful not to use the phrase BB-COW, as that upset the hierarchy of the Museum) for allowing us to use this wonderful Coe Auditorium for our meeting. Second, I'd like to introduce you to the man whose inquiry started all of this. You may have heard of him – Abdul Faisal, the founder and CEO of Crescendo Drilling, one of the most innovative drilling companies in the world. Stand up, Abdul. Mr. Faisal is a man with far-ranging curiosities, and he has visited Yellowstone several times because he's intrigued by the place, like many of us. Last year he came to me with a simple question about what he was seeing and what did it mean – that this long straight valley where Sunlight Creek runs lines up directly with the termination of some faults and seismic events. He questioned whether they might be related. My first reaction was that it could not be, that anything so apparently obvious to a curious mind could not have been overlooked by professional geologists. But then I thought about the apparently obvious matchup of the opposite sides of the Atlantic, and how professional geologists missed that for decades. I'd actually been up Sunlight

Creek about 20 years ago, so I went back to my field notes and found remarks I'd written then about unusual horizontal striations – I'd put glacial. Abdul's question got me thinking – could they be slickensides?"

Abdul leaned over and whispered into Husain's ear, "That's geology-speak for skid marks on rocks."

Rainey continued, "Could I have missed a strike-slip fault?"

Abdul again informed Husain, "That's a sideways-moving fault like the San Andreas Fault in California."

Rainey went on. "So, I called some people who love field geology. I asked Shive at Wyoming and Smithson at Bozeman to come join me. Shive picked up Barbara and John Vietti in Thermopolis on his way up. My colleague from the park, Steve Jensen, is here. The conclusion from the six of us was the presence of some weak evidence, certainly not conclusive. Now the reason you were invited here is to determine whether there is more evidence and if so, what is its importance. If there is a strike-slip fault here, then our understanding of the mechanics of the Yellowstone system changes. That would be truly significant. Most important it would make the prediction of the next major eruption more problematic. So, as the invitation said, we'd like you to examine what we've seen, and look for more, and think about what it means. We are grateful so many of you have come, but I wish to thank especially those two who came the furthest just happen to be perhaps the most renowned experts on strike-slip faulting, Dr. Johannes de Bruin of UCLA and Dr. Roberta Greene of UMass." Polite applause spread through the audience.

"Now I'd like to get right to work. I would like to think our good friends at the University of Utah for providing this map of the fault patterns in Yellowstone. Note the last caldera. Here's the Sour Creek resurgent dome, rising a few centimeters every year. Note how the Sour Creek faults stop along a line where these unusual northeast-striking faults are. Note how the faults east of Sour Creek seem to wrap around the Caldera and the resurgent dome. Note how the top of the Absaroka

Mountains seem to shift eastward at the place where those faults end. Is that a result of the caldera, or evidence of a strike-slip fault that runs northeasterly? Note the shape of Yellowstone Lake. I've always thought it appropriately looks like a backpacker. See how the strange straight line of the backpacker's pack goes right along the offset line of the Absarokas. Okay, okay, it could also be a result of the oblong nature of the caldera. But let's extend that line to the next map. It goes right down Sunlight Basin. Look at Google Earth or Bing Maps — whatever you've got. Take that line down Sunlight Creek. It intersects where the Clark's Fork makes a big left turn and goes straight into the canyon. The Clark's Fork goes in a straight line for nearly 14 km before the Clark's Fork makes that turn. Is the turn and the canyon evidence of a strike-slip fault? Maybe, maybe not. Is this proof of a fault running through here? No. But I think it's enough evidence to make a hypothesis we need to investigate. That's why the six of us came here last June, to check it out. I've looked at the literature for this area — it seems all the geologists who've ever been in here have been so focused on the Heart Mountain mystery that they have not looked at anything so mundane as the possible presence of a strike-slip fault. We had some volunteers to go up Sunlight Basin Creek and some go down. You all have been here for several days now, checking our evidence. I suspect that you guys who brought your fly rods and chose the Clark's Fork did check out the geology in between your fish taking." Several geologists laughed lightly and some pointed fingers at others. "Now, I'd like to open this meeting for comments before getting to the presentations."

Gene Trowbridge, a bald, gruff-looking bear of a man and a professor at Montana Tech, growled. "People, this hypothesis is so weak it should not even be called a hypothesis. We have nothing that could conclusively be called evidence. We have no clear offsets. Where are the offsets?" Abdul did not understand the geologic jargon, but from the response of the other geologists, he could tell some felt the remark was damning.

Trowbridge continued, "We have a canyon running in a straight line – nothing unusual in these elevations. The earthquakes stop along a supposed line. So what? They have to stop somewhere. The fact that they line up with a straight canyon which is not quite so straight is coincidental. This is all easily explained by the chaotic behavior common in such a complex environment. You all know my reputation for looking for alternative explanations of geologic phenomena. Here we have no geologic phenomenon to resolve. We are wasting our time with this idea."

Johannes de Bruin, the ancient white-haired professor at UCLA often called 'The Dean of Structural Geology', stood and pulled his pipe out of his pocket, and began packing it with tobacco. Clearly, he was so preoccupied with his thoughts that he'd forgotten the restrictions against smoking. A story of struggles between him and the UCLA administration over his smoking in the classroom and his office had become apocryphal, with the legendary geologist threatening to go to cross-city rival USC. The dispute had settled into an uneasy truce. He no longer smoked in the classroom while the administration turned a blind eye to his smoking in his office.

Rainey watched, disbelieving the crime being committed before her eyes. When de Bruin struck a match, Rainey rose and shouted, "Dr. de Bruin." De Bruin dismissively waived his arm in her direction. Jensen grabbed Rainey's arm and pulled her down, shushing the agitated moderator.

"Gentle Geologists," he began with his famous salutation spoken with a Dutch accent. "We have heard all the talk about lack of evidence and the consensus seems to be headed toward the idea that there is no strike-slip fault. For many years I have been in my friend Dr. Trowbridge's camp, but now I fear that the lack of evidence provides the most dangerous situation of all." A murmur swept the audience. De Bruin was considered the world's greatest expert on strike-slip faults, having studied the San Andreas his entire career. He took a pull on his pipe. "What do we know? We know that the quake activity northeast of the lake seems to stop at a line, which extended, heads down Sunlight Creek. That much we know. All the other evidence, even the possible slickensides, is questionable. The lack of evidence may mean no fault exists. Or it may mean the fault is simply waiting, building stress, until it finally breaks in a massive release of force. You all know this. The San Andreas near Los Angeles creeps slowly, inching a little every year, displacing fence lines and streams, gives off lots of small fairly harmless quakes. But the San Andreas near San Francisco is stationary, building pressure until it gives violently, like the 1906 quake, then again in 1989 in the World Series quake. That was 83 years of silence. This Sunlight Basin fault could have been sitting here for 640,000 years, silently building pressure. When it goes, if it's real, it would release god-awful force. Maybe a magnitude 9 earthquake like the one in Chile. What would be its effect? I submit to you that we need to study this area closely. The only way to know is to determine what pressure, what stress exists."

Peter Shive, a thin, athletic-looking professor at the University of Wyoming, rose. He raised his fist like a boxer, and Abdul recognized the posture as the same that Dr. Rainey had taken last year. Shive spoke, "I think of the hot spot like this." He moved his other hand over the fist. "As the continent moves over the plume, the upward pressure from the magma and the motion of the continent creates its own strike-slip fault as it moves along. That's why, if you extend the straight line from Yellowstone Lake into Idaho, it runs right down the track of the hot spot all the way to Twin Falls. I think we are dealing with a critical fault for the super volcano."

David Hawk, a ruddy-faced and bearded Scot visiting at the University of Idaho, rose and spoke fiercely with a strong accent. "We all knae tha' Yella'stone is a livin', breathin' monster tha' someday will rise up and bite us on the arse. What deBruin and Shive have said is enou' for me. We must seek ever' bit of knowledge we can abou' this fault." Murmurs and some animated discussion followed.

"Quiet, everyone," shouted Dr. Rainey. The crowd calmed down somewhat, and she said, "I'd like to recognize Dr. Buck."

Abdul realized Rainey meant a woman who had been standing for several minutes quietly waiting her turn. Her body stooped with age; her sandy grey hair hearkened to what must have been flaming red hair years before. She was elegantly dressed in a coral-colored suit, with turquoise and silver jewelry displayed prominently on her chest and arms. He thought she looked more like a jewelry dealer than a geologist, but from the way the crowd reacted, they profoundly respected her. They knew her record: Arizona State's first female Ph.D. in geology, its first female faculty member in geology, a member of Tanya Atwater's team at MIT that had proven seafloor spreading and continental drift during the 1960's. She had taught and inspired generations of geologists. Her voice was as elegant as her dress, soft but clear. "I have a graduate student whose work bears directly on this discussion, particularly on its urgency." She turned and pointed toward the far aisle, where two students sat separated from the rest of the group. "Anna?"

A young woman stood, wearing a long richly embroidered dress that hung from her neck to the floor, with her dark brown hair pulled back into two long braids that reached to her waist. The large round glasses on her round face allowed Abdul to recognize her as the geologist whose work he had contaminated, and the young man next to her was Ricardo, in a suit and tie, unlike the other geologists. She looked strikingly different from the field geologist on the lava bed in khakis and a large hat. Here, she looked like one of the art students or humanities majors he'd met in London and College Station. She appeared intimidated by the giants of geology in the room, almost embarrassed to speak, and it showed in her soft weak voice. "Ladies and Gentlemen." People strained to hear.

Dr. Buck leaned over and spoke loudly but gently. "Speak up, dear." Rainey walked over and offered a microphone.

"Sorry," said Anna weakly. She took a deep breath and seemed to grow more determined. "We have some pertinent results but I don't know if they are true yet. I'm doing my best to try to prove my first year's work wrong, as it seems crazy."

"Don't apologize, dear," coached Dr. Buck. "Just tell them what you have found so far." She turned to the audience. "I want you to know that Anna is one of the most careful and conscientious researchers I've ever taught. I came out of retirement to be her advisor, so pay attention to what she has to say." She turned back to Anna, "Just say it, dear."

Anna seemed strengthened by the praise and spoke clearly into the microphone. "I-we-have been measuring the Lava Creek Tuff in order to determine the movement of the magma immediately prior to the last big eruption 631,000 years ago."

Trowbridge interrupted with a verbal sneer, "Don't you mean 640,000 years ago?"

Anna looked first to Buck, who nodded, and continued, "Sorry, Dr. Trowbridge. The faculty at ASU has been studying the timing of the eruption with a variety of radiologic measurements at Yellowstone and comparing them to layers of ash throughout the Midwest. We think we can demonstrate with near certainty that the date was 631,000 years ago, plus or minus a thousand years."

Buck added, "I apologize for just tossing the number out in this manner. The abstract and paper for that research should have been on the internet for your review this week. We are confident in the results but welcome your criticism and insights. Anna, please go on."

"From crystals in the lava bed we can infer temperature and pressure at the time of flow, and how quickly it occurred. It appears about 640,000 years ago," she nodded toward Trowbridge as she used the rounded number, "that we had a situation similar to what Yellowstone is like today. That is, with a relatively cool layer of magma on the top of a large chamber, with much hotter magma, the hot magma required for an eruption, deep below. We were expecting to demonstrate that it took hundreds or thousands of years for the hot magma deep to move up to the top and displace the cool magma, to a position that enabled the eruption. Instead, our data indicate that the movement occurred in a matter of two to three decades." Dr. Buck was smiling sweetly as her graduate student clung solidly to her knowledge, with her voice growing stronger as she did.

Murmurs of shock and disbelief rolled through the audience. "But how?" asked Trowbridge. "How can you move that much magma that quickly?"

"We don't know, Doctor, but it is a significant question, and others at Arizona State are looking at the issue. As for this research, we can't answer the question how, only that the results indicate that the incredibly rapid movement happened."

"That's an incredible volume to move," stated Trowbridge emphatically. "It is impossible." Several geologists nodded in agreement.

DeBruin arose, and in his gravelly voice commented, "Dr. Buck, I suggest your people look at strike-slip faults such as the San Andreas, and how they can open holes. I think they will find a strike-slip fault can provide a superhighway for the magma."

Abdul felt a sharp slap on the back of his head. He turned and looked. No one was there, but he recognized the slap. It was his father, slapping his head when the man wanted the boy's attention. Suddenly he knew why God have placed him here in this room. Everything fit. The Sunlight Basin Fault could provide the "superhighway" for the magma. Make the fault move and the magma would move, and the eruption would occur! He realized the atomic bomb could supply the trigger for the fault movement. He hoped Husain realized the implication.

Dr. Greene rose and spoke. "Our modeling at UMass shows what Dr. DeBruin says is correct. A strike-slip fault provides many spacious avenues for the magma, although we question whether there's enough room for a 20-30 year time frame."

"I know there are questions we can't answer and it seems improbable. All I can do is show my first year's results. My second year's field work is being done to try to disprove the first. Dr. Buck says that's how to do science. However, although my analysis is so far not complete, the second year has confirmed the first year. When our work is published, please examine it carefully and let me know where I've gone wrong."

Buck was reveling in the memory of the uproar and outrage when her and Tanya's work on sea-floor spreading and continental drift was first published. The Q&A sessions were brutal, with some mean and derisive objections centered on the fact that this work had been done by women. Once she even broke down in tears, but they learned to stick to the research and ignore the rest. Today no one had denigrated Anna's results simply because she was female, as happened fifty years ago. That was progress, definite progress, and she was pleased that her life contributed to that. Even more satisfying was the fact that her students were doing real science, upsetting the consensus, expanding the frontiers of knowledge. Their students would do the same, and science would continue for generations. That made Buck feel her life not just worthwhile, but glorious.

Rainey tried to gain control of the meeting, and used the microphone. "Thank you, Anna. Oops, Dr. Buck wishes to speak."

"Anna, tell them the possible lower time limit."

The graduate student seemed embarrassed. "If you take the error bars off and look at the central points only, they lead to the conclusion that the movement took less than ten years. I have not looked at all the samples of this year's field work, but of the ones I've looked at so far, all they've done is narrow the error bars."

Several members of the audience were clearly incredulous, and murmuring increased..

Buck smiled and said, "Ladies and Gentlemen, we look forward to your reviews of Anna's work."

Rainey used the pause to steer the discussion into what next. Shive stated Wyoming had money in its STEM funds to pay for a new array of seismometers across the fault. Greene said her group would get to work on the physical models UMass was famous for. De Bruin said he had some lasers that could be placed across the proposed fault to measure movement.

Abdul realized that, for the second time in his life, he was once again in that perfect spot, in the midst of experts arguing passionately over the evidence all focused on one goal: to find the truth. No politics, no personalities mattered; only the truth. He was transfixed and profoundly delighted. Hassan stroked his beard, sensing that Abdul was going on one of his quixotic ventures. He had never understood the diversions of his boss. He simply enjoyed the pleasure of drilling a clean hole, and could not grasp the other feelings that drove Abdul. Hassan knew that Abdul saw something in the world around him that he did not see, but that did not bother him. Like Sancho, he was content to carry his master's lance.

A consensus emerged that strain measurements on both sides of the proposed fault were necessary, but surface measurements might be insufficient. Abdul rose and went to the microphone. The talking of various people in the audience had gotten louder. Rainey was unable to get them to quiet down. Abdul had to shout to get their attention. He did with the statement, "I propose drilling a well and putting some strain-measuring instruments in it." Hassan was disbelieving at his boss's audacity, but not surprised.

De Bruin seemed intrigued. "But could a well be dilled inside the Park?"

Rainey replied, "Honestly, probably never." Several geologists nodded in agreement. The USGS would have to appeal to the Park Service, who'd reach out for public comment. Every environmental group in the country would rise up in arms against the violation of the pristine park by a drilling rig, the symbol of all the environmental ills of America. Rainey voiced what most thought inevitable. "Despite our best scientific arguments, The Park Service would capitulate to public pressure and decline permission, in my opinion. And I work for the Park Service." She continued, "Of course, if we can get permission from a private landowner, a well could be drilled just outside the Park."

A red-headed woman, slight of build, rose. Abdul recognized Dr. Laura Bigley-Puzio from television. Her show, "Quakin' & Shakin'" was a popular feature on one of the science channels, presenting geology, earthquakes and seismology in a way that engaged young people. She was an enchanting teacher, and many students switched majors to geology after attending one of her classes. Her status as a media star, plus her expertise that many of her colleagues interpreted as arrogance, angered many of her associates in the Michigan State geology department. They complained her television status demeaned her academic work, and seethed through their envy. Bigley-Puzio reveled in the controversy – she seemed to go out of her way to tweak the sensitivities of her colleagues. Her husband, also a geologist but an employee for an oil company, therefore naturally despised by many on campus, responded to the criticism of his wife with "It ain't bragging if you can do it." Despite complaints from faculty, the administration of the university loved her for several reasons. Her celebrity added glamour to the institution, a significant portion of applicants listed her as one of the top five reasons for wanting to attend Michigan State, resulting in the status of the university approaching its archrival, the University of Michigan. Finally, more science grants meant higher salaries for faculty, and larger alumni donations down the road. Bigley-Puzio asked, "So you'd have to drill on private land. Where?"

Rainey answered, "There's a shortage of private land in the area. Let's get together and find a spot. I have a map here somewhere."

She brought out a map that showed private land. There was some in Silver Gate, near the northeast entrance, but that was considered too far away from the suggested fault line. So was the private land along Crandall Creek. Somewhere on some private property along Sunlight Creek seemed best.

Bigley-Puzio objected, "That's too close to the fault. Drilling fluids might lubricate the fault and cause movement like what's happened in Oklahoma and at Rocky Flats." That caught Abdul by surprise. He hadn't thought of that. It was almost too delicious to contemplate.

Abdul broke in, "Look, we would not drill this without monitoring drilling fluids. If we start to lose too much we can shut down the operation and move further away. We are talking about one well here. In Oklahoma, there are thousands of wells – Rocky Flats, hundreds. We can monitor and control how much mud we lose." Abdul was pleased at how his mind swiftly produced effective counterarguments.

Bigley-Puzio shouted, "We don't know how much is too much." It was clear to the others that Abdul had carried the argument.

Abdul interjected, "Ladies and gentlemen, I suspect it will take 2-3 months to drill this hole, considering the rock we have to drill there and the size of the hole we'll need." He was imagining what diameter he'd need to lower the bomb, but had a ready excuse. "We don't know how much protective casing we'll need so we will have to start larger, perhaps even a 30" hole. More important, how big a hole is necessary for your strain detectors?"

Several people spoke, but de Bruin dominated. "Since we have some time, let's see what the equipment designers say about how they can improve our devices. How about Bob Malone at Los Alamos or Rock Bush at Berkeley or the guy at Cal Tech. What's his name? Walowitz?" The audience laughed at his joke.

Abdul stated, "In our research for the Saudi Arabian fracking project, we have developed some new strain-detection devices. I will check with my engineers to see if they can be adapted for this."

Rainey asked Abdul, "When can you begin drilling?"

"Nothing can be done until the snows melt, then I imagine there will be considerable road work required before we could move the rig in. It'll be a big rig. Might take a month of road work, so I guess a month after the snows melt." The fact that the geologists suddenly showed a strong sense of urgency after all the 'sometime-in-the-next-20,000-years' remarks made a strong impression on Husain, but a stronger one on Abdul, who realized he'd stumbled into something significant. He sensed that God had placed him here to do something powerful. "One thing, though, I will volunteer to fund the drilling myself – that's probably ten million dollars or more – only if I have complete control of the drilling. You tell me what size you need for the instruments, but everything else is up to me. Anyway, it's an offer for you to put several million dollars of my money to work."

More laughter. The geologists began to appreciate this guy from the drilling industry.

From the wing, a woman wearing a badge stepped onto the stage, held her arm up toward Rainey, and pointed at her wrist. Rainey grabbed a microphone but had to shout over the tumult. "People, our time in Coe Auditorium is up. We must be out of here in fifteen minutes. You can continue your conversations outside, but please keep your voices down in the museum. So please move outside the auditorium. Remember, we have the private room at Irma Grill reserved to tonight for those of you who can make it."

Abdul, Hassan and Husain rose and began to slide along the seats toward the aisle. Several people crowded around Anna and Ricardo, questioning every aspect of their work. At one point, Anna looked at Dr. Buck in despair, but the professor smiled and let the two endure their trial by fire. Finally, Anna grabbed a microphone and said, "Our research is not complete and possibly won't be ready for publication for two years. At that time you will be able to examine every aspect of our research thoroughly. You will find our measurements are accurate and our field work impeccable. If anything, our interpretation of the data may be in error. We will be eager to hear from you then. Now, excuse me." She left Ricardo in the crowd, then bounded up the steps, her flowery dress flowing around her, and extended her hand. "Mr. Faisal, thank you for paying our way here."

"You are quite welcome, Anna." He turned toward the others. "You know Hassan, my right-hand man." They shook hands. Abdul nodded to Husain, "This is Saleh Tawfiq Saleh, my Chief Technology Officer in Riyadh." After the greeting, Abdul said to Anna, "I see you have switched to a Latin lover."

Anna glanced back toward Ricardo and blushed. "Ricardo and I are much more compatible. And if I can keep the conversation away from the situation in Venezuela, he is a funny man."

"I caught that the night we met. It's a most important trait. I'm pleased for you."

"Ricardo got permission to stay for a Ph.D., but he desperately needs a job to stay in America."

"I don't think we have a need for a hard-rock geologist, but have Ricardo send his resume to Noor. She'll get it to the proper HR person."

"How about a consulting geologist on this well you're going to drill in Sunlight Basin?"

Abdul raised his eyebrows in surprise and smiled. "Of course, we will need a hard-rock geologist for drilling through the volcanics. Good thinking, Anna. Have Ricardo put on his resume that he is applying for that specific job."

"Oh, thank you, Mr. Faisal. Come, I want you to meet Dr. Buck." She grabbed his arm.

Rainey was gently pushing people to the exits, but a few remained near Dr. Buck. Anna pulled Abdul toward the professor just as she and Bigley-Puzio greeted each other like old friends. They hugged. With arms still around each other, Buck said, "Laura."

"Binky," replied the other.

Abdul wasn't certain he heard the nickname right. "Binky?" It hardly fit the geology professor, except perhaps for her jewelry and outfit.

"Two redheads getting things done," said Bigley-Puzio.

"Except my red is becoming more like the color of sand."

"Oh, you will always be a redhead at heart. I wish to get your permission to talk to your graduate students so I can do an episode of Quakin' and Shakin' on their work."

"Laura, you have my permission, but on the condition that nothing comes out about their work until after publication."

"Of course, Binky." She seemed offended. "I would never jump the gun."

"I wouldn't expect you to, Laura, but this is dynamite stuff, and there will be temptations, and I want your promise that you will wait."

Laura sighed, somewhat indignantly. "I promise."

"Sorry, Laura, but I began my career almost sixty years ago with a revolutionary discovery, and now it appears I might end my career with another. I want it done right."

"It's okay, Binky," said Laura. "I understand completely."

Rainey arrived and pushed the group toward the exit. Outside the auditorium they found themselves near the museum's library and researchers' offices were located. "Dr. Buck," said Anna as she grabbed the woman's arm. Turquoise and silver jewelry flashed as she turned. "I'd like you to meet Mr. Faisal."

She extended her hand, and Abdul shook. "Mr. Faisal, I wish to thank you for your encouragement to attend this conference and your generosity in paying our way here. And especially for your great generosity in paying for this well."

"You are welcome, Dr. Buck. It is my pleasure. When I met Anna and Ricardo, I felt they had something important to add to this meeting."

"Oh, I think everyone will agree it was worthwhile."

"As for the well, I indulge my delight in science. God has blessed me with riches and I am pleased to help." Husain grabbed Abdul's arm and pointed at his wrist as if he'd been wearing a watch. "Excuse me, Dr. Buck," Abdul said, "this is my Chief Technology Officer, Saleh Tawfiq Saleh. He is reminding me our families are upstairs and we must fetch them."

"I do hope you will come to dinner," said the professor. "I'd like to talk more."

"Yes, do come," said Anna.

"Okay, we will try. But first we must see to our families," said Abdul. They went upstairs to the Plains Indian Museum and found the women and children there. Abdul spoke, "Saleh and I are going to dinner with the geologists. Hassan, what about you?"

"My head is spinning from all that talk. I'll stay away—a quiet night for me."

"Saleh," said his wife. "We have learned there is a rodeo tonight and the children wish to see it. But without you, how can we go?"

Abdul desperately wanted Husain to spend more time with the geologists. He turned to Hassan and asked, "Hassan, will you escort them?" Everyone knew Hassan, although a great friend, was not a relative, so this was a profound request. Hassan noted the significance, and nodded. Abdul and Husain left Hassan to handle the women and children, and walked to the Irma Grill a couple of blocks away.

Unfortunately for Abdul, the conversation was mostly about personal things, and nothing of geologic importance was added to what had been discussed during the conference. His mind, however, was burning with the insights that the day's session had brought. Immediately after they left the dinner, as they walked toward their hotel, Abdul pressed Husain. "You heard! The bomb will make the Sunlight Basin Fault move, and that will create superhighways for the magma. The hot magma will rise, and soon the super volcano will explode."

"I heard the geologists, Abdul. If the bomb works, it'll be 10-30 years before the volcano erupts. I may not have that long to live. I want to see the results of my revenge. I want to see dead Americans—I want to see their economy ravaged—I want to cut them down to size—repay them for their arrogance. I want revenge for my family. Now."

"But, at Yellowstone we are not talking about just a blow to the economy. The bomb would cause the destruction of the West. Famine like the world has never seen."

"But once the bomb explodes, the Americans will see what's happening. They'll know they have 10-30 years to prepare for the eruption. The country would go on a war footing—this is the strongest country in the world. It would find a way in those 30 years to prepare."

"Ha! Sixty million people live in just the states of the Great Plains and the Rocky Mountains. Where would they move them? Where would they build the cities to house them? Where would they grow the food to feed them, and the rest of America? We are talking about a meter of ash over most of the Great Plains. You can't just go out with a tractor and till that into the soil. The soil would be ruined for a hundred years. No wheat, no corn, no sorghum, no cattle, no chickens. Famine will ride in on his black horse and rule."

"That's all pie in the sky. I want something real. I want the destruction of Houston."

"Manzur, don't you see? This did not all happen by chance. God put you in my path. God put the uranium at Ras ed Dom in my hands. God showed me the pier at Halaib. God inspired me, through the death of my friend, to create the rig robot, which gave me all the money to do this. God put the geologists in my path, geologists who practically instructed me on what to do. God even took away my Yasmeen to motivate me."

"No, Abdul. You created the rig robot due to your own clever mind. You saw the rings at Ras ed Dom, the same rings seen by millions of people who'd flown over it, but you realized the possibility because your mind was seeking a solution to a problem. The same with the pier at Halaib. And the King put me in your path, not God."

"Ah, Manzur. You are so smart but so blind. The hand of God is everywhere, leading us onward, but you don't see it."

"Abdul, are you the Mahdi?"

"What?" Abdul was stung by the sacrilege. "Of course not. I am just a fellow being shown by God the way to destroy the West, if he so wills it."

"But would that not make you the Mahdi, the Messiah who will rid the world of evil and bring justice?"

"I am not the Mahdi. I don't claim it." He was defensive, and was buffaloed by the turn in the conversation.

"But whether you claim it or not, if you destroy the West, you would be the Mahdi."

"No! I have no intention of ruling anything."

"Why not? You are clever enough. You have proven you can rule a company. If the people knew you were the one who destroyed the West, they'd rise in acclamation and demand you rule until Judgment Day."

"This is all nonsense. I will destroy the West, God willing. Your bomb and Yellowstone will be my instrument. But no more crazy talk about the Mahdi. You have disturbed me."

"No, my friend. I say no. Houston is the place where we will explode the bomb. My bomb."

Abdul was silent, stunned. His mind rushed over his arguments for Yellowstone and the famine. He had been certain Husain would agree. He could not believe the physicist was not convinced. How could he have been wrong? He was perplexed. Finally, he looked up. "Okay, Manzur, it is your bomb. Houston it is. I will smuggle you and your bomb into Houston and leave you at the warehouse. While you are preparing it for the explosion, I will be flying to Denver. You must give me at least three hours after I leave the warehouse. I will not be a martyr. Instead, I'll buy some oil futures and watch my fortune grow as Houston burns."

"That is good, Abdul. I know your heart was set on Yellowstone, my friend, and that you are disappointed. But there are others in this conspiracy besides you, and they all want Houston."

"I am disappointed, yes. But I must accept the will of God."

Husain put his arm around the younger man as they walked through the lobby.

CHAPTER TWENTY-SEVEN

SUNLIGHT BASIN RANGER STATION, EAST OF YELLOWSTONE PARK

JUNE 2016

"**P**eople of Sunlight Basin, of Cody and Powell, of Cooke City and Silver Gate, of Montana and Wyoming, from all across the United States! Welcome to one of the greatest scientific adventures of our time. Citizens of this beautiful area, thank you for welcoming us scientists and drillers here. Be certain that we will definitely disturb your life for a few months while we search for answers for some great questions about the geologic complex that have made Yellowstone the magnificent place it is. We thank Mike Healy and his family for allowing us to drill on their land. We hope you all enjoy this building." Abdul waved his arm toward the building and the eyes of the small crowd followed to where it pointed. "It will be a small visitor center until we are through drilling, then it will be given to the Forest Service to use as they wish, so you can use it for years to come."

"Drilling is a noisy business," Abdul continued. "It occurs 24 hours a day, 7 days a week, and you will hear it and it's loud. Please tolerate the interruption of your idyllic quiet valley until the end of the summer, when we'll be done. Keep reminding yourselves it's for a great cause. Not just a good cause, but the greatest cause of humanity: knowledge of how nature works. People living here know something that most people in the world don't know — that Yellowstone is the caldera of a giant volcano that erupted some 640,000 years ago. What we will be trying to learn is the exact structure of the layers down to the mother rock that lies beneath us – the same hot rocks that create the geysers – the largest concentration of geysers in the world. We'll be measuring things like the temperature of the rock – how it varies with depths, and many other things. It's a grand adventure. Drilling is also dangerous work. So, we are putting a fence around the rig site. Please tell your adventurous boys not to climb over the fence."

"One thing you've probably read is that I am personally paying for this drilling. Crescendo is my drilling company. Some of the rig hands are Muslim. I know many of you are wary of Muslims due to the horrible actions of a few terrorists. You will see that these particular Muslims are just like you – hard working, sincere, and religious. I'm sure by end of the summer you will not be wary, but welcoming. I have been blessed by God with many riches, and my favorite way to share this wealth is by underwriting the costs of scientific research. Let us pray for God's blessings. You know I am a Muslim, but Muslims believe that Christians and Jews are also children of the Holy Book, so I have asked Pastor Coleman from Red Lodge to bless this venture and also this food. Pastor?"

The pastor prayed for God to bless the effort, all the people involved in the effect, the people of the town and everyone in attendance. Then he asked for God's blessing on the food. After, he shouted, "Let's eat!"

Cheers went up. Most people walked directly to the food tables, while a few lingered around the displays – some similar to the ones at Canyon Village illustrating the Yellowstone volcano, but some showing how the rig would drill through the rocks. Abdul and Rainey were pleased with the displays, and with how the reception went.

CHAPTER TWENTY-EIGHT

ON THE PLANE FROM HOUSTON TO DENVER

SUNDAY, BEFORE THE SUICIDE BOMBINGS

Husain sat in a cushioned chair, seething with anger, his dark eyes glaring at Abdul, but he said nothing.

"Sorry, Manzur, but it is my bomb now. You would not agree to take it to Yellowstone, so now I am taking it."

Husain leaned forward, and hissed. "You are crazy, Abdul. We could have already destroyed Houston. You betrayed me; you betrayed the Consul; you betrayed every person in our group."

"They will feel betrayed until they see what magnificent destruction comes. Then, as the West crumbles, they will praise me and celebrate what I've done." His confidence soared.

"Even if the geologists are right, it will be 10-30 years before the eruption. I probably won't live that long. You might not live that long."

"Ah, but what a delicious 10-30 years, anticipating, waiting, knowing the catastrophe about to occur, the famine to follow, the collapse of the West."

"No! Without me, you can't do it, and I will not help you."

"Oh, but I want you to have the joy of exploding the bomb. It is yours. You are the expert, and it's your right. It may not be your favorite choice of location, but it's still your privilege if you want it."

"No, I will not. And without me, you cannot explode the bomb. Take it back to Houston so we can carry out the plan."

"Manzur, if you do not wish to help, I have a couple of people who will."

Husain snorted derisively. "Where are you going to get experience exploding an atomic bomb?"

"Ah, do you think that Saudi Arabia was the only country concerned about Iran getting a nuclear weapon? The idea of a nuclear Iran has made many countries anxious. Did you not know that Turkey has been trying to buy a weapon? It already has some American nuclear weapons on its soil, but they are under American control and Turkey does not trust President O'Brien to use them to stop Iran."

"So what? Buying a weapon is not enough. You need to have experience making them explode. Turkey has never had a nuclear test."

"Maybe not Turkey, the country. Did you ever hear of the American program called Operation Plowshare?"

"Never heard of it."

"It was an attempt back in the '60s and '70s to find peaceful uses for atomic bombs. They tried fracking some gas sands in Colorado with nuclear bombs. It was not successful."

"So?"

"Two Turkish physicists who were graduate students at the University of Wyoming at the time exploded the last one at Rio Blanco. You can bet they remember every bit of that experience, and they are anxious to show their knowledge by exploding your bomb. They want to prove to their government they are ready to run Turkey's nuclear program."

Husain felt as if sands were washing away under his feet. He sat back in the chair and tried to fight back. "That was so long ago, and technology has changed."

"Their names are Haluk Beker and Burhan Oral. Ring a bell?"

Husain knew the first name from research literature and realized Abdul had won the argument. Beker was one of Turkey's most brilliant physicists.

"Does Turkey know what you are doing?"

"Not yet. Only the two physicists know. They are on their way to

Cody right now to take over if you decline."

Husain closed his eyes and paused a long time. His choice was to return to Saudi Arabia and an uncertain future, or to carry out Abdul's plan. "Okay, Abdul. You win. I will explode the bomb where you say."

CHAPTER TWENTY-NINE

DENVER AIRPORT, THEN CODY, WYOMING

MONDAY, THE DAY AFTER THE SUICIDE BOMBINGS

While waiting to change planes in Denver, Camille called Perez. "Where are you?" he asked.

"I'm sorry, boss, but I'm on my way to Cody. This Saudi connection has me thinking of nothing else. I must follow it to its conclusion."

"What?" Perez was incredulous. "You are supposed to be working on the Saudi deaths here in town."

"Chief, there is nothing I could learn at the Saudi embassy. The answer lies here, if at all."

Perez could not believe his ears. Anger rose in his chest at her insubordination. "Agent Richard," his voice becoming formal. "You work for me. You do as I direct you. I'm directing you to return to Houston and get back to work on your assignment."

"Let me explain, boss. There are two avenues we've discovered so far. One leads to Crescendo Drilling and its project in Yellowstone. The other possibly to China. I need to determine what the drilling project here means."

"You need to follow my orders, Agent Richard." He was shouting, but took a deep breath and his voice modulated. "Right now our job—your job—is to investigate the victims and find out who murdered them. That may lead us to the plot. Even if the Saudis are involved in the smuggling, they may have nothing to do with where the bomb is and what will be done with it. That is what you are supposed to be investigating."

"Chief, that's like asking me to check the fleas on a dog that's been bit by a water moccasin. Those two dead men were cast aside by the bomb smugglers like trash. They are irrelevant to finding the bomb and who's got it."

"You don't know whether they're irrelevant!" He was shouting again, and his fury was rising. "Those guys were with the suicide bombers. That's a fact. They may lead us to the clue we need. Now quit barking and get to work!" He hesitated, then said, "Besides, I talked to Agent Joffe and he is checking out the drilling rig as we speak."

"Does he have an Arabic speaker with him?"

Perez hesitated. He remembered something from Joffe's file. "I believe Joffe speaks Arabic, as he served in Pakistan and Afghanistan."

"Well, just in case, I drafted Farman Yousif to come with me to talk to the crew."

"You what?" Perez's voice rose to a shout again. "Yousif is needed here! Both of you get back here immediately."

"I hear you, Chief," said Camille in a soft voice. But when she turned off the phone, she waved to Farman and they headed toward the gate for the plane to Cody.

When Camille had called Farman a few hours ago and asked him to travel with her to Cody, he'd assumed she was as smitten with the stunning good looks that God had given him as most women. He was looking forward to fun with the energetic forceful young woman, but on the plane to Denver, she made it clear this was all business. So, he consoled himself with the thought of traveling to a famous place he'd never seen. As the plane was taxiing to the terminal in Cody, Camille turned on her phone and found a text message from Riley pleading for her to call and a voice message from headquarters informing her that Joffe had been hurt in a car accident but the Resident Agent in Billings would handle it. She was to get on a plane and return to Houston immediately. She ignored the message, determined to follow her hunch despite the consequences. Walking down the airplane's stairs to the tarmac, Farman raised his arms and yelled, "Feel that air!!" The air felt…delicate, so unlike Houston's. Camille was struck by the nearby mountains west of the airport. They looked like a giant loaf of bread that had been cleaved by some giant knife, leaving a sharp "V" separating the heel from the rest. The air was crisp and light, with a briskness she had not felt since March. Walking to the Avis counter, she called her Irishman. His voice was almost angry, "Cammie, darling, why are you on this crazy wild goose chase when we are desperate to find the damn bomb?"

Startled by his tone, her voice turned cold. "I'm following evidence."

His voice was despairing. "It makes no sense! Why would they take the bomb there away from all the cities and power structures?"

Her voice remained calm and cold, "I'm not trying to find a reason – I'm just following the evidence."

"What evidence, Cammie?"

"Ask your superior officer," she said and hung up, exasperated and angry at the man she loved.

As she handed her ID to the Avis agent, Camille dialed headquarters and asked Perez about Joffe.

Perez' voice was so icy she shivered. "Joffe had a car accident. He went off the road on the side of a mountain. We don't know the details of the accident, but he was in the middle of a phone call relating something at the drill site when he yelled and crashed. He's at the Cody hospital. The RA from Billings is on his way to check him out. Meanwhile, Agent Richard, I am ordering you to return to Houston immediately."

"Yes, sir. But there won't be a plane back to Denver for a while. I'll have to check when. While I'm waiting, please let me go see Joffe and find out what he knows."

"No, Camille. You have already violated my orders. Get your ass back here as soon as possible. Your job is on the line." Perez hoped that threat would bring her back to reality.

"Yes, sir. I understand." But she didn't. The sense of Saudi involvement, the overwhelming feeling that it all pointed to Abdul Faisal and his science project, drove Camille now. She had to follow through. Still, she knew Riley and Perez and the entire Bureau was against this endeavor. She felt like she'd stepped onto a glacier trying to see through a white-out blizzard. She felt helpless, with nothing to steer her by. She prayed for guidance, for calmness, for strength.

After getting car keys and directions to the hospital, Camille walked outside where Farman was enjoying another cigarette. She looked at the building. The walls were built of pale yellow bricks. "How ugly!" was her immediate reaction, but then wondered whether it was truly ugly or her anger with Riley and her battle with Perez had upset her that much. Was she taking it out on the building? Yellow bricks – name Yellowstone Regional Airport – is that why? No matter, it was just plain ugly. Farman called to her. "Breathe this fresh air!" he exclaimed. "Isn't it wonderful?"

Camille took a deep breath and had to agree. The air felt light. "Yes, Yes," she said, anxious to get moving.

"Come look at this," he said pointing to a mountain several miles away that stood isolated in the countryside. "Do you see the dead man?"

"What do you mean?"

"Look at the profile of the mountain. On the left is the head and in the middle are hands folded on its stomach. On the head, you can even see the nose pointing up."

It clicked. "Yes, I see it," she said. It seemed immaterial considering what was happening.

"Wait. There's another way to look at it," he said. "Make the mountain just a head facing the other way. The hands become his nose and the head becomes his chin. They say it looks like a dead Indian."

"Okay, I see it too," said Camille, but her eyes were pulled back to the tarmac as she saw a golden jet landing, its tires emitting small clouds of blue smoke as they struck the pavement. "What is that?" She asked an airport worker, who said that private planes went to the General Aviation terminal in the next building. He said it was the old Cody terminal. She turned to her companion. "Come on, Farman. Let's check that out."

She thought about the airplane. Completely gold! She'd heard about the plane but never seen it. It belonged to the extravagant Saudi Arabian playboy who lived in Los Angeles. The plane was a marvel of ostentation, bold and brash. Camille sensed the fact that it belonged to a Saudi could not be a coincidence. She realized that the gold plane was headed to another building about a quarter-mile away but there appeared to be no direct road from this terminal to that one. She'd have to drive out to the highway and back down another road to get to the other terminal. On an impulse, she tossed the keys to Farman, and ran directly toward the other building. A barbed-wire fence was in the way, and she ran to climb over it, grateful that she'd worn jeans. As she got closer, she realized it was constructed like a prison fence, and she would not be able to climb it anyway. She returned to the RAV4 and Farman drove them out to the highway and back to the other terminal.

The building was marked General Aviation. A television truck, with a CBS eye on the side and a satellite receiver on the roof, was parked near the entrance. Excited, she forced herself to walk slowly into the building so not to draw attention. Inside she realized she was looking directly down a low incline ramp at the entrance door for incoming passengers. A small banister separated the ramp from a surprisingly small waiting room. Lounging around on sofa chairs were several strong young men that appeared to be military, and near the banister stood a striking Saudi male. His confidence and power dominated the room. People were staring at him. Camille recognized him immediately from television – Abdul Faisal– tremendously smart and tremendously rich, and power seemed to ooze out of his pores. The TV crew meekly tried to get a few shots of Abdul but turned their focus toward the famous gold plane.

Abdul had been waiting anxiously in the airport, in a tiny lounge in a tiny airport in a tiny town. With the two Turks soon to arrive in his plane, he'd have the final pieces to his puzzle, and he was eager to finish. Then he saw a glistening golden jet landing on the tarmac, smoke jetting from the tires as they struck the pavement. Abdul was dumbstruck. There was only one bright golden jet in the world he knew of, owned by the man who owned a dozen golden limousines and lived in several golden palatial mansions scattered around the world: "The Playboy of the Eastern World," his own cousin, Moteb bin Said. They shared the same grandfather, brother to the King, members of the royal family, but the two could not be more different in personality, in outlook, in accomplishment, in manner, in anything.

Abdul did not notice anyone else – he was focused on the golden airplane and the rotten human who owned it. He could not believe that of all times, now, his cousin Moteb was here to antagonize him, the man he hated more than anyone in the world, the man who had taken his daughter Yasmeen. Anger rose in his chest, and heartbeats pulsed in his head. Abdul immediately recognized the hand of God testing him again. He steadied himself for the coming storm. "This too is the will of God," he told himself. "Submit, submit to the will of God."

Camille suddenly was hit by the thought that she'd left her bag at the other terminal, but her thoughts were interrupted by one of the military guys. "Hello, darlin'." He said, smiling. She noticed the tag on his black outfit that said "Teton Jump School" in red letters and realized the men were fire fighters.

"I'm engaged," she said curtly. "Go away."

"I saw no ring. Your man needs to get with it."

Camille glared at him. "Go away."

"Hey, no problem." He said. "You can't blame a guy for hitting on the prettiest woman in the joint." He smiled broadly. "We're going to the Cody Night Rodeo tonight. If you want to have some fun, join us. We're actually nice guys."

Camille scowled and flashed her badge.

"Sorry," he said, and walked back to his friends laughing at his striking out.

Down the airplane steps came Moteb, resplendent in total Saudi regalia, his headdress and robe flapping in the brisk Wyoming wind. The TV crew had moved outside and was trying to catch it all. At the base of the steps he threw back his arms and head, and made a show of breathing deeply. "Marvelous air!" he shouted. Then he waved his arms as if creating the mountains and exclaimed, "Beautiful mountains!" Behind him a group of gorgeous women followed – the men guessed they were models or actresses. The firefighters in the waiting room crammed around the window. The TV crew was obviously enjoying the performance and the reporter pushed a microphone at Moteb and asked, "Welcome, Moteb. Why have you come to Cody?"

"I hear my cousin Abdul is performing a great contribution to science and I want to watch him. Plus, I've never been to Wyoming – such beautiful country."

The TV crew backed into the building continually filming Moteb, who was clearly enjoying the attention. Behind him walked about ten women in dresses designed to display their marvelous bodies. The fire jumpers ignored the two men and rushed to the banister and began talking to the women, delighted when the women spoke to them. The TV crew struggled to get it all, but dropped the lovemaking and concentrated on the two Saudis. Halfway up the inside ramp, Moteb stopped, stunned and surprised to see Abdul. Abdul thought Moteb looked ridiculous with his flowing white thobe, a white ghutra held on his head with the traditional black braids, and that irritated him even more. What would have looked normal in Saudi Arabia was as out-of-place here as a cowboy hat, jeans and boots would appear in the souk in Omdurman, but that was part of Moteb's flamboyance. "I'm sorry it took us so long to get off the plane. My camera man had to put his pants on." Abdul closed his eyes and steeled himself.

Moteb leapt the rail, walked directly to Abdul, hugged him tightly and kissed both cheeks. Abdul awkwardly stood stiff and still, clearly not enjoying the greeting. The two men's tension drew attention, like a campfire at night. The cameraman bobbed and moved, trying to catch one man, then the other, then both. Passengers by the baggage claim, the waitress in the diner, the diners whose vision was not blocked, the people behind the ticket and car rental counters were frozen, quietly watching, transfixed. Camille forgot about her bag and watched, fascinated. She knew Abdul Faisal, but had never seen the other man, the famous flamboyant one from the golden airplane. Moteb grabbed Abdul's arms, stretched them as is to enable a hug, and loudly said, "Cousin! I am so pleased that you came to greet me! I did not know you cared so much."

"I did not know you were coming or I would not have been here."

"Oh, dear cousin," Moteb leaned into Abdul and spoke softly into his ear. "I have come with ET TV so you can shine my star. And I will shine your star, too!"

"I have no need of that and no need of you."

"Oh, cousin! How that hurts me! It's so unlike a good Muslim to say that about his own cousin. Everyone loves me! What don't you like about me? Is it because I have fun? Because I enjoy this life and don't wait for the next? Is it because I spread my seed among all the infidel women? Tell me where the prophet says I should not do so."

"You blaspheme."

"Really? Do you think I offend God? Then why does God not strike me down? No, God wants me to enjoy myself completely. That's why he's given me such plenty. And the women I have are much better than virgins with no clitoris. The women enjoy sex, and women who enjoy sex make it more enjoyable for men too. That's one place where the prophet was wrong."

Abdul's anger rose precipitously. He was fighting his impulse to strike Moteb despite the fact he knew his cousin was purposely baiting him. Moteb could feel the tenseness in Abdul's arms and see the clenched fists. He leaned closely to Abdul's ear. "Want to hit me? Go ahead. It'll make great TV." Abdul then realized a cameraman was recording the meeting. That thought brought more control. He tried to squelch down his fury. He focused on the bomb and what it would do, and how much more important his goal was than this irritating, very irritating evil gnat. He realized that was why God was testing him.

"Forget that, Moteb. I am glad that you came so you can see what I'm doing. Perhaps you can learn that a man can do something useful with his life and not waste it."

Moteb smiled and turned directly to the camera, "Did you hear that, my friends? My cousin does not think the fun I have and the parties I throw are useful. Useful! What do you think? You know my Twitter account, my friends – let me know. What's your Twitter account, Abdul? He turned back to Abdul.

"I have no need for Twitter."

"Really? What do you think, my friends? He looked at the camera again and winked.

"You and I each started with a hundred million dollars or so – you've turned yours into a few billion. I, on the other hand, am down to about a million or so, and I'm going to run out of money way too soon. But I've got a plan – I'm already signed up for a reality show – the Arab equivalent of the Khardashians. Come join the show – you'd be great – the sparkling achiever contrasted with the dissolute rake. People will love it"

"No way. Get away from me."

"I knew you'd say that – never mind – it's already on camera."

He swept his arm toward the video crew. Abdul closed his eyes and concentrated on breathing.

Suddenly, the thought of Yasmeen flashed. His mind blackened in fury. He exploded.. He rushed Moteb, striking at the retreating man as hard and fast as he could. But Moteb, who'd trained under Luis Pacheco, 'Taekwondo Master to the Stars', parried Abdul's flailing arms easily and taunted the enraged man while doing so. Fire jumpers leapt the banister and separated the two men while security guards scurried over. One pulled some handcuffs as he approached Abdul. "No need for that," said Moteb loudly, clearly for the camera's benefit. "Just a family squabble. I won't press charges."

The security officer looked at the straining Abdul and back at Moteb and asked, "Are you sure?"

"Yes," he answered, and turned to the camera man. "Did you get all that?"

He turned to Abdul, "Fear not, cousin, I have brought you a present." He swung his arm toward the airplane steps. Abdul had been so absorbed with Moteb, he had failed to notice a young dark-haired woman in a plain summer dress that she had to hold down in the wind.

"Hello, father," she said, walking softly toward him. Abdul staggered, dumbstruck, flabbergasted. The anger and frustration that had compelled his attack turned to confusion and surprise. disbelieving his eyes that told him that his daughter was with Moteb.

"Yasmeen!" His chest felt like it would explode. Not thinking, he reacted and held his arms wide as he'd done for his eldest daughter when she was young. She rushed to him and they hugged, tears streaming down both faces. Abdul could not speak. He held – and felt her. The warmth of her body flushed his brain with memories of his daughter. He could hardly believe she was in his arms again. She was a grown woman, but she still seemed small and fragile to him.

Even the chattering women from the golden plane had stopped

talking, watching, and a few had tears in their eyes, as did a waitress in the cafe and one in the car rental booth. Moteb put his hand over the camera. "Let's let the father-daughter reunion happen in peace."

Abdul's emotions overflowed. He was a confusion of joy and grief and love and terror. His legs felt weak. Finally, Abdul pulled back and looked at his daughter, her face, her hair, her clothes.. His brain swirled with anguish and horror. "Your dress..."

"Oh, father, why must that be the first thing you mention? Do you think it means I am not a good Muslim? I am not one of Moteb's women. But he is my cousin and offered me a ride to see you. I want to see you. Do you want to see me?"

"A good Muslim woman would cover her hair and arms, as commanded by Sharia."

"Oh, Father, don't say that. In America, many good Muslim women dress just like this, many good Muslim women. I would not dress like this in Saudi Arabia but in America I can be free to dress the way I want, to live the way I want, and think the way I want." Irritation with her father rose in her heart. "That is why I love America – I am not bound by some 8th century notions of women." She knew that would sting, and it did. It also brought Abdul back to his reason for being here.

"You can't stay."

Yasmeen was astonished, disbelieving what she'd just heard. "Father! I came all the way to see you and you want to send me away?" She turned to run away. Abdul grabbed her arm.

"No, you don't understand. What I'm doing is dangerous." He tried to think quickly of an excuse. "Come look at the site, but you must promise that you will leave tonight."

"I don't understand. I am here to see you, to see your great science experiment. I won't promise such a thing."

Camille was astonished. What father would not want to share this work with his daughter? Her daddy had taken her to hundreds of drilling rigs – they'd looked at well samples together. She'd experienced his excitement as logs came out of a new well. She loved his teaching and he'd clearly loved sharing his world with his daughter. "Too dangerous?" She couldn't believe what she'd heard. Angered by Abdul's treatment of his daughter, Camille immediately disliked him intensely. Blessed by the loving hands of her own father, she could not fathom the harsh demands by Abdul directed to the girl, obviously crushed. Could he not see her pain? Suddenly Camille realized what he meant by dangerous, the bomb, the atomic bomb. Could he really believe he could cause the super volcano to explode? That had to be the plan.

Abdul hesitated, then said, "If you will cover your hair and arms and legs, you may come with me." Yasmeen turned and ran back to the airplane and climbed inside. Camille was certain the man had blown his chances with his daughter. She was disgusted, and looked for Farman, ready to leave. But after a few minutes, Yasmeen appeared in the doorway with her hair and arms covered, wearing pants. Camille understood. Yasmeen was willing to sacrifice part of herself to be with her father.

Driving to the hospital, Camille called Perez. "I just saw a bizarre scene at the Cody airport. That flamboyant Saudi from LA, the one who flies the golden airplane was there – his cousin is Abdul, the head of Crescendo Drilling. I don't know what it is, but something strange is going on," she said. "It was being filmed by a television crew from Billings. The truck had the CBS eyeball on it. Call them and get the footage and watch it. I think it'll show I'm on the right track."

Perez asked, "What do you mean?"

"I don't know for sure," Camille said. "Maybe it's just a family squabble – but I saw Abdul endure some terrific emotions when he saw his daughter with the playboy. They got into a fight. Maybe it is nothing but family. But in my gut, I feel like it's more than that. He said he did not want his daughter to go to the well because it's dangerous. That makes no sense unless he's got the bomb there."

Perez hesitated. "What do you mean, Camille? Drilling rigs are dangerous."

"Only if you are working on one," she answered almost breathlessly. "Visiting is not dangerous. My daddy took me to lots of drilling rigs. There has to be another reason that Faisal does not want his daughter there. The bomb is the reason."

"God, that is far-fetched," said Perez, exasperated.

"Okay, boss, but something crazy is going on. Maybe I just can't explain why."

"Okay, okay," Perez said, frustrated. "Just call me after you've talked to Joffe."

CHAPTER THIRTY
THE CODY HOSPITAL

MONDAY, SHORTLY THEREAFTER

The hospital corridor seemed to go on and on. "How could it be this far?" wondered Camille. She understood the long corridors in the Texas Medical Center, but Cody was a tiny town with what seemed to be an endless hospital corridor. The nurse had said Joffe was unconscious and couldn't speak but Camille wanted to see for herself. Entering the room, she saw a middle-aged woman, in disheveled clothes, sad with eyes reddened from crying – Joffe's wife, Camille imagined. It was. They introduced themselves and Camille expressed her regrets. Barbara said, "They don't know if he will make it, but say they are hopeful. Robby, our son, is driving up here from Laramie and will pick up his sister. They should be here tonight."

"What do you think? Could he have just driven off the road?"

"Leland was a careful driver – you gotta be to survive up here. The mountain roads are dangerous and there's no room for mistakes. There are rails that are supposed to keep you from rolling down the mountain but they don't always work. Headquarters said he was on the phone when it happened but would not tell me what he was talking about. No sense of what happened, just a yell and a crash. It could have been as simple as a deer. One could have jumped in front of the car and he just reacted. Lots of deer up there. Cattle too." Her voice drifted off.

"Did he tell you what he was doing there?"

"He said he was checking out the drill site."

"Yes, we are investigating some smuggled equipment and think some of it may have been headed here."

All Barbara said was "Okay," and Camille could tell she should leave the woman to her grief.

"Barbara, I'll try to learn more and will let you know what I can. Meanwhile I will pray for your husband."

"Bless you, Camille. I appreciate that." She returned to her vigil.

Walking back down the long corridor, Camille reckoned she was on her own vigil, waiting for her beloved Irishman to realize her strength and love. Then she caught herself and admonished herself for the selfish attitude. There was no comparison of her problems to those of Barbara, waiting and praying for the life of her husband. She felt ashamed of her feelings and how she had treated the woman.

Leaving the hospital, Camille realized she had exited through a different door and found herself looking at a statue of Buffalo Bill on a horse, holding his rifle in the air as he examined hoof prints on the ground. She recognized it from somewhere in her memory. She realized the car was on the other side of the hospital, and hoped Farman had not wandered too far.

At the car, she realized they had not gotten directions to the drill site and called Perez. "What was Joffe saying when he went off the road?"

"Turns out he was talking to Bob Janz – the RA in Billings. He said the signal was poor but he did learn that someone there pretending to be Saudi spoke Arabic with a Pakistani accent. He wanted us to review everyone at the drill site, but Janz was unsure of the name. Sounded like Sally something Sally."

"OK. Text me Janz's number."

She called and he answered gruffly, "Janz."

"Camille Richard of the Houston office. I just left the Cody hospital. Where are you?"

Janz smiled. No nonsense, he thought. He liked that. "Just leaving Billings. How is Joffe?"

"Not good," answered Camille. "Unconscious."

"Sorry," said Janz. "They say he was run off the road by a drunk driver. It happens, unfortunately. What are you investigating?"

"I'll fill you in when I see you. I'm driving a rental black RAV4. I have a person from the Houston Police Department with me as translator. Do you have firepower?"

"I'm bringing what I keep in the office. I'll stop at my house for more. I should be at the drilling rig in about 2 hours or so. Let's meet at the Sunlight Basin Ranger Station--that's close to the rig site. I'm driving a blue Yukon. What's your idea?"

"Just checking out some discrepancies. I'll fill you in when I see you. But first tell me exactly what Joffe said to you before the accident."

"He said that there was something suspicious going on. He could not tell what, but did say there was a guy who said he was Sudanese but other workers told him was Saudi, yet the man spoke Arabic with a Pakistani accent. The name was Saleh Something Saleh, but I did not hear the middle name clearly. Joffe said he had taken a picture surreptitiously and was going to transmit it to me when he hung up, but then the crash happened while we were still on the phone."

The nape of Camille's neck tingled. "A Pakistani working with a Saudi?" she thought. On the list of countries potentially involved, Pakistan and Russia topped the list. "Too many coincidences," she thought. "You say there's a picture on his phone?"

"That's what he said."

"Then we've got to take a look at it. I'll get the phone and send it to headquarters. There must be some paperwork on him with a passport photo."

"The Highway Patrol should have been at the drill site by now," Janz said. "And looked at the workers files. I'll give them a call on the way. See you at the Ranger Station."

Camille ran back into the hospital, leaving Farman standing

beside the car wondering what the FBI agent was doing. Once inside, she slowed to a swift walk, lest she disturb patients, but when she got to the room, she dashed inside. It appeared that nothing had changed. "Barbara, do you have Leland's phone?"

Barbara looked dazed for many seconds, as if she hadn't heard. Then, she raised her hand and looked at Camille, and said, "Of course. Sorry." She reached beside the chair and pulled up a white plastic bag, and began extracting bloody clothes. Her hands started shaking and she began crying. Camille's heart sank.

"Here, let me help," said Camille, gently taking the bag and sorting the clothes. She found the phone not in a pocket, but simply laying in the bottom of the bag. It was an iPhone, not glamorous. The battery shown red--it would soon die. She had to hurry. "What is his password?"

Barbara seemed far away, as if she had not heard. Camille repeated the question, "Do you know his password?"

The woman seemed to agonize over the answer. Finally, she said, "Most of the time he uses the name of his favorite dog, Ranger, plus 17. That's how old Ranger was when he died. One or two of the letters was capitalized. Maybe the R's."

Camille typed the password in, capitalizing the R's. The phone rejected the password. "Any other letter possibilities?"

Barbara looked stunned and lost. "That's what he uses at the house. I don't know about his work stuff." She began to cry again.

Camille, torn between her drive to find the bomb and her feelings toward the grieving woman, realized the coarseness of her interruption. "That's okay, Barbara," Camille said, wanting to end the woman's ache. "I am so sorry to have bothered you."

CHAPTER THIRTY-ONE

THE SAUDI ARABIAN EMBASSY, WASHINGTON, D.C.

MONDAY

After finally accepting that the bomb had been stolen, the Consul had called the Ambassador on Sunday and asked for a meeting the following day. He told the Ambassador they needed a place where spies would not be listening. In D.C. that would be difficult, but it was arranged. The Consul entered the designated room in the hotel and was greeted by a concerned face from Khalid Al Nami, the rotund Saudi Ambassador to the United States. "How did it happen? What do you know about the suicide bombers?"

"Please, Mister Ambassador, get the King on the phone. I have much worse news than the two suicide bombers."

Al Nami was startled. "My secretary is already calling. What is it?"

"Please let me say it to him and you listen."

Al Nami's eyes narrowed at the insubordination and the mystery. A buzzer rang, and the secretary's voice announced the King's secretary was on the line. "Please tell your secretary not to listen, Mr. Ambassador," spoke Mohammed in a depressed voice.

Al Nami glared at the Consul, but spoke in to the phone and instructed that no one was to listen. "Not even the King's secretary," said Mohammed gloomily.

"What?" puzzled al Nami, but he relayed the message. Finally, the

King's secretary stated the King was on the line, and his face appeared on the screen. "Majesty, I invited Mohammed here so we could speak to you together about the suicide bombings, but he says he has worse news."

"Very well, Mohammed. What is the worse news?"

"Majesty, I must confess that Saleh Tawfiq Saleh, Abdul Faisal, and I conspired to steal one of the atomic bombs and explode it in Houston." Al Nami gasped in horror and disbelief.

The King closed his eyes and rolled his head around as if his neck was hurting. He wondered how people could be so short-sighted, how they could put their own selfish agendas above the needs of Saudi Arabia. But it happened. No time to ponder their foolishness, he needed to focus on what to do now. After a half-minute of silence, he asked, "Where is the bomb now?"

"I do not know, Majesty. The bomb was stolen Sunday morning in Houston. The two men who were supposed to be the drivers were murdered and the two suicide bombers were part of the group."

"Who stole it from them?"

"I don't know. I suspect it might be Abdul and Saleh. Saleh is missing, too, although I talked to Abdul, who said he was in Denver on the way to that drilling rig in Wyoming near Yellowstone."

That struck a nerve with the King. Yellowstone was where Abdul had taken Husain last year. Was it a coincidence or was there a connection? It sounded too coincidental. "Is Saleh there? I did not give him permission to leave." He realized he had heard nothing from Saleh's wife. Had she turned on him too? He forced himself to concentrate on the present issue.

"Tell me about how Abdul is involved."

"He volunteered to smuggle the bomb out of Saudi Arabia and into Houston. He told everyone that was all he would do-smuggle-that he did not want to be a martyr. He even told me and Saleh to wait until he was out of Houston before exploding the bomb."

"What about Saleh's role?"

"He wanted to repay America for killing his first family in Afghanistan. He was ready to be a martyr. He said he had trained people in Saudi Arabia to take his place in the nuclear bomb program."

After a hesitation, the King spoke, "Is Abdul really in Denver? Could he be taking the bomb elsewhere?"

"He is definitely in Wyoming, near Yellowstone, Majesty. He got into a fight with Moteb Said at the local airport there."

"Was Saleh with him?"

"I don't know," moaned the Consul.

"Is it possible that Saleh stole the bomb to use elsewhere?"

"Certainly, sir. He's the one person critical to this operation. If we find him, we find the bomb."

"Ambassador," said the King. "Can you get someone to Abdul's drill site to see if Saleh is there?"

"Certainly, Majesty. I just can't promise how long it will take."

"Of course," said the King. "Do your best. We will find him and the bomb, God willing. Meanwhile let's think about where Saleh might have taken the bomb if he decided against Houston. I'll call my Council and we will discuss it."

"Yes, Majesty," replied Al Nami. "We'll call if we think of something."

"And you, Mohammed," said the King. "You know the punishment for theft." Mohammed's wrist tingled when he heard the words. "That will come in time, God willing. For now, let's find the bomb."

"Yes, Majesty," he managed to say meekly.

CHAPTER THIRTY-TWO

DRIVING NORTH FROM CODY

MONDAY AFTERNOON

Camille spoke with a little edge to her voice, anger at Riley and others. "He's much too close to smuggling – I'll bet it was his ship. I know it sounds crazy – but just too many things are pointing his way. Too many coincidences. And a man claiming to be Sudanese but speaking Arabic with a Pakistani accent? Something is going on."

Despite his anger at the woman, Perez gave in to his determined agent. "Just investigate the drill site and give me a report."

"I will, as soon as I can."

Realizing she did not know how to get to the drill site, she stopped at a convenience store for directions and to pick up a charger for the iPhone, then headed across a river northward out of town. Almost immediately cultivated ground turned to arid land. A few scraggly trees were scattered along a creek bed, but mostly all they saw around them was pale brown grass and grey-green sagebrush. It seemed very dry and boringly dull. She noticed occasionally makeshift signs along the road demanding "Stop the drilling" or "Save our wilderness" or "Save Sunlight Basin". They drove beside the mountain Farman had said was shaped like a dead Indian. A sign indicated its name as Heart Mountain. Camille vaguely remembered something about a Heart Mountain somewhere, but there probably were several with the same name and she couldn't remember the significance. Farman played with Joffe's iPhone, trying all the combinations of capital letters he could imagine, then tried different symbols before the 17. He wished he could just hand it to one of the FBI techies who were magicians at this sort of thing.

At the turnoff from Highway 120 onto 296, the road leading to Sunlight Basin, they noticed a bunch of similar "Stop the drilling" signs in a pile being dumped by a man wearing a cowboy hat and boots. A bearded, long-haired man was yelling out his car window at the cowboy, but did not get out of his car. Probably, Camille thought, because the cowboy had a rifle in his pickup window.

Shortly thereafter she saw a formal sign stating Open Range. Presumably those signs being dumped had been placed on private land. The road started heading up a hill, with a few switchbacks, though not as daunting as she expected after talking to Barbara. As they climbed through the hills the scenery became more palatable as a blanket of fir trees covered the dull gray sagebrush-a pleasant benefit to the eyes. Sharp peaks rose above the trees. Farman kept up a running commentary. "Look at that." "Wow." "Beautiful." Camille's brooding lightened with his enthusiasm and she began to enjoy the scenery. Suddenly they turned a corner and were startled by a wall of red rocks jutting out of the hillside like a karate master's stiff fingers thrust out of the sagebrush. "Amazing," yelled Farman, and she agreed. The contrast of the red rocks to all around was sharp and the red colors changed the ambience of the entire scene.

A couple of switchbacks later, and she had to slow down due to many black cows bunched together in the road. A couple of young cowboys, maybe teenagers, were herding them. "Wow! Real cowboys," yelled Farman, excited. The closest cowboy certainly looked the part, dusty grey hat, dirty jeans on a worn saddle. He squinted at them and did not respond to Farman's smile and wave. The Toyota was clearly just a nuisance to him.

At the top of the hill, the scenery opened up to a striking panorama. "Stop the car! Stop the car," shouted Farman urgently. A sign indicated 'scenic overlook', so she pulled into the parking area. "Wow!

Look at that," said Farman as they walked the railing and took in the magnificent scene. The mountain they were standing atop continued to their right and seemed to wrap around the scene. The same happened to their left, like two arms lovingly embracing the basin, with another mountain in the center. Signs identified the various mountains and identified Sunlight Basin and the Clarks Fork Canyon. Another set of signs explained the historical significance of this place named "Dead Indian Pass," how Chief Joseph of the Nez Perce made the U.S. Cavalry look like fools in its attempt to capture him and his tribe in 1877 by escaping over this seemingly impassable mountain. Camille was amazed that people on foot and horseback could cross this mountain. As she looked down this mountainside she realized that the ribbon crisscrossing the mountainside below them was the road they were going to travel. It appeared much steeper and more difficult than what they'd driven. Farman pointed to a sign that showed a truck on an incline with a 7% grade indicated. He could see her apprehension and offered to drive, saying he'd driven in the mountains of Kurdistan often, on much rougher roads. She readily handed him the keys.

Riding down the mountain, they noticed a rail on the downhill side of the road almost everywhere along the roadway. A long steel bumper ran along the road, attached to short wooden posts, about 6 or 8 inches in diameter, every few yards. Along most of the road she thought it would be difficult for a car to go over the solid-looking rail, but occasionally there were places where the posts were below the roadway and so the rail did not seem such an obstacle. Then they saw a section that was heavily bent, with yellow tape drawn along the rail and orange cones in front. Farman slowed, looking for a place to pull over, and saw an area at the corner of the switchback with a Wyoming Highway Patrol vehicle parked there. Farman parked behind. Initially the patrolman, who appeared to be of Asian descent, told him to drive on but Camille showed her badge and they introduced themselves. His name was George Sumida.

"Sorry to hear about Joffe," Sumida said. "I've met him a couple of times."

"I saw him in the hospital – looks pretty bad, but doctors are hopeful."

"Did he tell you what happened?"

"No, he's been unconscious since the accident."

"He was doubly unlucky," said the patrolman. "Let me show you."

The three walked to the damaged rail. Sumida began by saying, "First of all Joffe was unlucky to get hit here. 95% of this hillside has guard rails. He got hit in one of the very few spots where they don't protect the driver well. See the tread marks? They are headed about 45 degrees to the road all the way to the edge. To make skid marks that long and not stop he'd have to have been going very fast, much faster than anyone travels on this road. So, the second way he was unlucky was that the drunk must have hit the accelerator when the accident occurred."

"Why would he do that?" questioned Camille.

"Cause he's drunk," answered Sumida. "He may have thought he was stepping on the brake when he actually was hitting the accelerator. Or he could have thought he wanted to get away from the scene of an accident as quickly as possible. I've seen lots of nonsense like that at accident sites." Whatever had happened, the force had bent the rail badly. There were some scattered pieces of metal and grass and some damaged trees below them. Camille looked over the edge down the hillside. The Jeep and another car were still on the hillside, obviously having rolled several times. "I suppose Joffe was unlucky in another way, too. If he'd been driving in a Volvo or Mercedes, he could have survived that roll, but he was in his favorite Jeep, always ready for some back-road adventure."

"The drunk must have been attempting to pass when he hit Joffe. Then, instead of hitting the brake he hit the accelerator. That provided the force to push Joffe through the guardrail. Then the drunk kept going up the road but failed to react when he hit the switchback." The patrolman pointed to the torn-up dirt at the switchback. "He went straight into the dirt and rolled down the hillside. No trees to stop his roll."

"What next?" she asked.

"An autopsy is being performed on the drunk. That's procedure. Where are you headed?"

"To the drill site," Camille said. "That's where Joffe had been before the accident occurred."

"Be extra careful, Agent Richard, and let your people know what I think about this accident."

"Will do," she said. "Thank you, officer. Why do you call him 'the drunk'?"

"When we finally pried the door open, the cab stunk of whiskey. There was an open bottle of J&B on the floor. Plus, how else could you explain such reckless driving? Obvious. Sad to say we see too much of this sort of thing out here."

"Wasn't he one of the Muslim crew on the rig?"

"Yes, but I hear they are not all strict about their religion. Some of them have been in the bars in Cody with loose women."

Camille was amused by the old-school description, but said nothing. The tragedy weighed on her humor.

Camille and Sumida traded contact info, then Farman drove them down the mountain. Despite what she'd just seen, she could not help but marvel at the scenery.

At the bottom of the mountain was a small creek and a campsite with a sign marked full. Camille pulled into the area and got on her phone to Perez. She told him about Joffe and the drunk driver and the Highway Patrolman's analysis. She told him to expect the last photograph Joffe had taken, the one of the Sally character, as soon as they could get into the iPhone. In her mind, she was now convinced that all the coincidences were connected and they all led to the nearby drill site. She asked Perez to send a radiation sensor. "The only thing that makes sense of all this is that they are going to try to set off the super volcano."

Perez said, "Camille, until today I've thought you a terrific agent, but I think you're way off in this case. But because of all this screwy stuff, and the fact that you disobeyed my orders and are already there, I'm letting you run — but I'm under a lot of pressure — your career is hanging on this."

"Chief, I know it's crazy, but it all fits. And if you saw Abdul Faisal you'd realize he is crazy too and capable of something wild like this."

"Okay. I'll try to get a sensor flown over. You be careful."

"Okay, Chief."

Camille drove on, but didn't need the Sunlight Basin arrow to tell her where to turn. There was a wide area at the intersection crowded with cars and signs, including several like the ones she'd seen driving north from Cody.

CHAPTER THIRTY-THREE

THERMOPOLIS, WYOMING

MONDAY AFTERNOON

The Suburban in front of them pulled off the highway near the edge of town, and headed up a steep hill. As they eased out of town, with the truck struggling a little, Dolecek and Kern got a little apprehensive. "Might want to have your friend handy," said Dolecek. Kern said nothing, then saw a sign that showed an airplane. Were they nearing an airport? They relaxed when they saw the airport, and the three vehicles pulled into a parking area.

The leader handed them their phones and said, "Gentlemen, we have reached our stopping place. You have accomplished all that we asked. Please check your accounts to see that we have fulfilled our part of the bargain." They did, and both were pleased with the size of their accounts. The leader handed each an envelope and continued, "In each envelope is a thousand dollars. That will pay for an air taxi from here to Casper and a plane flight home. Before you rush off, though, I recommend that you make your reservations for tomorrow, then go down to the hot spring in town, what they claim is the World's Largest Mineral Hot Spring. I can guarantee it's a wonderful place to relax after your long journey. You should have enough left in the envelope to pay for a nice hotel. Spend the night, relax, then go home to your families tomorrow feeling terrific. But it's your choice. Our business is finished. We thank you for your effort. Do remember not to tell anyone where you've been. That's part of our bargain, too."

Dolecek and Kern assured the man they would honor the bargain, and walked into the air terminal, still somewhat apprehensive. Upon checking that they could not make the late flight from Casper to Houston, they decided to follow the Leader's recommendation, and later, soaking in the hot spring, agreed it was a fine way to recover.

What they did not expect would happen the following day. As each man walked to the front door of his home in Houston, he would be cut down by a "random shooting".

CHAPTER THIRTY-FOUR

SUNLIGHT BASIN RANGER STATION

MONDAY AFTERNOON

As Farman drove up the lonely Sunlight Basin road, Camille's thoughts kept returning to what Riley had said, and the whole idea seemed more and more ridiculous. Holland had said that a U-235 atomic bomb would create an explosion that could wipe out a city at the surface but when exploded underground would result in something around 5.6 on the Richter scale. He said that would only rattle teacups and perhaps shake pictures off shelves. He said bombs set off by Pakistan and North Korea had proven that several times. So how could setting off an atomic bomb set off Yellowstone's super volcano? Looking at a map, she had wondered whether it was possible. Now, surrounded by giant mountains on both sides, she felt the idea more and more preposterous. Even an atomic bomb would not do much to these mountains. Now she understood why Riley was so upset with her, why everyone thought she was wasting her time and the Bureau's money. She felt foolish. She felt small. If she weren't meeting Janz at the Ranger station, she'd have turned around right then.

As she drove along, she noticed the creek wandered back and forth across the valley floor, sometimes near the road, sometimes by the mountains on the other side. Along the creek she recognized willow trees plus there were large gnarly trees that seemed to grow only near the creek. Their branches were large and varied, and Camille thought they'd have been fun to climb when she was young. At one point, another small valley opened to her left leading up into the mountains. In many places along the valley, fields had been cleared and planted, with giant rotary irrigation arms. What would they grow up here?

Finally, they noticed a sign that pointed the way to the Sunlight Basin Ranger Station. The ranger station was comprised of three buildings, one of which appeared to be a house for the Ranger's family. Another larger building clearly sheltered fire-fighting and road maintenance equipment. The third was an office and visitor center. A yellow flutter caught her eye. Camille looked up the mountainside and saw a grove of yellow aspens amidst the green pine trees. "Quite beautiful," she thought. Farman stopped to enjoy a cigarette while she entered and introduced herself to a Ranger, a tall young woman with glistening black skin, decidedly healthy-looking, with a generous smile, wearing the light green Forest Service uniform. "Welcome to Sunlight Basin Ranger Station. I'm Leona Richardson."

"Camille Richard, FBI," she said, showing her badge. I'm expecting another FBI agent, Bob Janz. Is he here yet?"

"No, he's not. Do I hear a Cajun accent?"

"You do. I didn't think it was that strong."

"A person from south Louisiana has a fine-tuned ear." She smiled that big smile again. "I'm from Houma."

"Houma! You've got to be kidding me," Camille said, astonished. "I'm from Lafayette. What is a girl from Houma doing up here?"

"Quite a story. It was not my intention when I graduated from Southern, believe you me. My degree is in Forestry and I thought I might go as far as the Piney Woods in Texas, but this is where I got assigned. My first winter here was a struggle. I'd never seen snow before," she laughed. "It took some adjusting."

"I'll bet," Camille smiled. "I'd like to hear more, but I'm afraid I'm here on business. Let's talk about down home later. What can you tell me about the drilling rig and its people?"

"Okay," Leona said. "The rig is first class – I've seen a log of rigs back home – I bet you have too."

"Yes," said Camille. "My daddy was a geologist."

"Mine worked on the rig floor most of his life," said Leona. "Did you know the guy drilling this well is the guy who invented the rig floor robot?"

"I heard that," Camille said.

"My daddy says it took away a lot of good-paying jobs. He was kicked out of high school. They said he was disruptive. The word they used was incorrigible. He went to work on drill sites as a gopher hauling stuff around. When he was 19, he was hired as a roughneck on a workover rig, and he worked on those rigs for 30-some years. The thing he was most proud of was that he never lost a finger on a rig."

"Yeah. I remember all those guys hanging around town missing a couple of fingers or more. It was a badge that they'd worked on a drilling rig."

"Daddy would hold up his hands and say, 'See? Thirty years on a rig and I still have all my fingers.' For a retirement project, he bought a little service station in Houma and worked on cars. He'd only had it three years when there was an accident and he lost three fingers on one hand. He thought it was a big cosmic joke played on him by God that he lost fingers at a service station."

"Ironic, for sure."

"Now this Abdul Faisal guy comes along and makes it much safer, but Daddy says the robot takes away jobs. Used to be 20 men on a crew. Now there's like five. So, guys who used to have good-paying jobs are now on welfare hanging out at the ice house playing checkers with the guys missing arms and hands. Daddy says they'd rather be working, but I'm glad more men don't have to lose fingers and arms. Anyway, the robots made this Abdul guy insanely rich, so why is he up here drilling for a science project?"

"I saw him on TV," Camille said. "He says it's a hobby. He's interested in science."

"I heard the guy speak here a couple of times. Quite an impressive person. He certainly stirred up the geologists. The drilling crew is really quiet, though. Not like the normal oil field trash we get in Louisiana. Only a few drink, for example."

Just then, Farman entered the building, his strong features catching the Ranger's attention. "My, my, my!" gushed Leona. "What have we here?"

"Leona, this is Farman Yousif. He's a translator for us — originally from Iraq, now in Houston."

Leona smiled widely and remarked, "Oh, I bet he can do more than translate."

"Farman," Camille said, "this is Leona Richardson, the Forest Ranger here."

Farman knowingly smiled and looked mischievously at Leona.

Camille rolled her eyes. "We're going over to talk to the members of the drilling crew. Anything you can tell us?"

Leona's eyes lingered on Farman, then looked back to Camille. "Oh, they're not as rowdy as a normal drilling crew back home. There are a few hell-raisers but most are very religious — no alcohol, no women, a lot of praying. Kind of weird to hear the call to prayer five times a day, but I've gotten used to it. The ranchers have not complained to me, at least.

"Have you met Abdul, the owner of the drilling company?"

"Yes, once. No, twice. When they first arrived, he came and explained in detail what they'd be doing. A bigwig like that but he was generous with his time like he wanted me and the other rangers to have no concerns. I was impressed. He flies in and out on a helicopter. Quite sleek — shows what a big shot he is. But yesterday he went crazy over something, yelling and screaming. I could hear him all the way over here -- but it was in some other language."

A blue Yukon pulled into the parking lot. A tall barrel-chested guy with a round face and thin hair got out and headed for the door. Muscular arms, both women thought.

"I'll bet that's your man," said Leona. It was. After introductions all around, Leona went back to work and the other three walked outside. Camille was deflated by the message she was about to give. She looked up at the mountains and seemed to gather strength. Her problems seemed small in comparison.

"Bob, I'm afraid I might have brought you here on a wild goose chase."

Janz said, "Camille, I've had a lot of fun chasing wild geese over the years. Tell me about it." Camille relaxed with a smile. She laid out the history of what she knew and the questions about Abdul. Then she got to the doubts that Riley had expressed and what Holland had said and how preposterous it all seemed now. The only thing in her favor, she said, was the strange news about the Sudanese/Saudi/Pakistani.

Janz said, "We're here now. Let's go find out what we can. But first, let me show you the toys I brought." He opened the rear door of the Yukon. Camille gasped, Farman whistled. It held an amazing arsenal of rifles, shotguns, several automatic weapons, plus one other unexpected treasure.

"Is that a rocket launcher?" Farman asked, incredulous.

"A precursor to the RPG. It's called a bazooka. This one is from the Korean War."

Farman picked it up and examined it curiously.

"Is that legal?" he asked.

"What? I don't know what you're talking about," he said. "You must be hallucinating."

Camille chuckled. "Do you know how to fire it? Do you have ammunition for it?"

"It would be useless to have an imaginary weapon without imaginary ammunition and imaginary ability to fire it, now, wouldn't it?"

Camille laughed. Janz continued, "I'm joking. I'm legally allowed to have it as long as I don't use it. But don't ask me to explain that logic."

"What's that?" she asked, pointing to a pile of clothes. "Doing your laundry?"

Janz laughed. "I reckoned you two didn't come prepared for the mountains, so I brought some extra coats. Might be a bit large, though."

"Agent Richard!" Leona yelled from the door of the Ranger station. "There's a phone call for you. It's Highway Patrolman Sumida."

Camille was nonplussed. Why didn't he call her cellphone? She went inside and picked up the phone, attached by cord to a pay phone. "God," she thought, "I'm really in the boonies."

"This is Agent Richard."

"Ms. Richard, this is George Sumida. I'm glad I caught you. I've got some news that confirms what I thought happened at the accident."

"What is it?"

"The coroner always does blood analysis on drunk drivers. But this one had zero alcohol in his blood stream."

"Zero?"

"Yes, that means this was a set-up made to appear like a drunk driver. Either another person was driving and jumped out, or the dead man committed suicide disguised as a drunk. The accident is now attempted murder."

"Holy shit." Camille's mind raced. "Clearly something is going on. Okay, Agent Janz from Billings is here – we are going to the rig site now to investigate."

"Bob Janz? I know him. Tell him 'Hi' for me. Tell him to aim the bazooka high. That'll make no sense to you but it will to him."

"Oh, it makes sense," said Camille, astonished at the nonchalant breaking of federal gun laws by law enforcement out here. "Thanks, Leona. Call me if something new comes up. If you think of anything else, call Bob's phone." She gave Leona his number.

Then she burst out of the door and yelled to Janz, "It's no longer a wild goose chase."

Camille told Janz what Patrolman Sumida had said about the

deceptive drunk. Janz grunted in surprise, then asked, "Did you get Joffe's phone?"

"Yes, but we have not been able to get in. Barbara was unsure of the password."

"Have you tried connecting it to Headquarters?"

"Shit," thought Camille to herself. She should have thought of that earlier, and felt liked she'd slipped up. "No, I don't have a good connection. Would your phone work , or could we use the Forest Service phone?"

"Let's try mine first." He called a friend at FBI headquarters who arranged the use of a technical analyst. He listened to instructions, pulled a connector from his glove box, and fastened the iPhone to the satellite phone. Soon, he hoped, the digital wizards would be into Joffe's phone and downloading the last photo for input into the facial recognition software. The man said he did not know how long it would take, so Janz, Camille, and Farman got into the Yukon and drove toward the rig.

Janz mused out loud. "Sumida is a Japanese name. Do you know why there are so many Japanese names around here?"

"No."

"In WWII Roosevelt rounded up all the Japanese-Americans living within 120 miles of the Pacific Ocean and had them shipped to makeshift concentration camps. He said it was for their own protection but really it was for fear they might aid a Japanese invasion. One of the camps was the Heart Mountain Relocation Camp, and it was located on the other side of Dead Indian Pass, between Cody and Powell. About 13,000 people were incarcerated there." Camille realized that was why the name of Heart Mountain rang a bell. Janz continued, "George Sumida's grandfather was one of the people from Oregon confined here. He was one of the many in the camp who volunteered to join the US army. They were sent to Italy to fight. Their regiment, the 442nd, was the most decorated unit in the war. George's grandfather was wounded in battle. He returned to Wyoming and decided to make his life here. Turned out there were already plenty of Japanese-American farmers in the Bighorn Basin, and many of the ones confined at Heart Mountain stayed in the Basin and farmed after the War. One of them, Kaz Uriu, later became Secretary of Agriculture for the State of Wyoming. He said he stayed in Wyoming because he did not want to return to the prejudice in California, but the real reason was because he fell in love with a local girl."

Camille smiled. "Love rules," she said.

Farman asked, "Were the prisoners treated well?"

"Okay, I guess. They were given lots of freedom in the camps, and land to grow crops. One of the interesting things was that the people in Powell welcomed the residents of the camp, while the people of Cody were anti-residents to the point where they had signs on the stores like 'No Japs Allowed.' Opposite reactions from two towns just thirty miles apart."

They had to stop talking, as they had already arrived at the gate to the rig site, where a trio of guards loitered. Camille rang Riley.

"Callahan."

"Riley, I can't talk long. Just listen. You were right – this whole thing seemed preposterous – I was ready to turn around and go home, but just found out something strange is going on. The agent who reported a Pakistani trying to pass as Saudi or Sudanese was murdered by a Muslim suicide."

"What?"

"I can't explain now. We have just arrived and I have to call Perez. Just know I love you and can't wait to see you."

"I love you too, Camille." He was puzzled, trying to figure out what she meant.

"Okay, bye, Riley."

AT THE DRILLING RIG EAST OF YELLOWSTONE

A FEW MINUTES LATER

Camille turned off her phone as Janz was showing their credentials to one guard through the window of the Yukon. The men guarding the gate appeared to be private security, but much more professional than Camille expected. "Definitely not locals," she thought. The guard asked whether they had an appointment. Camille explained that she was investigating yesterday's accident. They turned to some raised voices.

The other two guards were arguing with an older red-haired woman in a flannel shirt, jeans and hiking boots. A younger bearded man in similar attire stood beside the woman and appeared to be supporting her. Camille immediately thought "hippie" but then noticed Michigan State University's logo on their pickup.

"But Abdul promised me," the hippie-type woman demanded. Camille thought she looked familiar.

"The boss said you violated the agreement when you helped the protestors and specifically forbade your entry."

"I was helping Abdul, not the protestors," she yelled dramatically, incensed. "If he'd just talk to me, I could explain."

The two FBI agents and Farman got out of the Yukon and stepped closer to the arguers.

"Excuse me," said Janz in a deep booming voice practiced from high school debate and his law studies, startling Camille as well as the others. They all turned to look at him. "I am FBI agent Janz and this is FBI agent Richard. Please explain what's going on."

Farman thought, "What about me?" He felt like an afterthought.

The woman saw an opportunity and spoke first. "I'm Dr. Laura Bigley-Puzio of Michigan State University and this is Dr. Leonardo Danielli from the National Institute of Geophysics and Volcanology in Italy. He's comparing the Yellowstone super volcano with one there."

Camille finally recognized the woman and interrupted, "You're the "Quake & Shake" lady from TV?"

The woman smiled but the Italian rolled his eyes. "Yes. The head of this project, Abdul Faisal, promised that I could monitor his fluid loss, but through a misunderstanding he won't let me in to do my work. It's critical work."

"Sorry," said Janz. "Could you explain what you mean by fluid loss?"

"Yes. When a well is drilled, chemical muds are pumped down the hole to remove rock cuttings from the drill bit. Some of that mud is lost during drilling, going into cracks in the rock and elsewhere. Too much fluid loss can cause earthquakes like what is happening in Oklahoma now. The last thing we want is for fluid loss from this well to cause the Sunlight Basin fault to activate. That would be horrific. Might even cause the super volcano to prematurely explode. That's going to be the subject of my next episode on "Quakin' and Shakin'."

Camille vaguely thought she understood, remembering she'd watched her dad take samples from drilling mud, but was not certain of the implications here. Janz looked at her inquisitively. He knew almost nothing of what had been going on in Houston except what he'd seen on television. Camille interrupted the professor. "What is the Sunlight Basin fault?"

The professor's voice deepened, as if lecturing a class. She faced west up the canyon and raised both arms, aiming them toward the mountain. "Some people think there's a fault running down Sunlight Basin that connects to the north end of Yellowstone Lake, to the core of the volcano." She turned to the east and pointed her arm down the canyon. "They think the fault might run all the way through the Clarks Fork Canyon. We are not sure the fault is here, so we want to measure the stress in the rocks to verify its presence and to see if it's anywhere near cutting loose. That's what the well is for. Abdul has invented some new stress measuring equipment for fracking that he will put in the hole."

"Have you seen the equipment?" Camille asked.

"No, he says it's a trade secret for his oil production research." Camille recalled something like that from the TV show she'd seen.

She looked at the professor intently. "Could an explosion cause the fault to go off and the volcano to explode?"

Bigley-Puzio laughed. "It would have to be a mighty big explosion. And where would you put it? An explosion here would just echo down the canyon."

Camille held her hand up and closed her eyes, questioning whether she should break the rules and tell the professor. But the immensity of the problem overwhelmed the rules: she had to know the answer. She spoke softly. "Professor, come with me and Agent Janz – we must get away from all ears."

They began to walk into the field and Danielli followed.

"I'm sorry, Professor, but your companion must stay with the others."

Bigley-Puzio stiffened. "He is with me. Anything you say to me you can say to him."

"Sorry, Professor. No games here. He is a foreign national and cannot hear what I am going to tell you."

"Nonsense," said Bigley-Puzio. "He is a trusted colleague."

Camille pulled open her jacket and showed the professor her pistol. "Please don't make me get mean. This is a matter of national security. What I am going to tell you will require the utmost secrecy from you. Agent Janz has not even been informed yet. "

Bigley-Puzio looked hard at the woman, saw how deadly serious the agent looked. She noted Janz had a quizzical look on his face, strongly curious.

"Okay," she relented. "Leonardo, stay with the guards."

Camille spoke to Farman, "Farman, stay here and make sure nobody comes close to us." He nodded and looked at Danielli and the guards, who did not seem inclined to move anyway.

"Have them try Abdul again," Bigley-Puzio said to the Italian, then walked with the agents through the sagebrush until about 80 yards from the gate.

Camille said, "Professor, would an atomic explosion in the well set off the Sunlight Basin fault?"

Bigley-Puzio and Janz were startled by the strange question. "What do you mean?" he asked. It was as if her first mention of the bomb had not registered. Meanwhile, Bigley-Puzio appeared to be having difficulty comprehending the idea.

"We think an atomic weapon was smuggled into Houston yesterday, just before the suicide bombings." Janz snorted in surprise. "We thought it was intended to be used in Houston, but we really don't have a clue where it is. It could be anywhere in the country. All the experts in Washington think it's headed there or New York, but it's unknown. One of the clues led me here to Abdul's operation. I suspect his company smuggled the bomb. But it didn't make sense – all the government experts have said it would be like a firecracker in the volcano – that the bomb must be going elsewhere. Nobody in Washington said anything about this Sunlight Basin fault."

"That's because it's just recently been postulated. Only a few academics know of it. We aren't sure it's even here but it's possible. That's why we are drilling this well. What about this bomb?"

"You said you were worried about fluid loss causing the fault to go. What about an atomic explosion in the wellbore?"

"First, what do you mean, atomic explosion?"

"Like at Hiroshima. Little Boy they called it."

Janz interrupted. "The Little Boy bomb at Hiroshima was designed like a rifle-barrel tube with the target on one end and the bullet fired from the other end. When they collided, critical mass was achieved and the atomic explosion resulted. The Nagasaki bomb was spherically shaped and caused a bigger explosion. It was called Fat Boy but is more difficult to construct. The Little Boy would be the shape for a well."

"I don't know how big that was," the professor said. "And I wouldn't know how that translates to the underground."

"An expert told me it would cause about an earthquake about 5.6 on the Richter scale," said Camille.

"5.6? That's not much. Let me think it through." The woman began pacing back and forth, concentrating. She began speaking slowly. "If no Sunlight Basin fault, it would mean nothing. There was an earthquake at Hegben in the '50's. That was about magnitude 7.5, say 60 times more powerful than what this 5.6 bomb would cause, and it had no appreciable impact in the Park itself. That's maybe 40 or 50 miles from Yellowstone Lake. If the Sunlight Basin fault does exist, though, the bomb could only affect the fault if it were close. Then it might cause it to slip." Suddenly she stopped. "God! O God!" shouted the professor.

Danielli, Farman, and the guards looked over. Danielli asked loudly, "Are you all right?"

"I'm okay," she shouted back, then turned to the agents. "It would be like the atomic bomb used In the Rangely shale experiment in Colorado many years ago." Her eyes seemed bigger, like fear was intruding. "The Rangely experiment crumbled the rocks into rubble. If an atomic explosion reached the fault, it'd be like marbles on a dance floor. The fault would give. The only question is how far it would travel, how far the movement would be. If it reached the core of the volcano then who knows? It just might set off the super volcano. Oh, shit! Why would anyone do that?"

Bigley-Puzio was pacing back and forth, kicking the dirt. Camille said, "Professor, would you explain more clearly what you mean?"

The professor realized these folks did not know geology, so she tried to think of an analogy. "If there is a fault, it's stuck now, but a bomb might weaken the friction that holds it together, and it would move, like lubricating the fault." She was thinking out loud now, trying to work through what it might mean. "If it does move, and the guys from Utah are right, then it might connect to the magma chamber." She hesitated, as if she remembered something significant. "But even if it does, the magma is not very hot, so it could not be a very big explosion." Suddenly she seemed composed and less worried. Then her eyes widened, and she became concerned again. "If the grad students are right, the explosion could cause the eruption in only 10-30 years."

"Sounds like a lot of if's," said Janz.

"Yeah, I think it unlikely," said the professor. She seemed to relax. "But let me call some of my colleagues, some of the modelers, and get their opinions."

"No," said Camille emphatically. "I've already violated a rule from the Director of the National Security Agency in telling you. You can't mention this to anyone, not even your husband. Even the governors of the states don't know."

"Agent Richard," said Janz. "Let's think about this. It's critical that we understand exactly what this means. We can't rely on one person's opinion. Let's get other people involved."

"You are right," she agreed, and thought a few seconds. "But it needs to be kept in the inner circle. Professor, would you call our experts in Washington and talk to them? Explain what your thinking is, and what we need to understand?"

"Of course," said the geologist. Camille gave her the phone numbers and told her whom to call. She also gave her Bradley Holland's number for more information about the bomb.

"What can we do?" asked Bigley-Puzio.

"There's still a chance to stop the bomb, I guess. At least it hasn't gone off yet. Actually, we don't even know if whether it might be coming here. We don't know whether it's on site. Bob and I will investigate. You and the Italian stay here at the gate. We'll use you as an excuse to talk to Abdul. I'm going to leave my satellite phone with you. See if you can make it work. If so, call Bob's phone to check on us. But remember – do not tell your colleague any of this."

"Understood. I'll give the phone to him. He likes to tinker."

"Good. Wish us luck." Camille blessed herself, and she and Yousif and Janz got in the Yukon and headed for the gate. One of the guards held up a hand, Janz rolled down the window and showed an ID.

"You can go in," the guard said. "I just wanted to inform you that the boss is not here."

"When will he return?" asked Janz.

"I don't know," said the guard. "But he always arrives by helicopter, so you'll know when he's close. I'm sorry to hear about your fellow agent. Is he okay?"

"In bad shape," Camille said, "but doctors are hopeful."

"I hope he recovers soon," the guard said. "He seemed like a nice guy. Head on up. The drill site is a mile up this road. You go up the hill through the trees and when you go down the hill you come out of the trees at the drill site. Dirt road all the way."

Riding with her dad going to well sites, Camille had seen lots of dirt roads, but this one was in pretty good shape. It must have been maintained for the ranchers in the valley and the ranger station, she thought. She noticed a sign warning about grizzly bears. She wondered whether noise from a drilling rig would keep grizzlies away.

She called Perez and related the news about Agent Joffe's accident, and the strange name confusion, and the reaction of the professor. "Have you checked out the people on the drilling crew?" she asked him.

"We're checking now. The drilling company gave us their names. They are mostly Saudis, but we hadn't got through them all last I checked."

"As the FBI?" Her question's implication was clear – wouldn't using the FBI cause suspicion by those people at the drilling company?

"Through the ICE. The company says they'll cooperate, but at this time they don't know for sure who exactly is at that drill site. They have several crews in this country that are always moving around. But they promise to get the list to me tomorrow."

"Did you watch the videos at the airport?"

"Yes, but I don't see what upset you. There were two men who obviously hated each other and a man reunited with his daughter. So what?"

"Did you hear that man Faisal tell him tell him tell his daughter it was too dangerous to visit the rig?" Her voice rose in anger. "The only reason he'd say that is because he has the bomb here!"

Perez cautiously responded. "Camille, you are imagining things. Listen, I'm getting a lot of pressure to bring you back to Houston. Most people don't know yet that you have violated my orders. They simply think you're on a wild goose chase." The phrase struck a chord, but now she had an answer.

Camille closed her eyes and sighed, then spoke more calmly but urgently. "I had come to that conclusion myself, boss, but the strange goings-on here make me now think I might have guessed right."

Perez continued, "The people in Washington think the driller, the Saudi Faisal, is a charitable man, smart and wealthy, so what would he be doing with an atomic bomb in a National Park? Even if he had it and wanted to us it, certainly he'd use it in a more effective place like a major city."

"I understand, boss. This sounds crazy, but it doesn't matter what we think. It only matters what he thinks."

"I've given you all the rope I can, Agent Richard. Report

immediately if you learn something."

They drove out of the trees into an open area with the drill site. A board road ran from the dirt road to two acres of boards, the drilling pad, upon which sat several silver and green trailers with green Crescendo logos, several large pickups and the drilling rig.

The drilling pad sat in a field between two lines of pine trees. One line, the one they'd just driven out of, covered the ground unending from there up nearly to the mountaintop. The other line of trees ran along the creek and included some of those gnarly trees they had noticed before. The derrick towered above the trees like some mechanical monster growing up in the forest. The rig was much bigger than she expected. She'd heard the well was drilling to a depth of about 6,000'. This rig looked like one of the big ones she'd seen in south Louisiana that drilled to 20,000'. It had a massive base about 40' above the ground, straddling a giant blow-out preventer sitting atop the hole.

Janz asked, "What now, kemo sabe?"

Camille shrugged, "Let's just check things out. I'll try to get Farman to talk to the crew, to see if he can find the Pakistani. First, though, we need permission from the tool-pusher."

She climbed up the iron steps corrugated with steel chips to enable cleaning of mud and ice off boots, and tapped noisily on the door.

"Come in," said a gruff voice on the other side. She swung the door open. The trailer looked like every tool-pusher trailer she'd ever entered, a beat-up desk near the door, a countertop with rows of monitoring devices and printers, and a cork bulletin board with obligatory directions from OSHA and the Department of Labor haphazardly tacked on it. She stepped inside and motioned the other two in. As she entered, a short man with skin like leather and forearm muscles like iron stood up. Another man, who appeared to be Middle Eastern, continued to sit.

In as cheerful a voice as she could muster, she said, "I'm Camille

Richard, Special Agent for the FBI, this is Robert Janz, another Special Agent, and our assistant Farman Yousif."

The standing man grinned a welcoming grin. "Richard? Missie, are you from Cajun country? I'm Terry Boudreaux, late of Lake Charles. How you do, miss?"

Camille had to grin back. Wherever the oil business went, Cajuns were sure to be there.

"I'm fine, Mr. Boudreaux. I'm from Lafayette. My daddy is a geologist – you may know him. Terrance Richard."

"Unusual name like that is hard to forget. I believe he's sat on a logging run on a few wells of mine. What can I do for you, Missie?"

"We're here to talk to you and the crew about the recent accident involving an FBI agent and one of your crew members."

"Of course, you're welcome to our help, Agent Richard, but the police were already here just a few hours ago and talked to just about everyone."

"I understand that, but it seemed your workers didn't speak good English, so I've brought an Arabic speaker." The man in the chair glared at Farman.

"Oh, of course. They don't understand the English too good when I'm chewing their asses, either." Smiles all around except for the man sitting.

"You're in luck, too. I had to get all the crew's paperwork out for the police and hadn't put it back." The stack of folders was conveniently on the desk-top. "Let me round up some hard hats for y'all, and I'll show you the layout." He pointed to the man on the couch, who finally stood.

"This is Waleed Moqed, my second in command. He'll be taking over for the next shift, which will happen whenever the boss gets back."

Moqed shook the hand of Janz and Farman, still staring intensely, but did not extend his hand to Camille. "You'll have to forgive this idiot's refusal to touch a woman," explained Boudreaux. "He says a matter of religious principle."

"If he doesn't want to shake mine then I don't want to shake his," Camille responded.

"He's the loser," said Boudreaux. He pulled some hard hats out of a cabinet, handed them out, then stepped outside and walked down the steps. "Come with me," he said.

Camille hesitated, recognizing the antipathy Moqed had for Farman, then handed the stack of folders to Janz. "Bob, perhaps you ought to assist Farman. We'll send the crew into you individually. Will that be okay, Mr. Boudreaux?"

"Makes sense to me," he replied, and called some workers over.

Janz went back into the trailer, where it seemed the other two men had gritted teeth already. "Good call," Camille said to herself.

Boudreaux yelled instructions to the men to line up for interviews, then turned his attention to Camille and began pointing things out. "The mud logging trailer is next to mine – the closest to the rig. Over there are the two crew trailers. The extra trailer is for all the professors and geologists who've been up here, although not too many have shown up since the first hpydrogen sulfide scare."

"What was that?"

"Oh, volcanic rock is loaded with tiny pockets of trapped gasses. Sometimes they have H_2S in them. Because of that we have lots of alarms set up and everyone has a gas mask handy at all times. All the academics had to sign a waiver about the dangers on a drilling rig but I don't think they realized what it meant until the first scare or two. Since then, not many have shown up except that TV lady."

"So why don't we have gas masks?"

"Cuz we're pulling out of the hole for the last time. The final equipment is supposed to arrive any time. After the last logging run it'll be installed."

"What is it?"

"Some device that measures the strain on the earth, whatever that means. The geologists say it will tell them whether there's a big fault here and whether it's about to go off."

"What you mean, whether there's a fault here? Don't they know?"

"No, that's part of the controversy. Some of the geologists say there's no evidence for a fault and this is all just a waste."

"You're kidding."

"No, and this is one expensive well. More expensive than a 24,000' well I drilled in Cameron Parish a few years ago."

"Why so expensive?"

"First, we're drilling through volcanic rock, all the way, top to bottom. They're expensive bits, and they're huge. This hole had to be almost perfectly straight and 18" in diameter at the bottoms. That's a helluva hole, Missie, but I did it. Hardest hole I ever had to dig, but we got it done and before the big snow."

Camille pointed to a large truck. "Is that a cement truck?"

"Good eye," said Boudreaux. "It is indeedy."

"My daddy said the cement truck came for two reasons, good to put the casing in a good well, the other bad to plug a dry one."

"True enough."

"Are the instruments being put in the hole going inside casing? That doesn't make sense to me."

"No, it will be in open hole just below the casing," said Boudreaux, "That's what we're doing. This special new equipment was developed in Saudi Arabia specifically for measuring stress in a fracking environment, but apparently it can measure stress anywhere."

Camille considered the idea of a bomb placed in the hole. It would make sense to put cement above the bomb to plug off the top of the hole to keep as much blast as possible in the ground. Without a plug, some of the power of the blast would go straight into the air. It fit her scary idea of an atomic bomb, despite what the experts had told her. "Are those pumps for the cement?" she asked.

"No," said Boudreaux. "the Boss wants extra fluids pumped into the hole to keep it clean and drill faster. The earthquake lady was monitoring the fluids but stopped for some reason and the Boss jacked up the amount of fluid."

"Isn't there a mud logger on the well?"

"There was a young Venezuelan just out of college here the entire time we were drilling. Worked his butt off. But as soon as the Boss said stop drilling, he hightailed it out of here." She wondered if he left quickly because he knew what was about to happen.

"How's the owner been to deal with?"

"I've never had a boss who didn't put pressure on me, but I gotta say the Prince applies pressure more politely than anyone I've dealt with. Until yesterday, that is. Since that car accident it's like something snapped. Now he seems frantic, almost unbearably frantic. Yells when he never yelled before. Actually, when that happened he said stop drilling – the equipment is almost here. We're only a couple hundred feet off scheduled Total Depth, but whatever the boss says, I'm good to go." Camille pondered the reason. Could Abdul have determined that the identity of his man Sally been compromised, and that's why he went berserk and stopped drilling?

"How's it working with Waleed Moqed back there?"

"He's about the only one I can't stand. Most of the crew is rock solid. Hard working, stoic even. And most don't drink or do drugs so that's a relief right there. Fewer problems to deal with. And I understand Waleed, really. He's a highly competent and experienced driller and he's pissed off because he's second fiddle to an American on an Arab rig. He feels he should be in charge, and he takes it out on everybody. He may be good at his job, but he's unprofessional."

"What about Ahmed, the driver of the car that hit the FBI agent?"

"That surprised me. I'd never known him to take a drink – he had always been a teetotaler, as far as I knew. Religious. Not all the crew said their prayers, but he did religiously, so to speak."

"Anybody else that's unusual?"

"We've had lots of visitors, usually escorted by the boss – politicians, ambassadors, that sort of thing. Plus, all these crazy geologists. Come to think of it, the first time Abdul went crazy was before the accident, when the other FBI agent left. His big research guy from Saudi Arabia was here, Sally – something - Sally. After the FBI guy left, Sally and the Boss talked hotly and the Boss went stomping off shouting in Arabic. That's it. That was the trigger."

"Is the Sally guy here?"

"No. He was, but he left on the helicopter with the boss. I understood he's the guy who invented the strain device we'll put in the hole."

CHAPTER THIRTY-FIVE

SUNLIGHT BASIN RANGER STATION

MONDAY EVENING

"Gumbo," exclaimed Camille as she entered the house. Leona was at the stove stirring the pot, wearing a red apron stating, "Warning: Cook is hotter than the stove."

"Unfortunately, everything has to be frozen before shipping to Cody, but I think you'll like it. If not, there's plenty of Tabasco."

"If it's half as good as it smells, I'll love it."

"Where are the boys?" asked Leona.

"They decided to stay in the trailer, maybe learn a little more."

"Too bad, they'll miss tonight. But there will be leftovers for lunch tomorrow." She spooned some rice in a bowl and poured steaming gumbo over it. Camille inhaled deeply and said, "Ahhh."

"There's a guy in Cody from Thibodaux, so I have some competition that spurs me to my best."

Camille took a taste and said, "I can honestly say this is the very best gumbo I've ever had in the state of Wyoming."

They both laughed. The conversation started off about gumbo and variations thereof, then to Cajun and southern cooking in general, then to growing up in South Louisiana, then to the men in their lives.

"Up here you can go places where you don't see a trace of civilization," said Leona. "You feel like you could be a Shoshone Indian or something, like you belong here but only as a small piece. Stand at the base of a cliff and listen to the wind rushing in the trees, and hear an eagle cry. You feel like a small speck of a much greater nature. Now that I've been here, I feel that way in the swamps back home, too, but here it's even more powerful. Like humans are just, uh, a passing fad. Like the houses scattered around here will just melt away like icicles someday. When I was in school, I kind of thought that history began when Jesus walked the earth, or maybe with the Egyptians building the pyramids. Then you learn that was only 6,000 years ago, and that 10,000 years ago there was no civilization at all. Then you learn that homo sapiens has been around for something less than a million years. That seems like forever until you hear the numbers these crazy geologists toss out, numbers I can't conceive of. Blows your mind. Like Yellowstone blew up 640,000 years ago, as if it were yesterday, but 64 million years ago was when the dinosaurs were killed off, and they ruled the earth for 200 million years, makes the 640,000 number seem small, and especially when they say Yellowstone will explode "any day in the next 20,000 years." Makes it seem just around the corner, and that's twice as long as civilization. Humans seem like smaller and smaller specks. Listening to them talk, and it makes the feelings I get up here more real. It isn't just a feeling – someday nature will take over and there will be no more humans up here, just the mountains and the birds and the bears and the forests. For some reason I love that feeling, part of why I love being a forest ranger."

"How did someone from Houma become a forest ranger?"

"Well, first it was because I like trees. That simple. I had a couple of great-uncles who worked over in East Texas logging trees. I liked being in the woods with them. The trees intrigued me. It was like the trees became my friends."

"Once, when I was a teenager, I met an Australian named Glen something who was canoeing down the Atchafalaya alone. He tied up near our cabin and was sleeping in his canoe. I thought he was crazy insane—I grew up there and I wouldn't have dreamed to doing such a dangerous thing. He talked about something he called a walkabout, how he was learning his place in nature. I didn't understand what he was talking about until I came up here. I feel like I know my place in nature now. And being here made me appreciate the swamps more too. Now I can get that same feeling when I'm back home."

Camille noticed a picture of dark-skinned Leona hugging a white man, appearing much in love.

"Leona, tell me about your man."

"Okay, about Marshall. He played on the Southern basketball team. He was a junior when I was a freshman and I didn't know him but everyone knew who he was. There were very few white faces on campus and one 6'7" tall really stood out. But I had zero interest in meeting him-I could tell he was a cocky rooster. The basketball team had its groupies, of course, and they all wanted a taste of vanilla. Can you imagine what it was like for a white guy to try out for the Southern University basketball team? A lot of guys thought it was a black athlete's sport and they didn't like even the idea of a white kid on the team, especially since it might take away a scholarship from a black kid. He had to prove himself over and over. He claims he wasn't any good, and he couldn't shoot worth a damn, but he was a great rebounder. Seemed to have a sixth sense about where the ball was going. That's why the coach wanted him on the court. My cousin once played in a pickup game with him and just bumped into Marshall. He said it was like bumping into a Mack truck. He called Marshall 'stolid', which he said meant he was solid like steel." Leona laughed again, a big hearty laugh. "Oh, he is mighty big and mighty strong but his cocky trash talking got him into trouble one time while they were playing Texas Southern in Houston. A fight broke out and the teams got into a free-for-all on the court. Cops had to be called and the game stopped. Marshall said that's when he learned the only colors that mattered were the colors of his jersey, because the guys wearing blue and gold were fighting the ones in maroon and white, and the fans. His being a teammate was what counted, and all that crap he'd endured made him a Southern Jaguar." She sighed. "The day he turned

21 he dropped out of school 'cause he got a job on an offshore rig. He wasn't a good student anyway, just a jock. We met a few years later at a Southern alumni function in Baton Rouge. I wanted nothing to do with him then, either, but he persisted and persisted and wore me down. Partly because I was laughing so hard at his attempts to impress me. One time he dropped a pizza into my mail slot at 7 AM for breakfast. After six months of that sort of stuff I finally agreed to go on one date. One date led to another, and here we are. It's been a thrilling ride but when he's gone it hurts. That'll be over soon. He's going to quit going offshore at the end of my tour this summer. We're going to have a baby in January." She glowed with pride and joy as she spoke.

Camille gushed in happiness for her new friend. Leona took Camille's hand and put it on her belly. She felt a kick and they both yelped for joy.

Leona continued. "Marshall loves the outdoors and the mountains, too, but I think it's just that he is no longer confined to the drilling rig for four weeks surrounded by the ocean. He flies into Billings instead of Cody just so he can drive over Beartooth Pass although every time we go over it, I'm scared to death. It's a beautiful mountain and he adores it, but its straight down a long way. He likes to camp up there too, and in the Absarokas. He says he found the place where Earl Durand, 'The Tarzan of the Tetons', held off the cops and the National Guard. He works on oil rigs offshore or sometimes overseas. He's four weeks on, four weeks off. While he's gone I miss him so much that when he gets back we're like a couple of rabbits—that's how I got pregnant." She smiled. "I like to do my field trips and when he goes with me we're always taking our clothes off and going at it on mountain tops, on dirt piles, granite rocks, and behind bushes. One time we stepped off a hiking trail and were pounding away grunting and moaning with me on top when I heard some bells tinkle – you know those bells back-country hikers use to warn bears? Then I hear a voice, "Is that a bear?" I lift my head up and see this old couple. She sees my black face and thinks she sees a bear and jumps and yells, then realizes what's she's seen and starts laughing and the old man starts laughing and I start and Marshall doesn't know what's up. They turn and walk away but the old man yells, "Use some bells."

Leona howled at her own story. Camille laughed mildly, not the way Leona expected. "Okay, honey, something's wrong. What is it?"

"Oh, Leona. There's so much." Tears formed and Leona saw them. She moved and sat next to Camille, put one arm around her shoulder, placed one hand over Camille, and said, "Tell me. We have all night."

"Riley. He's a DHS agent. We're living together and I expect the question any day. Then this case comes up, it's terrible, people are treating me like I'm a second-rate agent – after I found the major clue – and now they ignore me. They think I'm crazy and on a wild goose chase. And Riley – I want his support, but he's just all business. All the Top Gun Agent. I want him to hold me and cuddle me and at the same time I want to beat the crap out of him."

"Oh, all us women know that feeling."

"Then there's the case. It's unbearable. Leona, someone's smuggled..." Camille hesitated. "...a bomb into the country and we have no idea where it is!"

Leona looked confused. "What?" she asked.

Camille stood and paced as she spoke. "Oh God, you've heard about the suicide bombings in Houston. This case is related to that. I think I've figured out who smuggled it, but no one likes my idea – there are holes in the theory – but the only evidence we have leads to Abdul Faisal, the guy drilling this well. But it makes no sense. Everyone, including Riley, thinks it's a crazy idea, but today I learned it might be true and it depresses the hell out of me. "With what I learned from the earthquake lady makes it all make sense. She says the explosives could cause the fault to move and the volcano to explode. I told the guys in Washington and their experts say it's nonsense – there's no fault here. That's the consensus of all the experts. The earthquake lady says it's a new theory and not everyone believes it."

Leona put her hands up to get Camille to stop talking. "Camille, last summer and this spring there were geologists crawling all over this area like flies at a barbeque. They said they were looking for the fault. They told me they were drilling the well to find it. Come with me to the visitor's center." Leona handed Camille a jacket and led her through the chilly air to the new building. The Ranger showed Camille the displays. One compared of the size of the past eruptions and showed the far-reaching effects of the ash cloud. Leona explained, "Look at how the ash cloud blanketed the entire Midwest from Chicago to Houston. It would wipe out the grain harvest. We'd lose all our gain and corn. They say the Tambora volcano caused a year without a summer around the world. A Yellowstone eruption would cause many years without a summer. Not just America, but Europe would lose its crops, too. And Asia would lose its rice. Think no wheat, no corn, no rice. People around the world would starve. That would mean famine, world-wide famine. Do you remember the Four Horsemen of the Apocalypse?"

"Yes," answered Camille, "When the priest read from Revelations."

"One of the Horsemen was War, and the third one was Famine. I don't remember the other two. Death and Destruction, maybe. Anyway, famine would mean people killing and eating each other."

"That's gruesome," said Camille, and wondered whether that was Abdul's aim. "Fortunately, twenty thousand years is a long way off."

"Ha!" replied Leona. "The geologists say, 'anytime in the next twenty thousand years'. That could be tomorrow, too. That's why they are monitoring all the minor quakes and such, and why they are urgently drilling this well."

Leona showed Camille the second display, an illustration of the geology of the volcano and the fault, and how the fault could reach into the magma chamber. The last showed how the new well's instruments would measure the strain on the fault and provide early warning of an eruption.

"My God," exclaimed Camille. "Now I understand what the earthquake lady meant. Jesus! My stupid idea about Faisal might make sense."

"It's stupid no more," said Leona. "But let's not think about this now. It's too horrible and I don't want to upset the baby."

"Yes, let's go back. I want to call Riley." Returning to the cabin, Camille remembered from her Sunday School lessons that the first time that the Lord destroyed the earth was by water with Noah's flood. The second time was supposed to be by fire, and the Yellowstone super volcano might be that tool.

A chilly wind blustered and Camille shivered. Leona laughed, "It takes a little while for a Louisianan to get used to this country. It's supposed to get down below freezing tonight."

"Brrr. I haven't been that cold in a long time."

"Let's get warm and go to bed. I'll make up your room."

Camille used Leona's phone to call Riley. He seemed off-putting at first. Camille told about the displays she'd seen and how it made sense – what Abdul was trying to do. Riley cautioned her on jumping to conclusions, and Camille got angry. She shouted, "Look at the evidence!" and hung up.

She then called Perez and explained what she'd learned. She could hear clicks – someone was trying to call and she prayed it was Riley. She asked Perez to call Washington and to try to send troops here. Perez said he'd talk to Washington but was afraid troops were premature. They hung up, Camille wondering who else to call when the phone rang. It was Riley.

"Camille, darling." His words were imploring. "Please don't get upset with me. I love you. Your mind works so much faster than mine. Give me time to catch up. You say it's Abdul but we don't have proof, do we?"

"All the evidence points here. Who else?"

"Could there be anyone with his group that could have stolen the bomb?"

"I don't see it. Abdul Faisal runs everything. He's like a god in this company. Look, when the local RA was here, he must have learned something. Faisal went ballistic and apparently sent a worker to kill Joffe and make everyone believe it was a drunk driver. That would not have happened unless something terrible is happening here."

"Do we have any evidence of the bomb?"

"Not yet. But if they drove it up from Houston, it could be here tonight or tomorrow."

"Yes, I suppose that timing works."

"Oh Riley, now I know what he's trying to do. We have to stop him. Has the earthquake lady talked to you guys?"

"Yes, the professor has talked to several people here and some are paying more attention. But they still say it's unlikely. They don't think even the bomb could cause an eruption of Yellowstone. Something about the temperatures not being hot enough."

"Maybe that's what they think. But that's not what Abdul thinks and he's got the bomb!"

"The consensus here is the bomb is coming to Washington. That would be the most logical target – to cut off the head of the enemy."

"Those guys always think Washington is the center of the universe. What the geologists here say is that the Yellowstone eruption would eviscerate the country, and perhaps destroy most of civilization."

"Camille, doesn't that seem far-fetched to you?"

"Riley, it doesn't matter what I think. Only that Abdul thinks so."

"Okay, Camille, maybe you're right. I will do all I can to get the NSA to pay attention to you. But right now they still think you're wasting your time."

"Ok, please try, Riley. And I do love you."

"I love you too, Camille. I want to hold you again soon."

"Thank you, Darlin'," she said, and hung up.

Leona looked at a smiling Camille. "Better?"

"Better," she answered.

"I have your room ready. Let me show you."

As they parted company in the spare bedroom, they hugged strongly, "Oh, Leona! I can't thank you enough."

"Just two South Louisiana girls sticking together," Leona smiled as she closed the door.

"Amen," said Camille. She prayed the rosary before going to sleep.

Camille was awakened by the sound of Leona in the kitchen. The weak light of pre-dawn came through the window. Snow was falling softly. "It's September," she thought to herself. "it'll reach 95 in Houston today." She cleaned up and got dressed.

"Coffee's ready!" yelled Leona, as Camille walked out of her room. The aroma struck her. "Chicory!" she exclaimed.

"Yes. I finally have someone to drink it with."

Camille breathed the aroma deeply, took a sip of the strong bitter coffee and added sugar.

"I can't believe it's snowing in September."

"Oh, it'll be melted by noon. But this is the mountains. It can snow anytime."

Camille's thoughts gathered around the bomb coming to this place. Her hands shook, and she spilled coffee. "I've got to get to work."

As Camille headed out the door, Leona called her back. "One more thing," she smiled. "Keep that Farman away from me. Being pregnant makes me hornier than a tomcat on the back fence."

Camille grinned back. "Right," she said.

CHAPTER THIRTY-SIX

AT THE RIG SITE

TUESDAY MORNING

Outside the sleeping trailer at the rig, Camille asked Farman and Janz. "Did you learn anything?"

"They are done drilling the well and waiting for the stress monitoring equipment to arrive so it can be put in the hole," replied Janz.

Farman added, "The workers are eager to be done so they can return home. Most have been here since June and miss their homes and families."

"What about their feeling toward the head of Crescendo, Abdul Faisal?"

"Each one I spoke to was shocked by how Faisal exploded in anger Sunday," said Farman. "They said he's a stern boss and gets upset if they make a stupid mistake, but they'd never seen such a violent reaction before, as if his world was coming apart. I talked to about six and they all said essentially the same thing."

"Bob?"

"I could not get as close to the men as Farman could. They were comfortable with him in Arabic, and I gained nothing."

"Farman, any idea when the stress equipment is supposed to arrive?"

"They are hoping today sometime," he replied. "Two Turkish engineers arrived last night to help with the equipment, but they said they know nothing about the drilling, just the stress measuring equipment."

She turned to Janz. "Have you checked them out?"

"I've sent the information they supplied to Washington. No response yet."

"Have you heard from them about the photo Joffe took?"

"Nothing. Perhaps they had difficulty getting into his phone. Or perhaps there was nothing found by the facial recognition software."

"Is Faisal coming?"

Farman replied, "The workers expect he'll be here because this is his pet project. They say he's spent more time here this summer than working on the rest of his business empire combined."

"What do you think, Bob?"

"I'll be surprised if he doesn't come, for the reason Farman said. For a billionaire business owner, he's sure put a lot of time into one lonely science project."

"Which confirms to me that it is more than just that," said Camille.

Janz already was on his satellite phone. "Kruger, this is Bob Janz of the FBI. I have a serious problem and need your help." He paused while Kruger answered. "Can you get the airborne radiation sniffers down to Sunlight Basin immediately? We think we have a serious radiation leak."

"Great Falls? That's probably a minimum 2 hours. Please get them on their way as soon as you can. Do you know where the science well is drilling? Yeah, the science project near Sunlight Basin Ranger Station. That's where we think the leak is. Have them report to me as well as you guys. Ok, thanks."

"That was a quick response," said Camille.

"Kruger knows that I'm serious about work. Ha! No, the real reason is that all sniffer planes have been ordered to the cities, and his is headed to Denver. We're lucky we are on the path."

Camille's satellite phone refused to work again, so she borrowed Janz's and called Perez. She related all the facts then tried to express Bigley-Puzio's theoretical concerns about the implications. She told him what Farman and Janz had learned from the workers.

"Okay," said Perez, dazed. "I'll call Washington and alert the DHS. What are your plans now?"

"We don't know whether the bomb is actually on site. Agent Janz has called for the sniffers but that'll take a couple hours. Meanwhile he and Farman and I will hang out at the rig and try to learn what we can."

"Ok, be safe. I'll try to arrange some backup – get some troops there to capture the bomb if you find it," Perez said, and hung up. He took a deep breath and called Washington, trying to find a way to say what was needed without being laughed at by the experts.

CHAPTER THIRTY-SEVEN

RIYADH, SAUDI ARABIA, AT THE KING'S PALACE

TUESDAY MORNING

His usual serenity missing, the tall, heavily-jawed American Secretary of State was clearly angry. Spittle formed at the corners of his mouth as he spoke loudly. "You have betrayed an ally that has long protected you." He slapped his large hand on the desk.

The King did not rise from his chair. His voice was calm and firm. "Mr. Secretary, there is no betrayal. We simply did not inform you of what we are doing."

"But why? We have long protected Saudi Arabia. We have promised to continue to do so." The secretary shook his head.

The King replied calmly. "We have seen how the President O'Brien keeps his promises. Should I remind you of the red line in Syria? Now we must protect ourselves against Assad as well as Iran."

"It is in our interest to protect you," said the Secretary, "if only for the stability of oil supply. Look at what we did for Kuwait in the First Gulf War."

"Ah, yes. A war to protect oil supplies. But that was President Bush, not President O'Brien, the one who does not follow through on promises."

"We will withdraw our air bases!" shouted the Secretary.

"Mr. Secretary, do as you wish. Whichever candidate wins this election in two months, the former Secretary of State or the clown, will put them back. But I did not ask you here to discuss our nuclear program. I wish to inform you that our paratroopers currently training in Fort Benning have left the base to recapture our stolen bomb."

The secretary appeared stunned. "The bomb is yours?"

"Yes, it was stolen by extremists who wish to detonate it somewhere in the U.S. We do not know where yet but have an idea. We want our troops to recover it."

"I cannot – the President cannot allow foreign troops to carry weapons on U.S. soil. That is against the law."

"That is your concern. Let me state it this way. This morning I gave the order to increase our oil production 500,000 barrels per day. That ought to drop the price of crude oil about five dollars or more. If we do not have the bomb in our possession by this coming Sunday, we will increase that by another one million barrels. Then oil will drop at least another $15 per barrel. Think about what that will do to the American economy as those few oil companies left standing after last year's drop get hit again. If you don't know, ask Homer Knost, your Secretary of Commerce, what that would do. He will explain it in terms you can understand."

The Secretary glared. He'd never been so insulted by a foreign ruler. He was about to explode. During his entire career, he had been able to control his anger in negotiations, but not this time. His anger had already hurt him in this conversation, and now he felt as if he'd been slapped. It took all his energy to say nothing. He bowed his head slightly, turned and left the room.

CHAPTER THIRTY-EIGHT

AT THE RIG SITE AND NEAR GREYBULL, WYOMING

TUESDAY ABOUT NOON

An airplane, propeller-driven, was heard, then seen flying westward up the valley, the pilot keeping a safe space about the trees. It flew to the rig, then turned around and headed back down the valley.

Janz took the phone call a few minutes later. "That was Kruger," he said. "That was our plane. It reports no radiation anomaly."

Camille sighed. "Not surprised," she said, clearly disappointed. "The special equipment for the wellbore has not arrived. Let's bring it back when the delivery arrives."

"Could be tough," said Janz. "The plane's been ordered to Denver — all such planes have been ordered to major population areas. They went out of their way for us. I doubt we'll get them back."

"Shit," said Camille.

"We'll think of something," Janz encouraged, but Camille was deflated.

In Greybull, in a cavernous hangar originally built for C-130 tanker planes used in firefighting, Saleh Tawfiq Saleh, nee Manzur Husain, had been up all night, working like a demon, reassembling the atomic bomb. The bomb was lain gently on its side on a flatbed trailer and covered with a white fiberglass shell. The trailer was connected to a white Volvo truck. Husain elected to ride in the truck with his bomb rather than the more comfortable helicopter. Abdul was dubious. This close to his dream, he wanted Husain by him, but the man was supernaturally attached to his bomb so Abdul reluctantly agreed. The truck traveled west on fairly flat ground toward Cody along Highway 14, with Abdul's helicopter staying slightly ahead and above. As he reflected on the past few days, his anxiety level heightened. He was upset with himself over his reaction to the screw-up of the information given to the first FBI agent. He should have trusted the plans he had so carefully laid out. But so close to the end, that small error caused an explosion within him. Why had he reacted so violently? Subconsciously, was he uncertain? Was he doubting the way that God had prepared for him? He feared that was what had happened. To recover from the mistake, he had decided to press forward firmly without delay, and everything seemed to be working. Then, last night he was told of three more FBI agents at the well. A bad sign. Would three agents be sent just to investigate the car accident? They must be suspicious of something, but what could they know? Like a chess master, he mulled over all the moves he'd made: getting Husain into the game, the smuggling of the bomb, commandeering the bomb, arranging for its transport. He could not see where he'd made a mistake. But, like a chess master, he knew there were possibly dangerous surprises lurking. Something he might have overlooked. So close to the end, so close to the edge. He prayed for the peaceful acceptance of God's will.

Ronnie Schlup, the lanky co-pilot on the radiation detection plane, nudged his short-statured pilot. "Gary," he said. "Let's cut east and fly over our old stomping grounds."

"I don't think so, Ronnie. We've already gone out of our way to fly over that rig and we're going to be late for Denver."

"Whether an hour late or an hour and a half late won't make any difference. We've got an excuse."

"Okay," smiled Schneider. "I haven't seen Newcastle in quite a while," and he turned the plane southeasterly toward Bighorn Mountains, on the other side of which were their boyhood homes. "This is Searcher 47, we are diverting away from the Owl Creek

Mountains across the Bighorns. We want to come down the east side of the Front Range to avoid any disturbance between Laramie and Denver."

The ATC in Billings responded, "We see no problems at the Owl Creeks or the Front Range, but it's your call. Note there is a helicopter flying out of Greybull."

"Roger. We'll be increasing our altitude for the mountains anyway."

As the mountains became clearer he could see Sheep Mountain anticline in the foreground and Cloud Peak in the distance, also Bomber Peak, named for a WWII aircraft that crashed there. The thought made Schneider slightly apprehensive, but he concentrated on the scenery. "Beautiful country," he said.

A beep unexpectedly sounded on the radiation monitor, then another. Schlup turned and examined what the machine was reading. "Bingo?!" he said, surprised. "Gary, we got a hit! Where are we?"

"About 5 minutes out of Greybull. Let's circle back. The plane made a wide turn crossing over the Greybull airport.

"There it is again!" shouted Schlup, more incredulous than excited. "What's that doing here?"

"What are you seeing?" asked Schneider.

"U-235," said Schlup. "That's nuclear bomb shit."

"Christ," exclaimed Schneider. They circled and found the signal again, weak, but strongest when they passed over the airport west of town. They took wider and wider circles, going over the roads leading out of town, but found nothing.

Schlup radioed the DHS with the news while Schneider kept circling. The news shocked the men in the command room. "Wyoming?" shouted Bramwell. "What are they doing with it?"

"Sir, but we've circled the Greybull airport several times now. There's a small but definite signal when we pass over the airport. At first, we thought we saw a signal west of town, that's Highway 14,

I think, but we've lost that. The wind is blowing about 15-20 down there so a moving target may not be detectable."

"Okay, we will get the Greybull police working on it. Meanwhile, you get back on your course to Denver."

Schneider poked the pilot, thumped his forehead to mean "think" and pointed to the gas gauge. Schlup nodded, and said into his microphone, "Permission to land for fuel, sir. All this circling the airport has cut into our fuel and we might not make it to Denver now."

"Oh, of course, permission granted." The General sighed, exasperated.

On the ground, Schlup taxied toward a large hanger where Schneider had pointed out police cars. He radioed headquarters, "We can detect a weak source here, sir, as we approach the hangar."

The General replied, "Greybull police say a white Volvo semi pulling a flatbed trailer carrying what looked like a white shell left that hangar about an hour ago, heading west. After you refuel, head along that highway and see if you can catch up to it."

Bramwell, enraged, turned to the others. "It makes no sense. What are the targets west of Greybull, Wyoming? Zimmerman?"

Zimmerman spoke thoughtfully. "There are two dams nearby. Buffalo Bill Dam near Cody and Yellowtail Dam on the Big Horn River. Actually, that's north of Greybull, but they may be taking a different route. There's Boysen Dam south of there, but if they were going to blow that, it makes no sense to drive to Greybull. But let's say they blew the Buffalo Bill Dam. At most it would mean a few thousand dead, more likely a few hundred. Nothing like a bomb in Houston or any city. It would destroy the canal system that feeds some downstream farming, but that would be a drop in the bucket for the American farm system."

Rush, the head of the CIA, said, "Perhaps they wish to signal they can strike anywhere in the United States at will, that no one in any town in America is safe. That means terror everywhere. Like during the Cold War, when everyone was under the threat of nuclear war. That would be a great propaganda piece for them."

"Very well, get the Cody police or whoever has jurisdiction to get out there. How far is it from Greybull?"

"If they left an hour ago, they should be past Cody and already at the dam."

"Jesus," sighed Bramwell, rubbing his forehead.

The FBI Director Mason smiled and nodded his head, pleased with his agents, "Apparently Agent Richard was right. Let's get her on the phone."

His assistant reported the difficulty with her phone but said he was trying Agent Janz, who he believed was with Richard.

"Janz," stated the voice.

"Hold for the Director," said the assistant, and handed the phone over.

"Agent Janz, is Agent Richard with you?"

"Yes, sir. We are at the drilling site east of Yellowstone Park trying to figure an excuse to stay here." Janz's voice and manner oozed country insolence but the Director ignored it due to the urgency.

"Janz, I remember you," said Mason slowly.

"You should. I outscored you on everything, by a lot."

"And yet here I am in DC, and you're stuck in the boondocks."

"You were always an ignorant ass, Mason," said Janz. "You are the one stuck in the hellhole called DC. I'm in God's country. Got an elk this year along with my muley. How about you?"

"Bob!" pleaded Camille.

Mason responded, "I don't participate in that barbaric practice."

"Only because you can't hit the broad side of a barn."

Bramwell finally interrupted, shouting, "God damn it! Stop the trash talking! We have work to do. Janz, tell Richard a U-235 anomaly has been located east of Cody and we are trying to find its course."

Janz raised his eyebrows to Camille with some trace of delight. "Director, we can assure you its headed here," said Janz. "Richard concluded it's the only place that fits all the evidence." Camille looked intently at Janz, wondering what he meant. She leaned her head toward the phone trying to hear what was being said on the other end.

"You can explain that later," growled the Director. He somehow seemed displeased with this turn of events. "What is your plan?"

"Sir, there is not much we can do. We have some minor amounts of weaponry but we are greatly outmanned. I doubt they will listen to one word we say."

"Okay. Stall them anyway you can. We will mobilize some troops and get them there as soon as possible."

"Better make them paratroopers. It's a long drive." Janz's tone greatly irritated the Director.

"Of course," he replied, and hung up.

Janz relayed the information to Camille. She took a deep breath and asked, "How long do you think we have?"

"Well, assuming it's on a truck in Cody, we have about an hour and a half, no, at least two 'cause the truck will be slow going over the pass. But if it's already in Sunlight Basin we might have half an hour."

"Okay. Pull Farman out of there and think of how we can deploy our weapons," said Camille urgently. "I'm going to go over to the Ranger station and tell Leona to get out of here."

"No," said Janz. "Call her on my phone. We can't waste time."

"Of course," murmured Camille. She realized the shock of the news had stunned her – she wasn't thinking clearly. She forced herself to concentrate. She called Leona and told her there was a likelihood of gunfire and urged her to drive to Cody. "Do anything," she said. "Just get out of here for a while. Stay in Cody for the night."

Leona hesitated, but the urgency in Camille's voice was ominous, so she agreed, notified the other Rangers, packed an overnight bag and headed out.

CHAPTER THIRTY-NINE

WASHINGTON

AT THE SAME TIME, TUESDAY NOON

"Dr. Bigley-Puzio, are you there?" asked Bramwell into the conference phone.

"Yes. I am here with Dr. Mary Rainey, Chief Geologist for Yellowstone Park. Consider me the expert on earthquakes in general and her the expert on the super volcano in particular."

"Could setting off the atomic bomb in the well being drilled near the Park cause the super volcano to explode?"

"We think it unlikely."

"Come on! Unlikely? Is it possible?"

"Yes, it is possible." She looked at Rainey for some support. Rainey nodded, and Bigley-Puzio continued. "The bomb could cause the Sunlight Basin fault to move. The fault might reach into the magma chamber and provide a path for the magma to rise to the surface."

"So why do you say it's unlikely?"

Rainey responded, "We don't think it's hot enough to explode. We think that the core needs to get hotter to build up enough pressure to blow out."

"You mean enough pressure to blow the rocks off the top of the volcano?"

"Would it need to get to that pressure if the bomb gave it a path to get to the surface?"

"We think that because the magma is not hot enough, then all we would get are lava flows out of the volcano, not an explosion."

"You mean like the lava flows in Hawaii that merely flow down the mountainside into the ocean?"

"Yes, exactly like that. And if they occur at the drill site, it's likely they might fill up the Sunlight Basin, but hurt nothing else."

Tacawy interrupted. "Why don't you think the magma is not hot enough?"

Rainey answered, "Our seismic measurements give us the velocity through the magma, and that gives us the temperature."

"Isn't there some guesswork involved in calculating temperature from seismic, since you have another variable, pressure?"

"Well, yes," She hesitated. "There are certainly error bars on our calculations."

Bramwell cut in again, not understanding the science jargon, and clearly irritated. "So it could be hot enough?"

Rainey was defensive. "Yes, but we think not."

Bramwell exploded, "Think! Think! Don't you know anything?"

Bigley-Puzio attempted to rescue Rainey. "We are scientists, sir. We draw conclusions on what we know, but we do not know every-thing—we cannot see underground."

"Shit," said Bramwell loudly.

Rainey said, "Another reason we don't think Yellowstone will ex-plode is that we don't see precursor events."

"What does that mean?"

"Sir, have you ever seen Old Faithful explode? People are standing around, anticipating. Then there will be a puff of steam, then a spit of water with some steam, and that can go on for a couple of minutes before the geyser shoots off hundreds of feet into the air. Those puffs of steam and water are what we call 'precursor events'. They are signs of the geyser building enough pressure to blow."

"What about all this ground breathing and the earthquake swarms I've heard about?"

"Those have been occurring since Yellowstone was discovered, sir. We think that is normal activity."

"Have you seen anything unusual that might be a 'precursor event'?"

This time Rainey looked at Bigley-Puzio for support, then answered, "Yes, sir. One thing. We have seen an increase in the concentration of Helium-4. That happened just before a volcano exploded in the Canary Islands several years ago."

"Christ!" exploded Bramwell again. "So there may indeed be a signal of a coming eruption?"

Bigley-Puzio responded, "Sir, that was a minor volcano compared to Yellowstone. We don't think it a clear signal for a super volcano."

"But it is possible, is it not?"

"Possible, but the consensus of the experts is that Yellowstone is not about to explode."

"I thought science was not about consensus," he chided.

Riley jumped in. "To quote FBI Agent Richard, 'it does not matter whether we think the bomb will cause the volcano to explode, only that the terrorists believe it'."

Bramwell spoke in a tone that unmistakably gave the impression that he'd heard enough, "So, we must try to stop the bomb and recover it. General Ujifusa, do you have any paratroopers close to the site?"

"Mr. Bramwell, you know that we cannot order American troops to operate on US soil unless given permission by the President."

"General, you locate the goddam troops and Rosenberg and I will gain the President's goddam approval."

Ujifusa turned to the Army representative on the Joints Chiefs. "General Marietta, where are your closest paratroopers?"

CHAPTER FORTY

AT THE CATTLE GUARD ON SUNLIGHT BASIN ROAD

TUESDAY, TWO P.M.

When the urgent call came about the white semi and trailer, George Sumida was in the 120 Bar near the town of Clark finishing a late-lunch and talking to his favorite waitress, Susan. She was the daughter of Donna Wada, a classmate of his at Powell High School. They had gone out on a few dates then, but she was shy and quiet, and they did not have much in common. They went off to college separately. Donna came home and taught math at the high school, married an Anglo farmer, and had five children, of which Susan was the youngest. She was lively and loquacious, the opposite of her mother. George enjoyed talking to her and hearing a young person's take on life. This day, though, he rushed outside, got into his supercharged Dodge Charger, and headed south on 120, hoping he could beat the truck to the pass. If so, he knew where he could block it. If not, he should have no trouble catching up to it. Dispatch said the Park County Sheriff was heading north out of Cody. Sumida raced, thinking the Sheriff might find the truck before him. Regarding other Highway Patrolmen in section N and G, which covered all of the Bighorn Basin, Dispatch said the closest was Maurice Seghetti, now near Meeteetse, about 30 miles south of Cody, but on his way. Near the top the mountain toward Dead Indian Pass, Sumida looked down the mountainside and saw the white semi and trailer. It was moving up, but two cars were behind it, probably impatient at the truck going so slowly up the mountainside. Sumida stopped at his chosen spot, the second of two switchbacks. The truck would have to go slowly around the first switchback, and would not have any space to gain speed before hitting the second. Sumida parked the Charger perpendicular to the highway, so it completely blocked one side, and would force any car going around to drive with one side off the pavement. He notified Dispatch where he was, got into the trunk, pulled out his flak jacket and put it on. He moved to the side of the car opposite the arriving truck, put his megaphone within easy reach on top of his vehicle, pulled his pistol and braced himself against the side of the car. Immediately after the semi and trailer rounded the first switchback, a black Suburban, clearly impatient with the slowness of the journey, zoomed past the truck but had to quickly slow at the blocked switchback. Sumida waved the Suburban through, then returned to his braced position against the Charger. Semi-automatic fire from the Suburban behind him, surprised him, and he crumpled to the ground. Four men got out of the Suburban, backed the patrol car off the road, waved the semi and the Corvette past, then drove the patrol car back onto the highway, hearing a siren below them. They moved the Suburban out of sight, took positions behind some trees and waited. The Sheriff arrived, puzzling at the strange scene of a Wyoming Highway Patrol car sideways across the road. He immediately called for reinforcements, then opened his door and walked toward the Charger. The four men opened fire. Glass shattered and bullets pinged, and the Sheriff fell dead in the middle of the highway, with his pistol still in its holster and his hat rolled to one side.

The scene below the helicopter shocked Abdul. The Highway Patrol vehicle blocking the road could only mean they were trying to stop him. He stroked his eyebrows several times, trying to think clearly. The Patrolman must be just the tip of the iceberg. He must act quickly. He ordered the men in the Suburban to get the truck through, no matter how they did it. He wondered how much time before more law enforcement people arrived. Would he have time to get the bomb into the hole and explode it? He must try, then leave it in God's hands.

The Suburban caught the semi just as it was turning onto Sunlight Basin Road and was waved in front, just as Leona in her light green Forest Service pickup passed them in the opposite direction. Nearing the cattle guard, the four men noticed two mini-vans and a Sheriff's Department vehicle beside the road. As the Suburban approached, several agitated protestors moved to block it. The Deputy walked toward the group and spoke to one he knew. "Rafaela, what's going on? You can't block the road."

The short pudgy woman wearing a flowery shirt and faded blue jeans, tilted her cowgirl hat back, and responded, "The frack truck is coming! We can see it!" She pointed at the white Volvo truck headed toward them.

The Deputy shouted, "That's not a frack truck! It's carrying a stress-measuring device for the science well! Let the truck through!" The Suburban slowly drove through the protestors pounding on the sides of the vehicle and headed down the road. As the semi and the helicopter approached, though, the protestors became more agitated. Two laid down on the road, and one on the iron cattle guard. Seeing the happening at the cattle guard, the Suburban turned around and returned. The four men got out and shouted at the protestors to get up off the ground.

The large white truck approached, then stopped a couple of yards from the prone protestors. Several others with signs were standing nearby chanting "Stop the drilling." The Deputy Sheriff shook his head and walked over to the ones on the ground. "We've already told you that you are free to protest but not block traffic. I'll have to arrest you unless you get off the road now."

One of the protestors yelled, "This is Forest Service land and we have a right to be here. We're taxpayers."

Abdul's helicopter hovered overhead. The truck driver beeped his horn and shouted an obscenity out his window. The deputy put his hand up to quiet the driver then bent over the one closest to the cattle guard. "Get up right now." The truck moved a few inches and the engine revved, threateningly.

The deputy looked up and shook his head at the driver. Then he pulled out one set of handcuffs on his belt. When he did, the other protestors started shouting louder, and the ones on the ground started singing, "Tis a gift to be simple, 'tis a gift to be free." Some of the protestors had cell phones held high, photographing the incident.

When the deputy grabbed the wrist of one of the prone protestors, three others rushed him and began striking him with their fists and signs. He raised his arms to protect himself, and a wooden sign hit him in the side. He stumbled toward the fence with his arms up but the three continued to swing at him.

The leader of the four from the Suburban pulled a pistol and fired it at the ground. There was a brief silence, then one of the prone protestors stood up, but the one on the iron cattle guard smiled, grabbed the handcuffs that had been dropped by the deputy and, lying back down, chained himself to an iron bar in the cattle guard. Abdul viewed the scene from the helicopter, incredulous. His men had just killed the highway patrolmen. Police must be on the way. He had to get to bomb to the rig. His head pounding, he shouted into his radio.

The truck driver put down his phone. He honked the horn loud and long. He revved the engine and inched closer. He shouted out the window. The beaters ignored him, seemingly thrilled with their actions against the deputy. He struggled to pull his pistol out, but crashed into the fence and fell to the ground. The truck's engine roared. The driver lifted his foot off the brake. The truck crunched over the bodies on the ground, across the cattle guard and down the road, the helicopter following above.

The stunned protestors shrieked in disbelief and grief and rushed to the broken, moaning bodies. Some shouted, "Call the police!" In a few seconds, the videos of the incident were streaming into the world of social media.

The leader of the Suburban silently watched the helicopter fly off, paused, signaled to his men to get into the Suburban, and moved it to block the road. He realized that the Corvette had not followed the semi off the highway. Puzzled, he radioed the car, but no one answered. Later, when a troop transport plane and another helicopter passed over them heading for the rig site, the leader conversed with his men and a decision was agreed upon. He took a pair of wire cutters, walked to the fence beside the cattle guard, and cut the fence. The Suburban drove through the hole in the fence, passing the grieving and distraught protestors. As they turned north onto the highway, a fire truck and ambulance marked Crandall Creek Volunteer Fire Department was turning off. One of his men drove while the leader searched a map for the shortest way to Canada.

CHAPTER FORTY-ONE

AT THE RIG SITE

A FEW MINUTES LATER

Farman noticed the "thwak, thwak, thwak" of the helicopter first and pointed toward the east, nearly a minute before it appeared above the trees. A cloud of dust was rising on the road, caused by a large flat-bed truck. The helicopter with a Crescendo logo landed in a field away from the drilling rig. Abdul jumped out and walked swiftly toward the rig floor, ducking under the still-twirling blades.

The truck swung across the road near Janz's blue Yukon, then backed the flatbed trailer toward the rig and stopped a few feet from the rig floor. Everyone watched, intrigued, as the rig crane lifted the fiberglass shell and placed it aside, revealing a long cylinder with wires. Men attached the crane's cable to the cylinder and the motor roared as it lifted the long narrow object slowly, almost delicately. A couple of men pushed against the bomb, and a couple had a rope around it, steering it toward the hole.

"They don't want it swinging like a pendulum," thought Camille. "Is that it?" she asked, surprised at what appeared to be a simple device.

"Seems so," said Janz.

"Appears to have no lead shield. It would not block any radiation," Camille said.

"Not worried about that now," replied Janz. "Let's stop him."

The two agents ran toward Abdul, to intercept him. They stopped a few feet in front of him and lifted their badges. "FBI, Mr. Faisal," said Janz. "We need to talk to you."

Abdul was only vaguely aware of the two people standing in front of him. He did not break stride. He did not acknowledge their presence. His eyes were focused on the bomb being lifted by the crane, his mind concentrating on the climax of his plan.

Camille urgently pulled her pistol and raised it, thinking she had to get his attention. Janz grabbed her arm, not knowing whether she was going to shoot the man. "We can stop him with the bazooka." He turned toward the Yukon and walked swiftly that way. Farman followed.

Camille caught them, asking Janz, "Do you have authorization to use it?"

Janz just shook his head and said, "We don't have a choice."

The crew on the rig manhandled the device until it was centered over the hole; a raised arm provided a signal to begin lowering the bomb. Again, Farman's acute hearing picked up the "thwak, thwak" first. "Another helicopter coming," he said. "And more," he pointed up. Drifting down from the sky were a dozen or more tan parachutes. The troop-carrying helicopter got close, then hovered as if waiting for the tan-clad paratroopers to land.

"Who are they?" wondered Camille out loud. There was shouting from the gate and around the rig, as the drilling crew noticed the paratroopers. Then Abdul's voiced boomed in Arabic across the area.

"Something about guns," explained Farman.

Several men burst out of the crew trailer and raced to a storage shed. One began distributing what looked to be AR-15's. Other men continued to steady the bomb and the crane's engine roared as it lifted the bomb and moved it toward the hole.

All the agents were struck with the same idea: The way the crew awkwardly handled the rifles, it was clear they were merely rig hands, unused to weapons.

"Now, while they are distracted," urged Janz, "Farman! The bazooka!" The two men opened the rear door and pulled out the bazooka. Farman grabbed the rocket. Janz opened the driver's door of the Yukon and placed the bazooka on the frame. "Load," he said, and Farman placed the rocket in the weapon.

"Camille, get to that first tree. After we fire, cover us. We'll move along the trees up the hill."

"Okay," she said and ran to the tree.

"Okay, Farman, git!" Janz said, and Farman hustled toward the trees. Janz aimed the bazooka at the massive derrick, figuring any hit would disable the machinery. He fired. Flames leapt out both ends and the rocket zoomed through the derrick and into the trees beyond, with a loud explosion. The paratroopers flattened to the ground, weapons ready.

Janz was stunned, incredulous. Somehow the rocket had managed to find one of the few holes in the superstructure and had hit nothing. He simply could not believe his bad luck. But it did stir up a hornet's nest among the rig workers. Some shouted and fired wildly at the Yukon. Janz pulled his legs into the truck and crouched in the driver's seat, using the engine as a shield. Glass shattered, tires popped, bullets whizzed by the partially opened door, and whacked the sides. The paratroopers held their fire, waiting for a command, trying figure out who was the enemy.

Camille and Farman opened fire on the shooting workers, who stopped and scrambled for shelter behind buildings and trucks. "Now!" shouted Farman, and Janz jumped out of the truck and ran for the trees. He noticed the trees were not big enough for true shelter, as he was wider than most, making him uncomfortable. Gunfire from the rig area began to build in intensity. Farman yelled, "Camille, you are 1, Bob, you are 2, and I am 3. When I yell one, the other two give cover fire while one moves to another tree up the hill. Same with 2 and 3. Got it?"

"Got it," both said.

"Okay, one!" Bob and Farman stuck their weapons outside the trees and fired toward shooting workers. There was a brief pause in return fire, and Camille raced to the next tree. Shooting from the rig picked up again.

"Two!" shouted Farman, and Janz followed suit. He was grateful the next tree was bigger.

"Three!" shouted Farman, hesitated for the shooting of Camille and Janz took effect, then raced to the next tree.

"One," shouted Farman again, and Camille hesitated until the men fired, then ran again.

A bullet whizzed in front of Camille, coming from her left. "We're getting flanked," she yelled. She peered through the trees trying to determine the source of the shot.

"Okay," hollered Farman. "Hold your position until we can find them."

Then they noticed the firing dying down, and someone yelling into a bullhorn. They saw that the large helicopter had landed and two men in native Saudi garb were standing; one of them held the bullhorn.

Farman translated. "He says he's the Saudi Deputy Ambassador to the US, and the equipment being put in the well was stolen from the Saudi government. He's telling them to put down their weapons – that the only ones in trouble are Abdul Faisal and Saleh Tawfiq Saleh. They are the thieves and must deal with the consequences." The workmen seemed confused, unsure of themselves. Sounds of gunfire dwindled but a little continued from the trees along the creek, on the far side of the rig.

Three shots were rapidly fired from Camille's left. "Fuck!" shouted Janz. "Damn, damn, damn!" After spending two days with the man, Camille was certain the cursing meant he'd been hit. She scattered shots toward her left but could not see the assailant.

The Deputy Ambassador continued his pleas. Several of the workers put their weapons down and their arms up as the tan-suited paratroopers cautiously advanced toward the rig.

The rig engine roared again, Camille wondered whether the bomb was already in the hole. Abdul was at the control of the machinery he had invented. Another man was working on the wires, feeding it into the hole, with two other men hovering around him. "Those are the Turks," said Farman, "so that must be the Pakistani."

"Fire at the machinery!" yelled Janz. Farman and Camille shot at the stand behind which stood the operator. It seemed like a good idea, as the operations stand was not designed to stop bullets. However, it was designed to withstand falling drill pipe and lashing chains and exploding high-pressure mud, so bullets were as effective as mosquitoes.

Bullets pinged and ricochets scattered wildly.

The noise of another airplane arose, and people looked up to see a couple of dozen paratroopers dressed in black using black and red parachutes, floating down. "Who the hell are they?" shouted Janz. When he turned back, the bomb was already completely in the hole.

Farman yelled, "Cover me!" Camille responded, but first scattered more shots to her left, then toward the rig. Janz propped his rifle against the tree and fired solely with his right hand, his left bloody and useless.

Only a few rig workers still had guns, but a few took shots at Farman as he raced toward the rig, firing. The Turks dove for cover. Husain flopped down, apparently hit in his back. Abdul saw him fall but continued lowering the bomb. Abdul felt a spasm of despair. Then, inspired, he decided to trust his God who had brought him to this place and time. Whatever happened would be the will of God. He released the cable, expecting the force of the impact at the bottom of the well caused by the bomb falling 6000 feet would cause the bomb to explode. As he released the bomb, he stood, turned toward the charging Farman, raised his arms wide above his shoulders and yelled, "God is Great" as a bullet from Farman ripped through his heart.

Several other shots were fired at Farman as he ran. He crumbled. Pain in his gut screamed, his leg went numb. Camille and Bob looked at the rig and saw the wires falling into the hole and realized the bomb had been dropped into the hole, too. They hesitated, waiting for an impact of some sort. She whispered a prayer and thought of Riley, her Dad, and friends. Janz hoped the explosion would be confined to the basin, and said a prayer for Patti.

But no explosion occurred. She kept waiting, expecting it. Of all the living people there, only Camille, Bob, the Turks, the Ambassador and his cohort knew there was an atomic bomb in the hole. They realized that it had not exploded, and most breathed prayers of gratitude. As the rest of the workers put down their guns and surrendered, some of the tan suits were checking out the rig.

The black-suited paratroopers were gathered in a line at the fence, while several tan-suited ones were lined up on the other side nearer the rig. Both groups were eyeing each other, weapons ready. The Ambassador and the leader of the black paratroopers were talking loudly. Camille rushed to Farman, touched his neck and realized he was dead. "Oh, Farman. I am so sorry." She crossed herself, blessed his body, then returned to Janz.

A black-suited soldier approached, but Camille was working on Janz's bandage and did not look up. "I admit this was a lot more exciting than the rodeo." Camille looked up – the soldier's face was covered by his helmet and goggles but she recognized the voice from the airport.

"I didn't know you were a paratrooper," she said.

The soldier grinned broadly. "You call – we fall. No matter whether it's a forest fire or a firefight."

"Help me – we've got to get this man to a doctor."

"Let me look." The soldier squatted and readjusted the tourniquet. "Looks good. Ambulances are on their way."

"I don't want to wait – help me to that truck."

"Oh, I don't think you'll be going anywhere in that vehicle," he said. He pointed at several bullet holes in the front and at a flat tire.

Fluids dripping from the engine area.

"Stay here," he said. "I'll check out some of the pickups." Soon he pulled up in a white Dodge Ram 4x4 sporting a brush guard.

"Here you go," he said, and helped put Janz in the back seat.

"Would you help me put that body in the back?" she asked, pointing to Farman's.

"If it was a crime area, I couldn't and shouldn't. But it looks like a war zone to me." He waved Camille aside and picked up the body himself and laid it gently in the back. When he stood up Farman's blood was smeared across his shoulder.

"Thank you," Camille said. "You're a good man."

"You're welcome. Anything for a fair damsel from the South." He grinned again.

"God bless you, mister," Camille said and drove away, past the group of soldiers. The ones in tan seemed to have surrendered to the ones in black. The men in Saudi dress were arguing with the leader of the black troopers. Phones were held in the air, as if each side wanted the other to talk to someone on their phone.

In a few minutes, when Camille was approaching the protest area she saw the first ambulance and waved it over. After a brief explanation, an EMT examined Janz's hand and declared it okay to travel with the well-done tourniquet. He told Camille it would be better for her to drive Janz to the hospital, as he had an unknown number of injured to pick up at the rig. A truck was pulled off the road with what appeared to be bodies piled in the back. An ambulance was treating someone, and another zipped past her, toward the rig, siren wailing.

Driving as fast as she dared while getting used to the large pickup, it still took Camille ninety minutes to drive to the Cody hospital. On the way, she wanted to call Riley, but realized she had no idea where her satellite phone was, and Janz's was probably in his truck. The nurses at the emergency drop-off were at the door waiting for Janz, and immediately took him inside. They seemed to disappear instantly and she wandered inside, looking for someone to help her. She found a short older nurse, with skin that had experienced a lot of sun, and asked her about Farman's body. The woman went to the truck and examined the body, then turned to Camille. "Is he a friend of yours?"

"Yes," answered Camille, suddenly shaking, tears falling down her face. "A friend. He saved our lives."

The grey-haired nurse grabbed Camille by the shoulders and looked directly into her eyes with sympathy. "It's all right, child," she said softly in a wide drawl, "I'm from South Carolina. We know how to honor dead heroes."

"But he's Muslim. Do you know if there something special we should do?"

"I don't know, but I will find out." the nurse answered. "Do you know someone to ask?"

"Not really, but I will ask. Wait. There will be more Muslims brought here from the rig. I can ask them."

"Good idea, dear. I'll ask, too. I promise he'll be well taken care of. Where will the body be shipped?"

"Houston, I guess. I'll have to check on that, too. He worked for the Houston Police Department."

"I'm sorry, dear. Let me give you my number. Call me when you get the details." She gave Camille a card that read Jean Cox, Supervisor of Nursing.

"Thank you, Nurse Cox. I greatly appreciate your help."

"You're welcome, dear. Now you look exhausted. You get some rest and come see me tomorrow."

Suddenly Camille felt exhausted. "Thank you, thank you. Can you tell me where the Catholic church is?"

Nurse Cox explained that the hospital had a chapel, but if she wanted the church itself, it was within walking distance. She also showed Camille a telephone but said any long-distance call would have to be collect.

Camille realized that it had been so long, she'd forgotten how to call collect. But once she started dialing, computer voices came on and directed her through the process.

After he accepted the charges, Riley yelled "Camille! I've been so worried. I'd heard about the shooting and no word from you for such a long time." Simultaneously Camille was yelling "Riley. I needed to hear your voice. I was so scared."

Riley said, "you go first."

Camille spoke through her crying. "It all happened so fast. Bullets everywhere. I've never been in combat before. Farman had, and he saved us all. He kept the bomb from going off. But he was killed. Janz was wounded. I just dropped them at the hospital. I was fine through it all, until now. But now I'm scared and shaking and crying and want to hold you so much."

"It's okay," Riley soothed. "Take your time. Don't try to say everything all at once. We've got lots of time to discuss it all. I'm just happy you are okay."

"I'm sorry, darlin'." Tears began falling again. "I have so much to tell you. But mostly I love you. And I want to have kids now. I saw such evil today, and I want to have a family."

"Can we wait until we're married?"

Camille laughed while she sniffled. "I suppose the church would want it that way."

Riley laughed this time. "Okay, we will go see Father Phil as soon as you get back."

"Is that your lame idea of a proposal?"

He laughed again. Camille's spirit was intact.

Then Camille sighed. "Look, I have to do a few things here. I must pray for Farman and the others. And for us. I need to clean up some details here and get Janz out of the hospital. I'll be home in a few days."

"Call me every day, Camille. I need to hear your voice."

"Oh, you can count on that, mister. I need yours, too. I love you."
She hung up the phone.

A voice spoke behind her. "I'm glad that things are back on track."
Camille spun around and found a tall woman with a smiling black
face.

"Leona!" Camille cried, and they hugged.

"I figured you'd be here," Leona said. "I'm pleased that it's in one
piece."

"I have a lot to tell you. Come with me to church." They locked
arms and headed that way. Camille began crying again as she told the
story.

CHAPTER FORTY-TWO
CODY, WYOMING

AN HOUR LATER

"Where the hell have you been, Richard?" shouted Perez. "Sorry, boss. In church."

"No excuse!" he shouted again." No reports for hours, and I know you spoke to Riley an hour ago. You work for the FBI! You work for me! You've left me high and dry for all this time--and I'm the one who stuck up for you!"

"You are right, sir. I was derelict in my duty. But I needed to pray." Perez knew she was religious, but so was he, and he was furious. Duty to country came first in his mind. "I'm back on track now. I have a few things I need to clean up and then I'll be home."

"No you won't. The Directors of DHS and NSA not to mention the President of the United States want your full report... three hours ago. Sit down right now and write that report. Do not eat. Do not pee. Write that damned report and get it to me now."

"Yes, boss. I'll find a computer and get right on it."

"Find a computer?"

"Yes, sir. All my stuff is lost or destroyed."

"Okay, I'll put Heather on. You can dictate to her."

"Whatever you say, sir."

Perez then had the idea to connect everyone in, so he arranged that the people in DC could listen in to Camille's dictation of the incident. Soon questions were flying about from Bramwell and Mason and Ochoa and even President O'Brien. It took a couple of hours.

After the exhausting report experience, Camille called Perez again. "What next, boss?"

"They need to get the bomb out of the hole and into the arms of the Department of Defense. Then they'll have to decide what to do."

Camille responded, "The tool pusher who ran the rig before all the action started is probably somewhere in Cody, or perhaps on his way home. His name is Terry Boudreaux. He's from south Louisiana. His address will be on the crew documents. He could operate the rig."

"Okay," said Perez. I will find him through the Crescendo office."

CHAPTER FORTY-THREE

CODY, WYOMING

THURSDAY, TWO DAYS LATER

Camille decided to stay for Joffe's funeral. Many of the people she'd met in Cody were there: in a small town, everyone knew everyone, and attendance at a funeral was a show of respect for that person. Janz had gotten out of the hospital the first day, and his wife Patti had driven down from Billings to get him. They were there, along with Jean Cox and Leona Richardson, and several hundred from the town.

After the funeral, Bob and Patti drove Camille to the airport. As they approached, they could see a large C-130 transport aircraft. "I bet they are loading the bomb," Janz said. "Want to check it out?" Since she had a couple of hours, Camille agreed, so Bob turned into the General Aviation side of the airport. Patti stayed in the lounge with more fire jumpers, and the two FBI agents flashed their badges to get past the soldiers guarding the exit door. Another flashing was necessary to get past a cordon of soldiers surrounding the aircraft. They could see a large gurney-like carrier, with what appeared to be a lead sheet over it, maybe a half-inch thick.

"From what I've heard, I hope they have more lead underneath the sheet," Camille remarked.

Suddenly the ground seemed to shake a little. "What was that?" a soldier asked. They could hear some glass breaking inside the building.

"Earthquake," said a fire jumper.

Janz looked in the direction of Sunlight Basin, and could see a cloud of grey-black smoke rising above the mountains. Then they all heard a low rumble. Janz immediately walked to a man, dressed in an

Air Force uniform, checking the plane.

"Are you the pilot of this aircraft?"

"Yes," the man said, splitting his attention between the rising cloud and the man speaking to him.

Janz showed his badge. "I'm FBI. I need you to take off and to take this fellow FBI agent with you."

"I couldn't even if I wanted to. This aircraft is strictly military."

"Look at this," said Janz, and he held up his bandaged left hand. While the pilot's eye followed the rising bandage, Janz pulled his pistol from its holster. The pilot seemed bewildered, and as the soldiers slowly realized what was happening, aimed their weapons at Janz. "Listen," said Janz in a threatening voice, "this woman kept this bomb from exploding and saved all our butts. She is going with you. Or you are dying with me right here, right now. What's it going to be?"

"You're in trouble, asshole, threatening an officer in the US Air Force. I won't do it."

Janz hesitated, then said, "I'll make you a deal. You swear on your honor as an Air Force officer that you will transport her to safety, and I will turn myself in."

The pilot hesitated, but all he could concentrate on was the pistol pointed between his eyes. The barrel seemed to consume his world. "Okay, I swear. Since she's FBI, she can go with us." The pilot seemed to regain some composure. "But not you. I'm reporting you. What's your name?"

"It's Robert Janz, J-A-N-Z. FBI Resident Agent in Billings Montana." He turned his face slightly toward Camille. The pilot saw a chance to rush, but decided against it. "Camille, get on the plane. Now, you!" Janz turned back to the pilot and suddenly handed his pistol to him and shouted, "Get the hell out of here."

"What about you?" Camille asked.

"Don't worry about us. Patti and I will be on our way to Argentina shortly."

"Thank you, Bob. God bless you."

"And God go with you, Camille. Now git." She walked up the ramp into the plane's large storage cavity. The pilot looked at the pistol, puzzled, then handed it back to Janz. The pilot waved off the other guards, and climbed into the cockpit, cursing Janz. The pilot waved at the people on the ground. It took several minutes for the ramp to be closed, and the plane to warm up. Janz entered the building and hugged Patti, then the two walked swiftly toward their car, hand in hand.

Camille found a spot by a window between a couple of soldiers. More shakes occurred as the plane taxied down the runway. The plane shuddered, and the passengers gasped. It took off westward into the wind, toward the mountains. Camille looked out the window at the billowing dark gray cloud moving above Sunlight Basin and the Absaroka Wilderness. She marveled at the terrible majesty of the growing cloud, and remembered the geologist saying "any day in the next 20,000 years". She closed her eyes and began to pray, "Holy Mary, Mother of God, pray for us sinners ...."

THE END

ACKNOWLEDGEMENTS

First, many thanks to my editor, Kathy Dodge. She greatly improved the manuscript and tried to make this a coherent book. Any failures are mine.

The life story of James Houston Turner, a college classmate and now friend, inspired me to think I might be able to write. He and I had the same writing instructor, Thelma Morreale. I believe she'd enjoy this novel.

A big thank you to Elaine Simpson at Outskirts Press, always positive and always supportive despite my procrastinations.

Thanks, of course to my wife, Patricia, and to my family for encouragement and criticisms.

Of the thousands of people I've known in my life, the names of a few made it into this book. Some are heroes, some villains, by the luck of the draw, but thanks to all. Here is how I knew their names, in order of appearance:

Manzur Husain was a math professor who taught Partial Differential Equations in grad school. He drilled Fourier Analysis into my head, which enabled me to understand how seismic data processing worked.

Father Phil Lloyd is a wonderful priest with a great sense of humor.

Thomas Dickerson was a fraternity brother and a great fishing buddy.

Ron George was modeled on Ron Georgeoff, a man whose penetrating intellect I admired. Ron did not let his physical disfigurement constrain him. Once he traveled cross-country and showed up on John Updike's doorstep, and was able to have a conversation with that magnificent wordsmith.

Farman Yousif is not quite as attractive in real life as in the book, but he is good-looking enough to have been a kept man. An Iraqi, Farman helped the US forces during the war and is now an American citizen. I tutored him in algebra, helping him to overcome test anxiety, and he has since obtained a B.S. in Electrical Engineering.

Robert Perez is a fishing buddy and great friend.

Monroe Jahns was a radiation physicist at M.D. Anderson Hospital. He once built a house completely by himself. He and his lovely wife Ruth babysat our children.

Bradley Holland is taken from Brad Lee Holian, the most brilliant person in my high school. Brad earned a 4.0 at Cal Tech, got his Ph.D. in Nuclear Chemistry at Berkeley, and spent his career at Los Alamos.

Shih-Hua Wu, called Charlie, shared the Mossbauer laboratory with me in grad school.

Dave Bramwell was a fraternity brother. His has always seemed a strong name.

Amir Tacawy was in graduate school with me, and spent his career in California government.

Jeffrey Rush (CIA Director) was a roommate and fraternity brother. His degree was in music, but in army intelligence during the Viet Nam war, he was encouraged to go to law school. He did, and ended his career as Inspector General for the Department of the Treasury.

General Ujifusa is modeled after Grant Ujifusa, who was ahead of me in high school. Grant received an award from the Japanese government for his work to obtain reparations for those interned in camps like the one at Heart Mountain.

The Wyoming highway map is copyright by the Wyoming Transportation Commission and is used with permission.

The map of the Hot Spot through Idaho was compiled under the supervision of Paul Link for the Idaho Digital Geologic Atlas and is used with permission.

The map of the faults in Yellowstone Park was constructed by geologists at the University of Utah who made it available on the internet.

Dick Dolecek is a geophysicist with whom I worked at Exxon.

Jeff Kern is a geologist who attended grad school at the same time I did, and was Dolecek's business partner.

Saul Rodriguez, originally from Venezuela, is now an American citizen and a doctor. He is the uncle of my son-in-law.

Laura Puzio is a friend of mine, along with her husband, Michael, and I enjoyed turning her into Bigley-Puzio. They both studied geology at Michigan State.

Salih Tawfiq Salih was an accountant and office manager for Texas Eastern in Khartoum. I tried to capture in this book how he impressed me with his life and family.

Mary Rainey was a geologist at Exxon with whom I carpooled and built a sailboat. The book's MR does not have the same physical appearance as the MR in real life, but does have the same dedication to geology.

Theresa Mathis is my sister-in-law and a wildlife biologist with the Forest Service.

Homer Knost is a friend who built in Sudan the largest sugar mill in sub-Saharan Africa.

Barb and John Vietti are geology friends. John has the most amazing workshop I've ever seen.

Steve Jensen and I shared a lab in grad school along with Charlie Wu, and have remained friends.

Robert A. Greene was my housemate for several years during grad school. He was from Massachusetts, so it was easy to turn him into Roberta Greene of UMass, which really does have a proficiency in geologic modeling.

Cornelia Buck Allen is my sister-in-law and was the only female in the College of Engineering at Arizona State during her time there in the '50s. Her father worked on the Manhattan Project.

Marion Jones is a friend and fishing buddy who is the winner of a national award for teaching excellence. My children had the good fortune to have him as coach and teacher.

Gene Trowbridge was a consulting geologist with whom I worked for several years. I learned more about geology from Gene than from anyone else.

Johannes DeBruin was my study partner for the comprehensive exams in graduate school.

Peter Shive was my major professor in grad school. Still highly athletic, he is a champion Frisbee Golf player.

David Hawk is a geologist and friend who helped us make Idaho the 35th producing state.

Mike Healy is a friend from high school in Worland.

Haluk Beker and Burhan Oral, from Turkey, were fellow physics grad students. Haluk was a great help during a stressful time.

Luis Pacheco is my son-in-law's brother, and a champion in martial arts.

Robert Janz was my best friend in junior high and high school, and debate partner.

George Sumida was my supervisor when I worked in the laboratory at the Holly Sugar plant. He was in the Heart Mountain Interment Camp, served in the 442nd, and won a medal. He was kind, humorous, and helpful.

Leona Richardson was secretary for our group at Texas Eastern. She was a delightful person, and I hope I have captured her personality.

Kaz Uriu was as described. His daughter Donna was in my high school class.

Leonardo Danielli was a geologist at Esso in London. He introduced me to Italian wines.

Terry Boudreaux is a land broker in Lafayette, Louisiana. He and I once nearly froze our ears off fishing on Calcasieu Lake.

Ronnie Schlup and Gary Schneider were two of my best friends during grades 4-6 in Newcastle.

Maurice Seghetti was a high school classmate.

Jean Cox, who was married to my cousin, was a schoolteacher in Cody and was one of the most delightful people I have ever known.

Many thanks to all.